D1475025

A MOST SINGULAR *Venture*

Elizabeth and Richard in Jane Austen's London

PRAISE FOR A MOST SINGULAR VENTURE:

The latest outing for Donna Fletcher Crow's engaging pair of amateur sleuths takes them back to England – with Richard lecturing on the golden Age of British crime writing, while Elizabeth follows in Jane Austen's footsteps around the capital. As always, Crow's immersion in her subject pays off: a thoroughly satisfying mystery, peopled by an intriguing cast of characters, is wrapped up in an impeccably researched tour of London, as recognizable to the modern visitor as it would have been to Jane Austen herself. Yet again, a new Elizabeth and Richard story gives cause for celebration. More, please!
—Joceline Bury, Jane Austen's Regency World

"A delightful and engaging mini-course in British detective fiction, all wrapped up with a page-turning murder mystery and a modern-day tour of London that will have you literally walking in Jane Austen's footsteps. Janeites in particular will find much to admire."
—Syrie James, best-selling author of *Jane Austen's First Love*

Donna Fletcher Crow exhibits an impressive knowledge of literature, today's London, and Jane Austen's visits there more than two hundred years ago. Much to enjoy here for Janeites and mystery readers alike.
—Julie Klassen, Bestselling author of Regency fiction

Donna Fletcher Crow spins a tale of intrigue and murder in the middle of Jane Austen's London, with a backdrop of collectible first edition Jane Austen novels. Another great Elizabeth and Richard 'whodunit', this story is a cozy mystery and an entertaining lesson in history. What more could a reader want?
—Janet Taylor, More Agreeably Engaged

A Most Singular Venture is like going on a tour of London with two friends (Richard and Elizabeth). Readers get to learn about Jane Austen and the city during the Regency era, while becoming ensconced in solving a mystery.

—Eva Maria Hamilton,
Jane Austen's Colouring and Activity Books

PRAISE FOR THE ELIZABETH & RICHARD LITERARY SUSPENSE SERIES:

"Playful mystery featuring an engaging pair of amateur sleuths—It's great fun!"

– Jane Austen's Regency World Magazine

"I've always been a fan of the traditional cozy murder mystery such as Agatha Christie wrote, or Dorothy L. Sayers, or Margery Allingham—the sort of story portrayed on PBS Mystery Theatre. So I was excited to discover a modern-day voice that has captured that fast-paced and snappy dialogue that you would find in a Tommy & Tuppence whodunit. That voice is Donna Crow, award-winning novelist."

– Christine Lindsay, Twilight of the British Raj Series

"A charming page-turner that will keep readers on edge to the very end."

– Kathi Macias, *People of The Book*

"Entrancing moments and plenty of suspense. Crow provides plenty of suspects in her twisty murder plot, and the killer's identity remains in doubt until the very end. Crow's descriptions are delightful."

– Susan Fleet, Frank Renzi Mysteries

"An enjoyable read that will activate your 'little gray cells.'"
    – Janet Benrey, The Royal Tunbridge Wells Mysteries

"Excellent, light hearted, easy reading."
    – Dolores Gordon-Smith, The Jack Haldean Mysteries

"Looking forward to more in this series."
    – DeAnna Julie Dodson, The Chastelayne Trilogy

"A delight!"
    – A J Hawke, Cedar Ridge Chronicles

"Delightfully English."
    – Sheila Deeth, *Divide by Zero*

"An enjoyable read, with just enough plotting to keep the action going and the reader just a bit off guard. For a few hours one plunges into another world, and an enjoyable and believable one it is."
    – William Shepard, Robbie Cutler Diplomatic Series

"Highly recommended for those who enjoy the game of mystery solving."
    – Glenda Bixler

"Because of Donna's great knowledge and experience with England and Englishmen and travel in the UK, her story flourishes and almost dances on the page."
    – Maryanne Robinson

"Extremely well done and my evening of reading was very well-spent."
    – Clark Crouch, *Rustic Ruminations*

"This book will keep your brain active as you follow the complex plot and interesting characters."
– Hannah Alexander, The Healing Touch Series

"Engages the reader with a lively dialogue between the two protagonists in a complex dance of relationships."
– Gwyneth Bledsoe, *Death Before Breakfast*

ALSO BY DONNA FLETCHER CROW

The Elizabeth & Richard Literary Suspense Mysteries
The Shadow of Reality
Elizabeth and Richard at a Dorothy L. Sayers mystery week
high in the Rocky Mountains
A Midsummer Eve's Nightmare
Elizabeth and Richard honeymoon at a Shakespeare Festival
in Ashland, Oregon
A Jane Austen Encounter
A second honeymoon visit to Jane Austen's homes turns deadly
The Torch Ignites
Elizabeth and Richard look back to their first meeting
in a New England autumn

The Monastery Murders, Clerical Mysteries
A Very Private Grave
A Darkly Hidden Truth
An Unholy Communion
A Newly Crimsoned Reliquary
An All-Consuming Fire

The Lord Danvers Victorian True-Crime Mysteries
A Most Inconvenient Death
Grave Matters
To Dust You Shall Return
A Tincture of Murder

Where There is Love, Historical Romance
Where Love Begins
Where Love Illumines
Where Love Triumphs
Where Love Restores
Where Love Shines
Where Love Calls

The Daughters of Courage Family Saga
Kathryn, Days of Struggle and Triumph
Elizabeth, Days of Loss and Hope
Stephanie, Days of Turmoil and Victory

Glastonbury, **The Novel of the Holy Grail**

A MOST SINGULAR Venture

Elizabeth and Richard in Jane Austen's London

#5 The Elizabeth and Richard Mysteries

DONNA FLETCHER CROW

Verity Press

A Most Singular Venture
Copyright © 2016 by Donna Fletcher Crow

All rights reserved as permitted under the U.S. Copyright Act of 1976.
No part of this publication may be reproduced or transmitted in any
form or by any means, electronic or mechanical, including photocopy
recording or any information storage and retrieval system, without
permission in writing from the publisher. The only exception is brief
quotations in printed reviews.

Verity Press
an imprint of Publications Marketing, Inc.
Box 972
Boise, Idaho
83704

First eBook Edition: 2016
First Print Edition: 2016
ISBN: 978-1-53743-505-3

Editing by Sheila Deeth
Cover design by Ken Raney
Layout design by eBooks By Barb for booknook.biz

This is a work of fiction. The characters and events portrayed in this
book are fictitious or used fictitiously.

Published in the United States of America

Verity Press

Jane at Prayer

Give us grace, Almighty Father,
so to pray, as to deserve to be heard,
to address Thee with our Hearts, as with our lips.
Thou art everywhere present,
from Thee no secret can be hid.
May the knowledge of this, teach us to fix our thoughts on thee,
with reverence and devotion that we pray not in vain.

Above all other blessings, Oh! God,
for ourselves, and our fellow-creatures, we implore Thee
to quicken our sense of Thy mercy in the redemption of the world,
of the value of that holy religion in which we have been brought up,
that we may not by our own neglect,
throw away the salvation Thou has given us,
nor be Christians only in name.

Hear us, Almighty God, for His sake who has redeemed us,
and taught us thus to pray.

Amen

Jane in London

August 1788
Orchard Street   Dined with Mrs. Hancock and Cousin Eliza

August 1796
Cork Street   Possibly overnight with Tom LeFroy's Uncle

June 1808
Brompton   Visited Henry and Eliza at 16 Michael's Place

April 1811
Sloane Street   Visited Henry and Eliza

May 1813
Sloane Street   Visited Henry after Eliza's death

Sept. 1813
Henrietta St.   Visited Henry with 3 nieces

Nov. 1813
Henrietta St.   With Henry to negotiate with publisher

March 1814
Henrietta St.   Visiting Henry and working on *Mansfield Park*

August 1814
Hans Place   Visited Henry after his move

Oct.-Dec. 1815
Hans Place   Extended stay due to Henry's illness, visited Carlton House

Characters

Dr. Elizabeth Spencer, researching Jane Austen's London

Dr. Richard Spencer, lecturer at Queens of Crime course, University of London

Sara Ashley-Herbert, Public Relations manager, Hatchard's

Jeremy Turner, American student doing summer internship at Hatchard's and attending Queens of Crime course

Jack, Nilay, Stav, choristers from Headington School where Richard is housemaster

Babs Ellington, American woman attending Queens of Crime

Andrew Spencer, Richard's brother, head of Caudex House publishers

Bramwell Child, Banker at Chestermere Chartered Bank

Gerard Asquith, Fine Arts Appraiser

Clive Kentworth, Legacy House Auctions representative

Wanda, Susan, Al, Noboko, Eleanor, students at Queens of Crime Course

Constable Lambert, Holborn Police

Inspector Fulsom, Holborn Police

Lenore, Regency Realm editor

Bo Egelton, millionaire playboy

For Stan,
Who walked every step of
Jane Austen's London with me

And
For Kelly
Who took me to view the
First Editions of Jane's Books

And
For Stanley, Jr.
Who hosted the evening at Rule's

Chapter 1

"JANE AUSTEN AS A Queen of Crime?" Elizabeth looked up from her book with a frown. "Are you certain? I'm well aware of your fondness for the lovely Jane, but wouldn't it make more sense to speak on Dorothy L. Sayers for this particular course?"

Richard's craggy features softened into a smile. "Now that does take me back. As I recall we had a similar conversation twenty-some years ago when you insisted on dragging me off to that Sayers mystery week."

"Twenty-four years ago to be precise. And aren't you glad I did?" She reached out to him on the other end of the sofa, resting her hand lightly on his arm.

"Eternally grateful, my love." He covered her hand with his. "Who would ever have guessed that a stodgy ex-publisher, English professor would become the author of crime novels?" He gave her hand a small squeeze, then let go to hold up his just-released book.

Their reminiscence was cut short by a series of short raps at the door. Elizabeth rose with a sigh. "Or that we would become houseparents to twenty lively youngsters."

She opened the door to three of their charges from the

Headington Boys School where Richard's service as temporary housemaster had extended to a three-year contract. Jack, the sturdy blond who seemed to grow taller every time Elizabeth looked at him, strode in ahead of the smaller Stav, and Nilay, of the snapping black eyes, who was waving a book. "This is wizard, sir."

Richard let out his breath with a smile. Until that moment he hadn't realized how concerned he had been about his boys' assessment of the story that had included their adventure in Godmersham. It had seemed a good idea at the time to give them advance copies—only fair really—but if his three years of housemastering had taught him anything, it was that you never knew how the young would react to something.

"And you put us in it, too!" Stav and Nilay spoke at once.

Jack plopped down on the footstool without waiting to be invited. "It's really wicked how the bad guy turned out to be an international spy." He hesitated before going on. "But he wasn't really, was he? I mean, it's sort of that crime we helped you with, but it isn't. What—"

"My mum borrowed mine," Stav interrupted. "But I had to tell her you made up the stuff about our tackling the bad guys."

"Best that mums don't know some things," Nilay agreed. "Thanks!" He took one of the Penguin bars Elizabeth was handing round. "Our mum already knows, though. Sahil told." He made a face at the thought of his older brother who had graduated last year and returned to New Deli.

"Will you sign it for me, sir?" Jack held out his book with unaccustomed shyness.

"I'll be delighted to, Jack. But are you certain you wouldn't rather wait for the official signing? I understand Mr. Springer is making arrangements for your whole choir to come to the launch at Hatchard's before you go on to St. Paul's."

Jack lowered the book. "Sure, I'll wait. Ol' Springs is dead chuffed to be in the book. We even get to miss maths to go up to London early."

"Yeah, but we have to come back to take our exams before the summer hols," Stav reminded him.

The mention of summer holidays prompted a general conversation. Stav would be visiting Israel with an aunt and uncle; Nilay going to see his family in India; Jack was the only one who didn't seem excited about his plans. He shrugged when Elizabeth asked him. "I'll be in London with my mum." Then Elizabeth remembered hearing that Jack's parents were divorcing.

"Well, then you'd better be about your revising, hadn't you?" Elizabeth said with mock severity. "I trust reading Dr. Spencer's book didn't take too much time away from your assignments."

The boys took the hint and, with a chorus of additional thank yous for the treats, tumbled out of the room. Elizabeth shut the door behind them, shaking her head with a smile. "Youthful energy. Now, about this summer course you've agreed to teach at the University of London…"

"I'm really surprised at myself. Three years ago I didn't think I'd ever want to get back in a lecture hall. But I find I'm quite looking forward to it."

"Not sorry you gave up your position at Rocky Mountain, then?"

"Not for a minute." He shook his head. "Amazing, isn't it? A whole new life, a whole new career at my age."

"Well, Old Man, move over." She plunked down on the sofa next to him again.

"And how about you? Glad you retired when you did?"

"Um hum." Elizabeth nodded.

But Richard didn't miss the pause before she answered. Nor the tepid quality of her reply. "Elizabeth, what's the matter? I thought you loved living in Oxford."

"I do." Her response was quick enough. So why did he feel it should be followed by a 'but'? He glanced down at the top of her head. Only a few grey streaks in her still-shining black bob. And he didn't have to look to know her petite figure was still shapely. He stroked her cheek with one finger.

Goodness, these days fifty-eight was still young. He was five years older, and he felt young. But Elizabeth had been head of the English department at Rocky Mountain, chair of two academic committees, and served on how many more, besides her full schedule of lecturing. Was she bored with their new life? With him?

"You're sure you're not sorry you retired?" He tried again.

Elizabeth's chuckle didn't sound too forced. "If you can call my *de facto* position as Mrs. Housemaster being retired. Although I am looking forward to writing that magazine article for *Regency Realm*." Before he could probe further she changed the subject. "So, are you going to spend all three weeks lecturing on Jane Austen?"

"No, no. A week with Austen, then P.D. James...," he paused for dramatic effect, "and finally—Sayers."

Elizabeth gave a triumphant crow.

"Before you say, 'I told you so,' you need to know I'd planned it all along."

"Of course you did, darling. Which books will you have them read?"

"*Emma*, of course—having them read it as detective fiction should be instructive for the most hardened Janeite. I'm not sure about Sayers, though. Should it be *The Nine Tailors*, focusing on how Sayers' moral grounding dictated the outcome, or *Strong Poison* or *Gaudy Night* as a study of a strong heroine?"

"You're asking me?" Her tone implied there couldn't possibly be any doubt.

"Right. *Gaudy Night* it is."

Elizabeth gave a satisfied nod. "And James?"

"Hard choice. I'm tempted to do something really offbeat and have them read *The Children of Men*—again for its moral grounding—but it isn't a mystery as such, so I think I'd best stay with the canon and do a Dagleish. *Death in Holy Orders*, I think. It shows so well how James wrote out of who she was."

"Ah, author authenticity. I recall you giving me that lecture after visiting a certain backwoods poet in New Hampshire, long, long ago when you worked for Caudex. I wonder if he ever regretted refusing to let you turn him into a superstar?"

Richard shook his head, thinking of his time working for the Spencer family publishing company. "Not as much as Caudex regretted losing him after he won the Pulitzer Prize for Poetry."

"Which he probably wouldn't have won, if he had given up on his focus all those years ago. Do you ever miss the publishing world?"

Richard shook his head. "Boston seems like a million miles away. As you say, another world. I do miss darling Granny, though."

Elizabeth nodded. "Yes, Alexandra was a lovely lady— she ruled her world with a silver teapot. Rather like the Dowager Duchess of Grantham."

"It will be good to see Andrew again," Richard continued the train of thought.

"Goodness, I've only seen him a couple of times since our wedding. When is he coming to London?"

"I don't have the exact date, but it should be while we're there. I sent him our schedule. Thought it might make it easier to connect."

"How exciting for him to be bidding on those first editions of Austen's books."

"It's even more exciting for Caudex. They want to publish facsimile editions of the originals, then sponsor a traveling exhibition to bookstores and Jane Austen events to promote the set. It would be a real coup—probably the most exciting thing our hyper-traditional publishing company has ever undertaken. I guess I'll have to say that I'm surprised Andrew has the vision to take on the project. Maybe my little brother has more imagination than I gave him credit for."

"What are his chances of being the successful bidder?"

Richard shrugged. "I don't have any idea. I expect there could be a lot of competition. I think the set is supposed to contain one book actually signed by Jane. It all comes down to how much Caudex is willing to pay."

"Or how much they can afford to pay." Elizabeth added when Richard fell silent. "One reads so much these days about the publishing world being in such turmoil with all the publishers losing money."

Richard gave a rather sardonic laugh. "It always comes down to that, doesn't it? The almighty dollar. Still, into the third generation Caudex is managing to stay afloat. I'm just so thankful I'm not at the helm anymore. Reading the yearly stockholder's reports is enough for me."

Elizabeth returned to her book, but Richard found that his lecture notes for the up-coming course couldn't hold his attention. How long had it been since he had seen his little brother? How well was his family's publishing company doing? He had struggled valiantly to make a success of it all when it was thrust upon him, no matter how trapped he felt when his older brother was killed in a plane crash—even remembering those years working in a job he despised made his body tense.

And then Drew had, quite suddenly, dropped out of medical school, and Richard had been able to hand the company over to his enterprising younger brother, leaving Richard free to apply for the English professorship he truly wanted. Richard relaxed, his mind flooding with pictures of the contentment those twenty-some years had brought. Struggles too, of course, but one tended to dwell on the good times.

What he had said to Elizabeth was absolutely true—he was still a board member and stockholder in the company, but he had paid it very little attention beyond reading annual reports. So was he being absurd now, suddenly to think of taking an active interest? It wasn't likely that Andrew would welcome his interference. After all, Richard knew almost nothing about the current state of affairs at Caudex.

Still, no matter how he argued with himself, he couldn't make the tiny niggle of worry go away. He had seen an article recently about an uncut, three volume, first edition of

Sense and Sensibility being offered for sale for a hundred thousand pounds. If each of the six books was to be offered at that price—probably with increased value as a complete set— Richard wasn't certain of the current exchange rate but that must be getting close to a million dollars. Could Caudex afford such an investment? Plus the cost of producing facsimiles—complete with uncut pages and antique binding—was there a market for such expensive books? Had Andrew done his market research? Add to that the cost of mounting the traveling exhibit Andrew had so enthusiastically outlined in his last report to the board ... Richard shook his head.

All that would mean little to one of the big six publishers, but Caudex, small and safe, could hardly afford such risk. Oh, he and Elizabeth would be all right if the stock crashed, even if he had to give up his much-valued retirement and take a regular lecturing position again—assuming he could find one. But Richard's widowed mother was in an expensive assisted living home in California. Had Drew given any thought to how they were to pay such bills if his scheme failed?

Richard sighed, making Elizabeth look up from her reading. He forced a smile and she returned to her book, but Richard could find no such comforting distraction. He would have to confront his brother when they met in London in two weeks' time.

Chapter 2

RICHARD CAUGHT HIS BREATH when he saw the bay window of London's oldest bookshop, filled with a stack of books featuring an antique manuscript dripping with blood.

"Stand there and let me get a picture." Elizabeth pulled out her phone.

"Are you sure? Isn't that rather naff?" Richard looked around uneasily, hoping no one was watching them.

"Don't be silly!" Elizabeth commanded. Richard moved obediently and she caught the moment. "There. You'll be glad to have that later."

"I already am." He grinned at the admission.

"Great. One more. Under the royal warrants."

Richard glanced up at the single word Hatchard's in its graceful gold script surrounded by three royal warrants above the door. He tried to look like the serious man of letters he hoped to present, rather than the excited Alex in Wonderland he felt like.

Elizabeth snapped her photo, but didn't move toward the door in spite of the busy pedestrian traffic crowding the pavement. "They were established in 1797, and *Sense and Sensibility* was published in 1811. Do you think Jane might have come here to see her books on the shelf?"

Richard pushed through the mullioned French doors, and Elizabeth followed him inside. "Ah, research for your article on Austen's London? Perhaps one of their clerks can help you."

Before she could reply, a woman in an elegantly understated black suit with a white silk blouse, her thick blond hair pulled into a smooth coil at the nape of her neck, approached them. "Dr. Spencer, welcome. I'm Sara Ashley-Herbert. We are so happy to be presenting your debut novel. Your publisher seems most optimistic about your Austen angle with contemporary crime."

Richard chose not to mention that Enigma was an imprint of Caudex, the family publishing house that his brother ran. Instead, he muttered something he hoped exhibited an appropriately understated optimism and introduced Elizabeth.

"And this is Jeremy Turner, a countryman of yours. He's doing a summer internship with us, and I've asked him to help out today."

A twenty-something young man, with the needing-a-good-shave stubble dictated by current fashion, held out his hand. "Hi. Pleased to meet you Dr. Spencer and Dr. Spencer." He grinned at his witticism.

"Internship. That sounds exciting," Elizabeth said as she acknowledged the introduction.

"Yeah, it's super. I'm an English major at UCLA. Want to work in the publishing world, so getting to work in an iconic bookstore is great."

Ms. Ashley-Herbert led the way past tables topped with attractive book displays in front of walls of dark wood shelves filled with books. At the back of the store a wide, gold-carpeted stairway led to a balcony surrounded with a dark wooden railing. Everywhere stacks of books with intriguing titles and eye-catching covers took Richard's attention, tempting him to stop and browse. And overwhelming his earlier optimism. All these books. Why did the world need his? How would anyone even find his? Why would they want to?

What was he thinking to leave his comfortable, scholarly world? If Elizabeth hadn't been half a step behind him he might have turned and run.

"Here we are. Will this be comfortable for you?" His hostess indicated a walnut table with barley sugar legs, easily a Queen Anne original, piled high with his books. To the side, a tasteful, pale green placard displayed the cover of his book, announcing that the author would be greeting readers and signing copies from 12:30 onward.

Richard supposed the "onward" part meant until no readers cared to be greeted. It might be a very short signing session. He only hoped someone would show up. At least he could take comfort in the fact that the Headington boys would be coming. That should be a helpful boost to the numbers. He realized Ms. Ashley-Herbert was waiting for his reply.

"Oh, yes. Yes, certainly. Most comfortable. Thank you." Richard slipped behind the table, thankful for the barricade it offered, and sank into the leather winged-back chair. The smooth comfort of the Moroccan seat that had been filled by his illustrious predecessors reassured him. He might be a neophyte in this role, but he had spent his whole adult life in the book world, first as publisher, then professor, and now writer. He was a tiny link in a long procession of those who cherished the English language and wrestled with it to tell their story, hoping to grip readers' imaginations in a way that would bring it alive for them. Chaucer, Shakespeare, Milton, Brontë, Dickens, and, yes, Austen—all those whose words had been a lifelong love of his. Richard Spencer wasn't worthy to dot an "i" any of them had written, but he was here, surrounded by their work, and sharing a spark of the love of language and story they had given to the world. He reached into his pocket and took out his pen. An actual ink fountain pen given to him by Elizabeth for this occasion.

A pounding on the stairway that could only be a herd of elephants or an English boys' choir made him look up. "Sir, me first! Sign mine first!" Jack held out his book.

"I'm next! Mum's still reading the copy you gave me, so I

bought one for you to sign. With my own money."

Richard smiled at Stav, hoping he would later think the sacrifice of two weeks' worth of sweets good value for money.

The queue of boys, fresh-scrubbed and neatly combed in their blue blazers and green and gold Headington ties, snaked up the stairway, each one exhibiting, by their enthusiasm or by their shell of nonchalance, how impressed they were with their housemaster. Mr. Springer brought up the rear. "Sign it to Charlotte, if you don't mind. She says she's looking forward to spending the summer doing nothing but reading for pleasure—and decorating the nursery, of course."

Richard smiled at the obvious pride with which the choirmaster inserted the fact that he and his bride of three years were expecting their first child in August. A happy circumstance for Richard, too, since the newlywed Springers' desire to live in their own home and start a family had meant that the temporary housemastership he had stepped into had become a permanent position.

Springer asked Richard when he would return to Oxford, and Richard explained they would be staying at the University of London for the rest of the month. "The school has our address in case you need anything."

The efficient Jeremy Turner appeared at Richard's elbow with a fresh stack of books, and the Headington group moved on. Richard was delighted to see that his home-grown readers were not the only ones waiting to have a book signed. He was also pleased that the crush wasn't so heavy that he couldn't take time to visit at least briefly with each person. His stock conversation starters were: Which was their favorite Austen novel? Did they like murder mysteries? To which his respondents replied, then offered queries of their own from the other side of the table: Did he live in England? How did he like it?

He had been signing for perhaps an hour, when the attentive Jeremy slipped a cup of tea onto the table. "Thought you might be needing this."

Richard thanked him and leaned back in his chair as he

sipped, happy to give his hand a rest. He noted out of the corner of his eye that Elizabeth had also been supplied with a cuppa and seemed to be pleasantly occupied chatting with the young American intern.

"Dr. Spencer, how exciting!" A well-endowed woman in tight jeans and an "I heart Darcy" tee shirt presented him with a stack of three books. Before he could begin signing, she unslung the carrier bag from over her shoulder and started rootling in its depths. She emerged triumphant with a lavender pen. "You won't mind signing with this will you? It's my favorite color." She placed the pen before him, then extended her hand to shake, making the gold bands on her wrist clank. "Babs. Babs Ellington. But only sign one to me. The other two are for my best friends back home—Indiana, that is. Evansville. They'll be so thrilled."

Richard was struggling to keep up, but before he could ask her friends' names for the other dedications, Babs raced on, "And guess what? I have a surprise for you. I'm going to be in your class! I can't tell you how thrilled I am to be studying at the University of London—even if it is only for a three-week summer course. I'll have to tell you, though, I was surprised to learn that it was being taught by an American." Richard wondered if he should apologize. "But then I saw the sign in the window, and I recognized your name, and I realized why you were teaching the class. I really can't wait to hear who your favorite Queens of Crime are. I've read every single Agatha Christie. I think Jessica Fletcher is my favorite, though—"

Richard held the purple pen poised. "Names?"

"Oh, yes—how silly of me, babbling on like that. One to Julie Ann and one to Martha. Julie Ann and I were—"

"May I offer you a cup of tea?" Jeremy gathered up the signed books and presented them to their owner, forcing her to turn from the table.

"My goodness, I'm surrounded by Americans. Isn't this exciting!"

Jeremy took Babs' arm and steered her away, allowing the

queue of waiting customers to move forward.

Considerably later, long after the tea in his cup had gone cold and the line in front of him had dwindled to a straggle before stopping altogether, Richard replaced the gold cap on his pen and leaned back in the chair with a sigh. "Well done, you," Sara Ashley-Herbert seemed to appear from nowhere. "A very successful debut, I'd say. I'm sure Enigma Press will be delighted. Did you enjoy it?"

Richard blinked. "You know, I rather did." The note of surprise in his voice made him laugh with the others as Elizabeth and Jeremy joined them.

Sara said she was pleased it had been a good experience for him, then left them to Jeremy's care once again.

"Guess what, darling?" Elizabeth said. "Jeremy is signed up for your course, too."

"That's grand." Richard beamed at him. "That should give me a chance to repay the help you were today. Did you tell the enthusiastic Babs Ellington you were to be classmates?"

"No, I thought I'd let that be a surprise." Jeremy grinned.

"Jeremy is going to look up what he can find on any record of Jane Austen's books at Hatchard's for me, too," Elizabeth said.

"Great. That's very kind of you."

Jeremy shrugged. "Sucking up to the teacher. I'll get my brownie points early. Actually, though, the thought of working in a place where the very first editions of Austen's books may have been sold is rather romantic." Jeremy looked around at the antique shelves lining the walls. "One can almost feel the rough edge of the uncut pages, the texture of the paper bindings." He looked up, slightly embarrassed. "Sorry, I do get carried away.

"Not sure I'll be able to come up with anything useful, though. I don't know whether Hatchard's would have bothered with Jane Austen initially. You know, it's generally considered that *Sense and Sensibility* was published as 'by a Lady' because Austen prized her privacy so highly—which was undoubtedly true in part, although her family talked about her writing freely enough. But the fact of the matter is that it was standard practice in that day for what was considered a minor work—the author simply wasn't important enough to bother naming."

They were still shaking their heads over such an irony, when a hurrying footfall on the stairs made Richard look up. "Am I too late to get an autograph?"

Richard stood and threw open his arms. "Drew! Amazing! When did you get in?" The brothers embraced. Then Richard, remembering they were in England, shifted to a hand-shake.

"Actually arrived at Heathrow about 10:00 this morning. Would have called you sooner but, once I finally got to the hotel, the bed just looked too tempting."

Elizabeth joined them and embraced her brother-in-law. "How lovely to see you, Andrew. Where are you staying?"

"The Russell. It's where our family has stayed since Grandpa came over on the ark."

"That's perfect! We're in College Hall at the University of London. That's just round the corner."

Richard introduced Jeremy to his brother and explained briefly about Drew's coming to London to bid on the Austen first editions for Caudex House.

"That's cool! An uncut set! I have seen first editions at UCLA, but I'd love to see a set in the original publishers' bindings." Jeremy pumped Andrew's hand with vigor. "Good luck on the bid."

"Yes, I'm pretty excited. Certainly the biggest publishing venture I've ever undertaken." Andrew started to talk more about the project, while Richard looked at his watch.

"I'm famished. I'd love to grab a sandwich before Evensong." Richard explained that the boys' choir for which he served as housemaster were singing at St. Paul's that evening and invited Drew to join them. "You, too, if you're free." He extended the invitation to Jeremy.

"That's those energetic boys who were so eager for you to sign their books? Sure, I'd like to hear them sing. Five o'clock is it? That's when I get off work. Maybe I could get off a bit early if I invite the lovely Ms. Ashley-Herbert to come along, too. All in the name of good customer relations, of course."

"Great. Hope to see you there," Richard turned to his brother. "Drew?"

"Sure, love to join you. I don't see the banker until tomorrow afternoon. Wanted to have time to get my feet under me before I launched into an international business deal."

Elizabeth did a quick search on her iphone. "How about a Pret a Manger? Ten minutes' walk to Trafalgar Square, then we can take the tube from there."

In a little over a quarter of an hour Elizabeth, Richard and Andrew were seated at a small table with sandwiches, salads and tea in front of them. Elizabeth bit into her food first. "Mmm, this Asian wrap is delicious. Now, Andrew, tell us about this auction. You said you're going to a bank? I would have thought it would be an auction house—Sotheby's or something."

Andrew set his cup down. "No, it's not quite that straightforward. It's an auction, but it's not everybody sitting in a room holding up a card when an auctioneer calls out a number."

"Pity. Those always look rather exciting on TV shows. And the bad guy takes the bid for the Rembrandt, but pays for it with counterfeit money."

Drew smiled. "Far more controlled and understated, I'm afraid."

"So explain the procedure," Richard said.

"It's a sealed bid auction. Quite normal practice, I'm told. The books are being held in a vault in the Chestermere Chartered Bank. Bidders and their experts make an appointment to go in to see and authenticate the books. Potential buyers deposit the amount of their bid with the bank, so no chance of your counterfeit currency scenario. After three weeks the winning bidder is announced."

"And the winner gets the books, and the others get their deposit returned to them," Richard finished for his brother with a nod. "But do you know who the seller is? How can you be sure he's legit?"

"The representative for the owner is Legacy House Auctions. I checked them out. They're an international company—been doing this for more than half a century."

Elizabeth pulled out her phone and pushed a few keys. "Hm, this must be them. Legacy House, you say? Yes, they do look well established." She scrolled a bit. "I don't see anything about the Jane Austen first editions here, though."

"No, this is being handled privately. I think the owner wants to have a say in who the books go to. We have to submit a statement of what we plan to do with them as well as the money."

"Why's that?" Richard asked.

"I can show you the prospectus. There was a rather inspiring statement about the cultural importance of these books and the owner's desire that they be used for the promotion of our literary heritage. I think the seller is concerned that they not just be locked up in a private collection. That's one reason I think we have such a good chance of winning. We plan to keep our facsimiles as reasonably priced as possible. And then, there's the traveling exhibit—that will make the books really accessible."

In spite of Andrew's enthusiasm Richard frowned. "It all sounds a bit eccentric. Do you know anything about the provenance?"

"It's a wonderful story. Actually, I'm glad you asked because we'll want to have it written up for the exhibit. The books have been in the seller's family forever. Descendants of the Lloyd family that were such good friends of the Austens."

"Yes, there is a delightful letter where Jane warns Cassandra not to allow Martha Lloyd to read *First Impressions* again, because she is convinced Martha means to publish it herself from memory, and one more reading should allow her to do that."

Andrew looked impressed at Elizabeth's knowledge. "Wonderful, we might be able to use that in our narrative. Maybe you could help write it up."

"I'd be happy to help any way I could. This is so exciting! I would love to see the books. Are we allowed to go with you?"

"I don't see why not. We're permitted to take experts with us."

Richard was quiet for a few moments as he chewed thoughtfully on his balsamic chicken sandwich, his thoughts split between worry over the auction and pleasure in his food. He enjoyed the nutty crunch of the bread in contrast to the creamy smoothness of the avocado slices. "How will you determine how much to bid?" He hoped it sounded like a neutral question and didn't betray his concern over what he saw as his brother's scheme to "bet the farm."

"I'll take the advice of my expert." Then Drew burst out laughing. "You should see your faces. No, I don't mean you. I've secured the services of a qualified appraiser. From the International Society of Appraisers. He comes with all the proper letters behind his name. You really don't need to worry about my going off half-cocked on this, you know. I have been running the company for almost thirty years."

"I know you have, Drew. And with very little help from anyone else in the family. I didn't mean to question your judgement. I just wanted to understand how it all worked. It's a long way outside my academic field."

Andrew appeared mollified, and talk moved on to family news. "Thomas is doing brilliantly at MIT if I do say so myself. I had thought for a while he might take up the medical route I started out in, but of course it's all computer science with the young these days."

"You know I'm eternally grateful to you for dropping out of med school and taking over at Caudex, so I could get on with my life." Richard wondered if he had ever thanked his brother properly. "I hope you've never regretted it."

"Not for a minute. My first encounter with a cadaver and I knew that simply wasn't for me."

"And how is Molly?" Elizabeth asked.

"Blooming. It's frightening." Andrew pulled a photo from his wallet that showed off his daughter's snapping brown eyes and long dark hair. His own eyes softened behind his silver-rimmed glasses when he looked at her. "Just turned sixteen. She's considering Bennington and Smith, but says she'll apply to the University of Vermont for her safe school in case she doesn't make the top tier. She's got a good chance, though."

"And Caroline?" Richard decided he might as well name the elephant in the room. Andrew and his wife had been estranged for years.

"Finally decided she wants to marry her real estate tycoon in Miami, so she's asked for a divorce." In the silence that followed that statement, Richard reached for Elizabeth's hand under the table and gave it a squeeze. He was fully aware of how fortunate they were. "Probably best to get it settled. The kids are old enough to handle it all right now." Drew's voice sounded a shade too hearty.

Richard wasn't so much worried about how his niece and nephew were handling the divorce as how his brother was. Beside the emotional strain it was sure to be expensive. Caroline had never been low maintenance, and she was unlikely to walk away without what she considered her fair share of her husband's property and the publishing company.

Might that have any bearing on Drew's business decisions at the moment? In spite of his expressed confidence in his brother, Richard determined to stay close to him in London and keep an eye on this curious venture.

Chapter 3

"SO, DID JANE AUSTEN worship here?" Richard asked, as they climbed the broad front steps of St. Paul's Cathedral.

The softness of a June evening made Elizabeth smile, as did the anticipation of the pleasure ahead of them. Other worshipers and sightseers ascended the steps with them, and a flock of birds circled overhead. The tones of the great organ coming from the open doors drew them forward, away from the rush and noise of the traffic below.

Richard's question reminded her that, as pleasurable as the evening was, her time in London was to be spent on work, too. There it was again, the push-pull feeling of wanting to enjoy her retirement and yet wanting something more at the same time. If only she knew what. She turned to Richard to focus on his question. "If she did, it's not recorded. She would certainly have known it, of course, but the St. Paul's she's connected with is Covent Garden—I thought we could go there Sunday."

Richard made assenting sounds and came to a stop at the top of the steps on the broad terrace before the pillared portico. "I can add one bit of connection. You might find this interesting, too, Drew." He gestured to the stone-flagged churchyard below them. "From medieval times on into the eighteenth century, St. Paul's Churchyard was the center for book printing and selling. Jane Austen's great uncle Stephen was a bookseller here, and her father George was sent to live with him for a short time after his father died. Uncle Stephen, who sold his books under the sign of the Angel and Bible, soon packed the orphaned George off to his Aunt Elizabeth in Tonbridge, though."

Elizabeth replied, "What a useful tidbit, my love. Please remember to repeat it all to me when I have a pen to hand." Then she moved forward, concerned about getting a good seat amid the crowd of people hurrying up the steps.

A verger stopped them just inside the narthex. Richard assured him that they were, indeed, there for the service, and they were ushered forward across the black and white tessellated floor.

As always when she entered this magnificent building, Elizabeth felt overwhelmed and a bit confused. She would have liked to focus on the baroque ornateness of the architecture, the rows of white pillars and arches, the gold highlighting, the magnificent dome soaring overhead. She would have liked to make sense of it all. As she hurried down the long nave, drawn forward by the gleaming gold of the high altar, however, she knew no analysis of architectural detail could do justice to the impact of the total experience. Far better to give herself up to letting her senses be absorbed in the beauty.

They were not long in their seats before the introit began and the choir entered. The sight of the crisp, blue cassocks with white, pie-crust ruffs surrounding the cherubic faces made her catch her breath. For a moment she was back in Canterbury Cathedral, three years earlier when the Headington School Boys Choir had first processed into their lives. She swallowed down the lump in her throat when she thought of the changes that encounter had initiated—the joy, and challenges, it had brought them.

A short time later, with the golden light of the quire stall lamps shining on each face, her boys sang Psalm 113: "He maketh the barren woman to keep house; and to be a joyful mother of children." Elizabeth thought her heart would burst for gratitude. The emptiness left by her miscarriage and their childlessness had been filled in multiples. She slipped her hand through Richard's arm beside her. He responded by giving it a squeeze. Surely she was being ungrateful to think her life should hold something more.

The service moved through its stately procession of readings, canticles and prayers. In all too short a time Elizabeth was standing with the others, singing "Now Thank We All Our God." After the final blessing she moved back down the center aisle as the organ trumpeted a Buxtehude voluntary. Again, the desire tugged, to look deeply, to drink in every detail of the beauty that was already beginning to blur in her mind, but the ushers urged everyone along at a crisp pace, keeping a sharp eye out for any who might be treating this as an opportunity for free sight-seeing.

Back outside, Richard paused under the cover of the portico for Drew to give him the details of tomorrow's meeting with the appraiser at the bank, and Elizabeth looked around for her friend from Hatchard's. Perhaps he had needed to work late after all. Of course, it would be easy enough to miss someone in this crowd. She was just turning back to Richard and Drew's conversation when she spotted Jeremy leaving the church with Sara Ashley-Herbert. Elizabeth waved and they joined the little group.

"I understand that one of the features of the collection is that there's a misprint in *Mansfield Park*," Andrew was saying. "That's further evidence of it being a first edition, because there were very few of those copies published."

"I can't wait to see it," Elizabeth said. "Shall we bring gloves?"

"I'm sure the bank will have..." Andrew trailed off as he became aware of the newcomers.

Richard made the introductions. "Oh, I don't believe you met earlier at Hatchard's. Sara Ashley-Herbert, may I present my brother Andrew Spencer?" Ms. Ashley-Herbert offered a small white hand to a dazed-looking Andrew.

"Pardon our interruption, but did I hear you talking about a first edition of *Mansfield Park*?" Sara asked.

"That's not all. Haven't you heard?" Jeremy jumped in, before Andrew could answer, to bring her up to speed on the essentials of what he had been told earlier in the day, obviously happy to demonstrate his insider knowledge to his boss.

"How splendid! And you're going to buy them?" She turned her large blue eyes on Andrew. "I can't imagine that we haven't heard a whisper of this. It must be very hush-hush. But then, private collectors can be extremely capricious."

"I'm sure you'd know more about that than I do. We've always dealt with new manuscripts, but I'm anxious to see our house branch out." Andrew had found his tongue.

"You must let me know if I can be of any help to you in that department. You see, I worked for a rare book dealer in Charing Cross before I came to Hatchard's, so I've had a bit of experience in the field."

"That's very generous of you, but we couldn't impose on your time," Richard said.

Drew, however, wasn't listening to his brother. "Thank you. If you really mean that. Would you like to see the books tomorrow?"

Elizabeth wondered just how large the bank's examination room was. They were getting to be quite a party. But she supposed Ms. Ashley-Herbert could qualify as an expert. Certainly more so than Elizabeth was herself.

The last of the evensong congregation, those who had been seated in the transept, was exiting through the southwest door of the cathedral, when a wave of small figures emerged from the side. Members of the evening's guest choir had shed their cassocks and surplices, donned blazers and ties, and were anxious to collect on the pizza supper that had been promised them before their bus ride back to Headington. But not before they greeted their housemaster.

"What did you think of the service, sir?"

"Wicked, wasn't it?"

"Amazing echoes, huh?"

Elizabeth curbed her impulse to hug the youngsters. Wounding their dignity would be the last thing she wanted to do. "It was absolutely lovely. I've never heard you sing better."

She wanted to wish them a happy holiday, even leave them with a few words of motherly advice, since their summer vacation would start in two days and it was unlikely she would see any of them again until August, but before she could find the words a voice ringing with a mix of southern drawl and Midwestern twang struck her ears.

"Well, we meet again! Wasn't that just the most beautiful thing you've ever seen in your life? We don't have anything like that in Evansville, I can tell you."

"Good evening, Babs." Elizabeth pitched her reply several tones softer than normal, hoping Babs would follow her lead and lower her voice.

Elizabeth's scheme backfired. If anything Babs sang out more loudly, "I know we weren't supposed to record anything, but I'm so glad I cheated just a teeny bit. Julie Ann and Martha—"

At that moment Jack and Stav tugged on Elizabeth's sleeve, vying to tell her something, and the last of the congregation emerged onto the portico as the heavy doors clanged shut behind them, causing the exiting throng to surge forward.

Distracted by those seeking her attention and the movement of the crowd, Elizabeth was never certain what happened. All she knew was that a sharp cry, followed by a screech from Babs, focused everyone's attention on a male figure catapulting down the flight of steep stone steps.

The body came to rest on the landing halfway down. He lay motionless, sprawled at an odd angle. "Jeremy!" Elizabeth cried and started forward.

She was the first to reach him. She knelt on the rough stone. In spite of the blood pouring from a gash in his head, she put her face next to his, to listen for breath.

Richard grasped her shoulders and pulled her back. "I've rung for an ambulance. They should be here in a moment." Even as he spoke they heard the rise and fall of a siren approaching. "Is he breathing?"

Elizabeth nodded and pressed into Richard's arm to control her shaking.

The next minutes were a blur as medics strapped the limp form onto a stretcher and carried him down the stairs. Mr. Springer rounded up his choirboys who were enthralled with the blood, and police and cathedral officials made efforts to disperse the crowd of gawkers.

Richard offered Elizabeth a handkerchief to wipe the blood off her face as a policeman approached, pulling out a notebook. "Did you see what happened?"

She shook her head. "Not really. There were so many people around … It's all confusing…"

"That's all right, take your time." He looked at Richard. "How about you, sir?"

"We were chatting. All of us." Richard's vague wave encompassed Andrew, Sara, Babs and the departing choirboys. "He was standing beside me. And then he wasn't," he finished weakly.

"And you knew him?"

"Just met today. Jeremy Turner. He's an American student, here for a summer internship. At Hatchard's. That lady can tell you more," he indicated Sara Ashley-Herbert. "He works for her."

The policeman moved on to question the others, but Elizabeth couldn't take any more. She closed her eyes and turned her still blood-streaked face into Richard's chest, one question coursing through her mind: Did he stumble; or was he pushed?

Chapter 4

ELIZABETH WAS STILL ASKING the same question the next morning, when Richard clicked on the electric kettle to make the morning tea in their sparse, but efficient, student accommodation. "How are you feeling?" he asked.

She groaned and sat up in bed. "I don't know which was worse—the half of the night I spent awake tossing and turning, or the half I was asleep seeing Jeremy pitch down those steps in my dreams."

"Good news on that score. I rang St. Bart's. From what they said it sounds like he may have had a better night than you did. Of course, he was medicated, but they said he's resting comfortably."

"Can we see him?"

Richard poured steaming water over a tea bag and handed the cup to Elizabeth. "They said he can have visitors. I thought we could stop on our way to meet Drew at the bank."

Elizabeth blinked. "Goodness, I'd completely forgotten. What a pity. Jeremy was so excited about seeing the first editions. I'm sorry he'll have to miss it." She set her cup aside and pushed down the duvet as if preparing to rush right out.

"Whoa, plenty of time. We're not going anywhere until

we've done justice to that full cooked English breakfast in the dining hall."

Elizabeth settled back to enjoy her tea, but she was anxious to see Jeremy.

When they entered the hospital room a few hours later, however, Jeremy's cheerful countenance made Elizabeth feel better instantly. "Jeremy, you're sitting up. How are you?"

"Not too bad." He nodded at his right foot in a heavy plaster cast. "Broken ankle. I was lucky, though. Didn't need surgery."

"And your head?" She eyed the tidy white bandage covering what her memory continued to see as a gaping wound pouring blood.

"I've got a dickens of a headache. Seems English docs aren't as free with the pain meds as they are at home. But I'll survive. A cute little blond nurse seemed pretty relieved when I woke up right after they got me here. Of course, now I've got an excuse when I forget things."

Elizabeth handed him a bag of green grapes they had purchased at a fruit stall when they came out of the tube station. "I think this is the traditional hospital-visiting gift here. At least they looked good." Before he could thank her she rushed on. "But how did it happen? Do you remember anything?"

"I've been wondering the same thing. I'm not usually so awkward. Actually, I'm a rather good tennis player." He grimaced. "Well, I won't be for a while now."

"Do you think that's it? You were just awkward? Were you standing too close to the edge?"

"I really don't remember anything. I was interested in what your brother was saying." He looked at Richard. "Meeting a publisher is awesome. Actually, I was hoping to ask him if there might be a job opportunity with Caudex. I would love to work on his Austen exhibit."

"If Caudex wins the bid," Richard amended.

"I'm sorry you won't get to see the books today," Elizabeth added.

"Yeah, that's a real bummer. I worked in the special collections library at UCLA, did a seminar project on their Austen first editions, but these sound really—" Jeremy slumped back on his pillow.

"Are we tiring you?" Elizabeth asked. "We should be going."

"No, no. You're fine. It just came back to me. That's what we were talking about right before it happened." He blinked. "I think I was talking about my work on the Austen first editions. Or was I just thinking about it?" He looked at Richard for confirmation.

Richard shook his head. "Sorry. Afraid I was distracted by the Headington boys. And then that woman descended on us—" He paused. "I expect Drew would remember."

"Never mind, it's not important. I suppose it's a good sign that I remember what was going on, though. But it still doesn't explain how I fell."

"Will you be out in time for the Queens of Crime course?" Elizabeth asked.

"No problem. Doc said I could go tomorrow as long as my head stays clear. I guess it's not always straightforward with head injuries, but it seems to be a good thing mine bled—on the outside, that is. Internal bleeding is the danger.

"Anyway, I should be able to hobble in. I'll have this awful, heavy cast for a few weeks, but it could be worse. Good excuse to get more reading done, I suppose."

Jeremy's eyes lit up at the entrance of a small, blond nurse in a trim, blue uniform with white piping. Elizabeth and Richard waved farewell and left him to his flirting.

"What a relief that he seems to be all right."

On the street Elizabeth pulled out her phone and consulted the route. "Looks like only about a fifteen minute walk to Threadneedle Street. That will still get us to the bank ahead of schedule."

They were turning into Aldersgate Street when she returned to the topic uppermost in her mind. "So what do you think? Do you have any theories about what happened to Jeremy?"

"Probably what he said, involved in conversation—took a step backward when that rush of people, led by the charging Babs, came at us."

"Yes, I expect that's it." But her voice sounded unconvinced to her own ears.

Chapter 5

THEY WERE WELL ALONG Gresham Street, lined with the classic facades of the most established banks in London, when Elizabeth looked up. "Oh, what a magnificent building."

"Bank of England—'The Old Lady of Threadneedle Street.' She was here in Jane's day and must have been of interest to all the Austens because of Henry's profession as a banker. Only the outer wall would have been familiar to Jane, though, because the interior was rebuilt in the last century."

"My *London in Jane Austen's Footsteps* guidebook mentioned a museum there with lots of interest to Regency enthusiasts, so I plan to visit. I think that book will become something of a reference Bible for my research."

"We should have plenty of time to go there tomorrow," Richard suggested, as he directed her to a building with an arched entrance. A brass plate beside one of the pillars declared it to be the Chestermere Chartered bank, est. 1837. "Suitably understated." Richard held the heavy, beveled glass door for Elizabeth.

They were just inside the marble interior when Andrew and Sara Ashley-Herbert turned from the two men they were talking to and greeted them, Sara with a small smile and Andrew with a wave to join them.

Andrew introduced them to the portly, balding Bramwell Child who was handling the auction of the first editions for the bank. His friendly, round face and grandfatherly air made him appear as one who would be more comfortable in old tweeds and a fishing hat than in the three-piece suit encasing his rotund form. "How pleasant that you could join us. Quite an exciting offering we have, I believe."

Before Elizabeth could reply, a tall man with slicked-back, dark hair, who looked like he must have been born wearing his perfectly knotted silk tie, introduced himself in a slightly nasal tone, "Gerard Asquith, fine arts appraiser."

Elizabeth acknowledged the introduction with a smile as Andrew supplied her name.

"Well, if this is us, shall we begin?" Bramwell Child led the way to the back of the reception room toward a carpeted hallway.

"Do you handle many auctions like this?" Elizabeth asked.

"We often hold security for our clients' ventures, certainly. Although the auction aspect of this undertaking is somewhat unique."

"Yes," Elizabeth made up her mind to probe further. "That's what puzzles me—this business of requiring the bidders to pay ahead."

Child looked momentarily perplexed by the question. "Well, it's perhaps more usual to require a deposit as proof of the bidder's commitment and ability to pay, but in this case, requiring the full bid is entirely reasonable in light of the uniqueness of the items."

Halfway along the corridor he stopped before a polished mahogany door and drew a ring of keys from his pocket.

The wainscoted room had rich, green draperies at the window and a large, dark wood table in the center, surrounded by padded, leather chairs with brass studding. In unadorned splendor, five stacks of slim volumes lined the center of the table, their simple board covers reflected in the high polish of the wood.

"Only five?" Andrew's question mirrored the one in Elizabeth's mind. The six novels having been published in multiple volumes according to the fashion of the day, she expected six stacks.

"That, of course," Gerard Asquith spoke as if it were beneath his dignity to have to explain what must be common knowledge, "is because *Persuasion* and the previously unpublished *Northanger Abbey* were published posthumously as a set in 1818." He pointed to a four volume stack at the end of the row.

"I'm sure you are aware," Asquith continued, although his voice indicated that he doubted his hearers were aware, "Jane Austen sold the rights to *Northanger Abbey* for ten pounds to Richard Crosby & Son in 1803, but he never published it. Austen was required to buy the rights back—a considerable outlay on her meagre income since that amounts to about three hundred pounds in today's terms."

Bramwell Child donned a pair of white gloves from the eighteenth century sideboard against the wall and indicated that the others should do the same. Then he turned to the first set of volumes. "As I'm certain you know," he glanced almost uneasily at Asquith, "*Sense and Sensibility*, Austen's first-published work, was brought out in October of 1811 in a print run of less than a thousand, priced at 15 shillings for each volume."

Richard's eyebrows rose. "That doesn't sound like much, but when you consider that Bob Cratchit earned 15 shillings in a six-day work week, it must have been considerable."

"Around 24 pounds in today's buying power, I believe," Asquith replied. "Which, interestingly, is approximately the price of a hardback bestseller today."

Child gave a brief nod and picked up the first of the three volumes. He ran his hand over the cover in a caressing movement. "These are a truly rare survival, as the board bindings produced by early nineteenth-century publishers were relatively flimsy and not intended to be permanent. Those who could afford it usually sent their acquisitions off to a book-binder to have them bound in leather."

"It was common practice for collectors to have all the books in their library bound in matching bindings." Asquith inserted himself into the explanation, as if to remind everyone that he had been called in as the expert. "The uncut pages," he gestured toward the uneven, doubled edges of the sheets, "show that the books were unread. A reader of the period, if he was too impatient to read the book to have it rebound first, would have had his pen knife to hand to run it smoothly between each doubled sheet as he read. The pages would have then been trimmed smoothly and decorated by the bookbinder. Usually edging the pages with gold leaf."

"I've often wondered about that. Why did they publish books with uncut pages?" Elizabeth carefully directed her question to their host.

Child smiled as though he appreciated her turning to him. "Books were printed with eight or more pages on a single large sheet of paper. The sheets were folded into a 'gathering.' To save effort and money, and perhaps as a means of assuring buyers that they were receiving an unread book, the printers left the edges untrimmed. This allowed owners the freedom to choose the trim they wanted."

"These are also known as deckle edges," Asquith inserted. "The term in Italian being *intonso*."

Elizabeth had encountered books with uncut pages and was delighted to learn more about them, but before she could ask more Andrew spoke up. "Who was the publisher?" He inclined his head toward the volumes of *Sense and Sensibility*.

Child took a breath, as if expecting Asquith to step in, but then continued in his rightful place as presenter. "Thomas Egerton. He had previously printed a journal that Jane's brothers James and Henry authored during their time in Oxford, so it was natural for Henry to approach Egerton for his sister. As was common during the period, the author was asked to pay for publication on a commission basis. Egerton fronted the money, and the author was only paid after the publisher recouped his printing costs and commission. Jane's expectations were so modest and her concern about the sales not meeting the printing costs were so great that, according to James Edward Austen-Leigh's biography, 'she laid by a sum out of her very slender resources to meet the expected loss.'" Child gave a discreet cough to allow the quotation to register with his guests.

"The precaution was unnecessary, however," he resumed his discourse, "because the first edition was sold out by July 1813, and Egerton brought out a second edition in October of that year."

Child picked up the top of the three volumes next to *Sense and Sensibility.* "*Pride and Prejudice,* the novel Austen referred to as her 'own darling child,' was first published in January of 1813. We believe the print run was likely 1,500 copies, so you see how rare such a pristine first edition truly is." He couldn't keep a note of pride out of his voice at the prize he had been entrusted to present.

"*Pride and Prejudice* was Austen's bestselling book during her lifetime, and a second edition was published by Egerton in 1813—"

It was clear Asquith could tolerate being side-lined no longer. He picked up volume 2 of Austen's most popular work and opened it to the title page. After a quick scrutiny he gave a satisfied nod. "Quite. The publisher took the precaution of stating 'second edition' on the title page so there could be no question of confusion." Or of shysters trying to take advantage, his look at Child clearly implied, since the volume he held was obviously a first edition.

The bank's representative coughed and moved on. "Austen began *Mansfield Park* in 1811 and finished it in the summer of 1813." He rested a hand lightly on the stack of volumes. "Egerton published it in three volumes in 1814 with a print run of only 1,250 copies.

"That was probably only one of the reasons Austen was becoming unhappy with Egerton, who largely ignored her and paid very small royalties. So, accompanied by Henry, she approached the prestigious publisher John Murray. Murray printed a second edition of *Mansfield Park* and brought out the first edition of her fourth novel, *Emma* at the same time."

He cleared his throat. "Of course, I merely offer references to second editions as background information—we are concerned only with first editions here." He reached for the first volume of *Emma*. "This, as you undoubtedly know, is famously dedicated to the Prince Regent, the only dedication Austen made."

Child opened the top volume in the stack to exhibit, not only the printed dedication, but also, as he held the open volume before each viewer and Elizabeth saw in her turn, the delicate, copperplate signature, *Jane Austen*. It made her catch her breath. Not only a first edition of Jane's book, but also one that she had held in her own hand and inscribed.

But who had she inscribed it for? Elizabeth wondered. "When did the custom of authors autographing books begin?"

Child opened his mouth, but it was Asquith who spoke. "At least by Victorian times. Dickens inscribed a copy of *A Tale of Two Cities* to George Eliot. Jane, however, simply directed her publisher to send the dedicated copy of *Emma* to the Prince Regent, so that particular one would not have been signed. What was entirely commonplace practice, however, was for owners to inscribe their own names in books to identify their own library."

"So this could have been Jane's own personal copy?" Elizabeth could feel her eyes getting wide. That would certainly increase the value of the offering. "But surely she wouldn't have left the pages of her own copy uncut?" Elizabeth's brow furrowed with questions but Asquith merely shrugged. He was not going to be rushed into any unprofessional assessment.

Child continued his discourse. "Unfortunately, bringing out the two books simultaneously meant that they competed with one another. This reduced the number of copies sold and forced Murray to remainder 539 of the 2,000 copies of *Emma*."

This left only the four volume stack comprising *Persua-*

sion and *Northanger Abbey*. Elizabeth couldn't have been more mesmerized if she had been gazing on the Holy Grail. In a way, she supposed that was exactly what she was seeing—certainly the Holy Grail of English literature.

Gerard Asquith was far less romantic in his approach, though. He seated himself at the table and selected the first volume of *Emma*. Pulling each finger individually like a pianist preparing for a concert, he removed his right glove, then slowly ran his bare hand over the cover in a caressing gesture with his eyes half closed. Next he raised the volume to his nose and smelled deeply. He gave a little half nod. "It feels right. It smells right," then quickly added, "but that can be faked with walnut oil."

Next he drew a small black pouch out of the briefcase he carried and pulled out a large magnifying glass that surely Sherlock Holmes would have envied. "Mmm, yes. Rag paper. Consistent with eighteenth century practice."

Bramwell Child looked smug as the expert next opened the book to the page bearing Jane Austen's purported signature. He took a small vial of clear liquid from his case and proceeded to drop a single tiny pearl onto one letter.

After a few moments of observation Asquith gave a satisfied sniff. "Quite. Oak apple, I would say."

The blank look on the faces of his hearers produced a mini-lecture. "Ink is essentially created by the chemical reaction between tannic acid and iron sulfate. The highest concentration of tannin is contained in the 'apples' oak trees produce on their bark in reaction to attack by parasites. In order to make the colored solution flow for writing it is necessary to add a binder. Gum Arabic is the most efficient, but highly corrosive to more modern fountain pens. It would have been quite safe, however, for a quill pen such as we know Jane Austen used."

A quick vision of the quill pen on the tiny octagonal table where Jane sat to write her books at Chawton cottage flashed across Elizabeth's mind, but Asquith wasn't lingering. He moved on to the printed type. "By the eighteenth century all printers' inks were made from fast-drying oils and resins."

He applied a minute drop from a different vial, then once again raised the volume to his nose. "Linseed oil. Quite correct. The typeset page would have been inked with a mixture based on linseed oil and rosin, with the addition of waxes and other additives to improve printing quality.

"The lithograph came into use in 1796 ...," Asquith launched into an explanation of the mechanics of the printing process, but Elizabeth was drawn back to the books themselves as she picked up the first volume of *Persuasion*, turning the first few pages reverently. She went on to volumes two and three and found it interesting that, although issued at the same time by John Murray, Publisher in Albemarle Street, each volume was actually produced by different printers. She guessed that was a practical necessity for bringing out the volumes simultaneously. She would have liked to discuss her surmise with the experts, but felt Gerard Asquith would not be amused if she were to interrupt him.

She moved on to *Mansfield Park*. Published in 3 volumes by T. Egerton, Military Library, Whitehall, 1814, again from various printers. The uncut pages required Elizabeth to push the folded sheet open if she wished to complete reading a sentence carried from one page to the next, rather than just skim, skipping the two pages printed inside the fold. She was doing precisely this when Richard, reading over her shoulder pointed to the misprint. "Look," his finger touched the catchword set alone at the bottom of the page.

Elizabeth read, "'Within a few days ...,'" she picked up the catchword "'of'" and peeked into the top of the enfolded page. "Oh," she saw what Richard meant. "It should be 'from.' 'Within a few days from the receipt of Edmund's letter ....'"

Richard smiled. "If the purpose of the catchword was to help the reader carry the thought across the page this could be quite counter-productive."

"I wonder if there were many such misprints? If so, they must have distressed Austen to no end. She was such a perfectionist."

Asquith looked up from his examinations. "Indeed. When Egerton brought out the second edition of *Sense and Sensibility* he included the corrections and changes Austen had demanded, but also with a rather large number of textual errors. Austen blamed such misprints for the fact that the edition sold only slowly. Similar problems in *Mansfield Park* may have been the final straw in what was already becoming a strained relationship between author and publisher."

Asquith returned to his work, and Elizabeth turned to the posthumously published *Northanger Abbey* and *Persuasion*. She opened each page with some reverence and paused to read the moving introduction written by Jane's cherished brother Henry who also served as her literary agent: "The following pages are the production of a pen which has already contributed in no small degree to the entertainment of the public. And when the public ... shall be informed that the hand which guided that pen is now mouldering in the grave, perhaps a brief account of Jane Austen will be read with a kindlier sentiment than simple curiosity.

"Short and easy will be the task of the mere biographer. A life of usefulness, literature, and religion, was not by any means a life of event. To those who lament their irreparable loss ..."

Irreparable loss, indeed, Elizabeth thought.

Gerard Asquith closed the volume he had been examining so meticulously and cleared his throat as if for attention. "I am satisfied—to the extent I can ascertain here. If I were to be allowed to take the volumes to our own workroom, of course..." He looked at Bramwell Child.

"Quite impossible. I am certain you understand."

Asquith looked down the length of his considerable nose. "Pity. Our facilities rival those of the British Museum—including an electron microscope. Of course, the drawback is that one must extract a minute sample from the document being analyzed. Beta-radiography, however, can be done on a whole sheet to expose and record watermarks. The DY-LUX process.24 works by passing visible and ultraviolet light through ..." His explanation continued, but Elizabeth's mind wandered.

At last Asquith turned back to the book still in his hand. "I shall, however, be able to verify the authenticity of this volume. Of course, I need to examine each volume before I can give my imprimatur for my client to submit a bid on this property. This, of course, will take some time. I would suggest you might like to move on to other activities?"

Since Asquith had been looking directly at Elizabeth when he spoke, she felt thoroughly dismissed. She walked from the room with her head up and her shoulders straight. Once more out on the pavement with the June sun warm on her head she looked at Richard. "What now?"

"Food, I should think. Then I need to polish my lecture notes for Monday. What would you think of visiting that kebab van that seems to live outside our building, then reading in Russell Square?"

"Perfect." Elizabeth consulted her tube map. "Ah, a straight shot on the Northern Line."

It all sounded idyllic for a relaxing Friday afternoon but, even after she had finished her tender lamb kebab with vegetable chunks and settled herself comfortably on a blanket under a shady tree, Elizabeth found it impossible to concentrate on Deirdre Le Faye's edition of *Jane Austen's Letters*. Her mind kept going back to the earlier events.

"Richard, do you trust Gerard Asquith?"

Richard, sitting upright with his back against the tree trunk, paused with his pen mid-air. "Why do you ask that? He seemed thoroughly professional, if rather full of himself. I'm sure he knew what he was doing. And he's a member of the Antiquarian Booksellers' Association. That must mean something." He returned to the note he was writing in the margin of his paper.

Elizabeth rolled to a sitting position, took out her phone and searched for Antiquarian Booksellers' Association. After a few minutes of reading she had to admit their Code of Good Practice sounded comprehensive enough. It took a bit of searching under their Members section, but, indeed, she found Gerard Asquith, complete with a photograph, listing a speciality in antiquarian literature.

Surely Richard was right that there was no reason to doubt his authenticity. And, certainly, there was no reason to doubt the soundness of Chestermere Chartered Bank— all that marble and dark wood just down the street from the Bank of England, and they had been there since Victorian times.

So who else was involved? Aware of the importance of provenance, she had already checked out Legacy House which was representing the reclusive owner. Everything seemed to be absolutely top drawer. Since she couldn't imagine what could be wrong, she concluded that the sensible thing to do was to put the whole matter out of her mind. After all, it was Andrew's deal. It didn't really have anything to do with her.

That lasted almost long enough for her to read one of the letters Jane wrote to Cassandra from Southampton. When she reached Jane's reference to the progress of Henry's bank, however, it turned her thoughts again to Richard's brother's dealings with a bank. She looked up at Richard with his head bent so intently over his lecture notes. Nothing to be gained from disturbing him. The worry seemed to be Elizabeth's alone. And there was nothing she could do about it beyond keeping her eyes and ears open.

Of course, any business deal held an element of risk. Caudex might not make back their investment. Was it just that? Or was it more simply her own lack of expertise in the business world, having spent her entire life in academia? Or was it something more sinister?

At a minimum, there could be no harm in learning as much as possible about banking—particularly scams and failures. After all, it suited her topic, as Henry had owned banks at various locations in London and a branch in Alton. And his business had failed.

Chapter 6

PERHAPS IT WAS HER determination to look out for a scheme that could be perpetrated by a miscreant selling antiquarian books through a bank that made Elizabeth look over her shoulder the next day as they rounded the corner of Threadneedle Street into Bartholomew Lane: a hefty blond woman in the pelican crossing, a blue mini-cab in the street, a teenage girl in bright pink sneakers with a boy in a blue hoodie on the pavement. What could be more normal? She gave herself a little shake and entered the door behind the imposing row of Corinthian pillars.

Worries about possible ne'er-do-wells fled entirely once inside the restrained elegance of ivory walls with pilaster-supported arches beneath a light-filled dome.

Richard picked up the visitor's leaflet. "Ah, this room is a reconstruction of the bank's Stock Office designed by Sir John Soane. This is where the bank's stockholders would have come to receive their dividends."

"Stockholders?"

"Yes, the bank was privately owned from its foundation in 1694 until it was nationalized in 1946." Richard pointed to the information board on the wall. "It was started as a way for the government to raise private money to rebuild the navy after a crushing defeat by France."

"I don't think there's much chance Jane would ever have come here, but I suppose Henry might have." Elizabeth would have to consider whether or not to include The Bank of England in her article on Jane Austen's London, but she would take a few notes just in case.

They moved on to the next display, and Elizabeth read: "The bank moved to their current location in 1734. This was probably the first purpose-built bank in the world." She knew that Henry's banks, a generation later, occupied an assortment of buildings which she hoped to locate on her explorations of the city.

"That's a coincidence," Richard pointed to the next placard, recounting the history of London banking. "Francis Child gave up his goldsmith business to establish a bank at the sign of the Marygold in Fleet Street in 1681. He is known as 'the father of the profession.'"

"Child?" Elizabeth's eyes widened. "Like our Bramwell Child? Do you suppose it's the same family? Are they still in banking?"

Since the board offered no more information, Elizabeth pulled out her phone for a quick search. "Hmm, doesn't say about the family, but Child & Co. is still at No. 1 Fleet Street, now as a branch of the Royal Bank of Scotland. And look—" She held out the picture on her small screen. "They still have a marygold on their cheques."

Of course, that didn't tell her anything about Bramwell Child, but it did make her wonder. If he was of the same family, why wasn't he working in the bank that bore so much of his family's history rather than in a competitor's bank?

They moved on to the exhibit drawing the most attention from a group of children—a large Plexiglas pyramid filled with a stack of gleaming gold bars. The light in the display made the bars shimmer and reflect golden on the enthralled faces the children pressed to the case as they reached in to attempt lifting the ingots.

The sign explained the history of bank notes, which could formerly be exchanged for gold on demand. Banks were required to keep enough gold on hand to meet such possible demands in those days. But times have changed. "Bank notes are no longer exchangeable for gold. Trust gives them their value."

Richard nodded. "True. Now all one can do is withdraw one's deposit if one loses trust in a bank. I remember a few years ago when that happened. The government had to step in to keep the banks from failing."

"Hmm, yes." Elizabeth's answer was vague. She supposed she remembered, although it wasn't the sort of news she paid a great deal of attention to.

The exhibit moved on to show historic inflation rates. Elizabeth noted that inflation was 40% in 1800. Although she understood little of it, she was certain that must have been alarmingly high and surely would have impacted Henry's banking business. It must have made everything very expensive for Jane, living on a small income and watching her shillings and pence so carefully.

The next case showed the coinage as it would have been in Jane Austen's Day. Well, that was how Elizabeth identified it, although the display label read George III. Farthing, halfpence, penny, twopence, all stamped with the king's rotund features.

It was all very interesting, but Elizabeth didn't feel she was learning anything that she could use in her article or could help her spot a possible scam behind Andrew's transaction. Although she did give careful attention to the display on forgery in the nineteenth century, accompanied by graphic Victorian drawings of forgers hanging on a gibbet, and an explanation of measures to protect against counterfeiting today, including printing the notes on polymer... Ah, there was the ten pound note with Jane Austen on it, ironically immortalizing the words of Caroline Bingley, one of Austen's most deceitful characters: "I declare after all there is no enjoyment like reading!" Elizabeth smiled and moved on, still pondering.

No, considering the modern precautions against counterfeiting, that was unlikely to play any part in Andrew's enterprise.

In the rotunda they found a temporary exhibit entitled "As safe as the Bank of England," chronicling economic disasters of the past. Elizabeth gave this careful attention. Might she find something of interest here? She started with the South Sea Bubble. In its early years the South Sea Company, named because of its monopoly on trade with South America, was competition to the Bank of England. In 1720 the company was so successful it took over part of the national debt. Its stock rose exponentially, and speculation led to the notorious bubble. George Frederick Handel was one such investor, but fortunately he withdrew before the bubble burst in 1729.

A considerable number of people were ruined by the share collapse, and the national economy was greatly reduced as a result. It was later discovered that the founders of the scheme had engaged in insider trading, using their advance knowledge of when national debt was to be consolidated to make large profits from purchasing debt in advance.

Elizabeth drew Richard's attention to the exhibit. "Insider trading—one hears a lot about that today. Could anything like that be going on with the sale of the Austen first editions?"

Richard furrowed his forehead. "Are you still on about that?" But he didn't dismiss her question. "You mean like Child and Asquith conniving over the valuation with Legacy House, so one of them will be able to buy the books at a bargain?"

"Well, something like that…" She had to admit it sounded unlikely.

Unformed ideas buzzing in her head, Elizabeth moved on, lecturing herself not to get carried away with unfounded conspiracy theories. She walked past a timeline of more recent economic shocks, many of them headlines that she vividly remembered: the .com boom of 2000, the global crisis of

2007...

Her face broke into a smile, and she gave a sigh, finding herself at last on familiar ground when she came to a corner dedicated to Kenneth Grahame. Toad and Mole sat in a boat reading *The Wind in the Willows*. The exhibit commemorated the fact that Grahame joined the bank as a junior clerk in 1878, becoming Secretary of the Bank at age thirty-nine— one of the youngest on record. He retired in 1908, the same year *Wind in the Willows* was published.

One final story, one from Jane Austen's day, brought them to the exit: "Was there really an Old Lady of Threadneedle Street?" Elizabeth paused before the account. "You used that term yesterday, Richard. Did you know this?"

Together they perused the display. Yes, there was, indeed, an old lady, and her name was Sarah Whitehead. Her brother, a bank employee, was found guilty of forgery—Elizabeth felt she was surrounded by stories of forgery. Sara's brother was executed in 1811. Sarah became so disturbed she visited the bank every day for twenty-five years, asking for her brother. When she died she was buried in the churchyard next door to the bank. Eventually the bank took over the property, and the churchyard became its garden. The ghost of Sarah Whitehead has reportedly appeared on many occasions.

With a final nod to a depiction of Britannia seated beside a lion—the traditional guardian of a treasure house—their tour was completed.

Elizabeth and Richard emerged from the relative quiet of the bank to the buzz of Saturday afternoon London traffic. Automobiles of all sizes and shapes, stately black cabs, red double-decker busses, cyclists and pedestrians created a ceaseless panorama of humanity in motion. Elizabeth could never get used to how crowded the pavements always were wherever she went in England—a major hazard for one who liked to follow her own thoughts and gaze at historic buildings rather than watch where she was walking.

She just managed to step aside in time to make way for a mother herding three small children toward the museum.

"Yes, you can lift the gold bar. If you're strong enough," the mother promised the oldest boy.

But Elizabeth was still thinking about the reports of the ghostly Sarah Whitehead. Was there a cautionary lesson there for her? Did people see what they wanted to see or expected to see? Was that what she was doing in seeing pitfalls everywhere for Andrew's endeavor?

"Sorry." She looked up just in time to sidestep a young man in jeans with a rucksack slung over one shoulder. Unfortunately, in dodging the man she stepped directly into the path of a group of young Oriental tourists busy snapping photos of everything around them. They scattered like a flock of birds.

"Careful." Richard smiled and took her arm. "How about rounding the tour off with lunch at the Old Bank of England pub?"

Elizabeth laughed. "Always thinking about your stomach."

"Of course. I'm not taking any chances. I made a whole list of eateries we need to hit while we're in London."

"Wonderful, lead me to it."

The twenty minute walk to Fleet Street was just right for ensuring hearty appetites, but, even without that, Elizabeth would have been enthusiastic when they walked up the flower-box lined steps and entered the gleaming interior of red walls, gold marble floors and dark wood furnishings, everything accented with polished brass. "This was a branch of the Bank of England, built in late Victorian times to serve the law courts," Richard explained.

And, indeed, the restoration had perfectly maintained the distinguished atmosphere of the bank, with windows draped in heavy brocade, scrollwork balcony rail lined with lamps, and gold marble pillars leading to a moulded ceiling. Elizabeth was well into her beef and mushroom pie when two men who had been dining in the gallery came down the iron-railed stairs. "Look. There's Bramwell Child." She prodded Richard. Child bore the benign, avuncular expression that seemed to be characteristic of him, but his companion's scowling, furrowed forehead, above heavy black eyebrows, looked anything but convivial.

At that moment, Child looked in their direction and waved. Elizabeth was surprised that, instead of continuing to the door, he turned to come to their table. "Dr. and Dr. Spencer, may I present Mr. Clive Kentworth who is handling the Austen books for Legacy House Auctions."

The dark-haired man acknowledged the introduction with a stiffly military nod.

"You must be delighted to represent such a remarkable property, Mr. Kentworth," Elizabeth said. "We were thrilled to get to see the books yesterday."

"Yes, I believe I may safely say it's one of the most outstanding properties our book and manuscript department has been privileged to offer." His words were confident, but his voice seemed to carry a question.

"We look forward to receiving your brother's bid for his publishing house," Child said. "I understand his expert authenticated the books."

"Not that there was any doubt, of course," Kentworth added, perhaps with a bit too much bravado.

Child filled in quickly. "It was a pleasure to see you again." He extended his hand to Richard. "We look forward to doing business with your brother."

Elizabeth nibbled a chip, musing on the dynamics between the two men as she watched them depart. "Isn't it amazing—a city the size of London, yet one can bump into someone one knows. I did that once in New York when I was there for a conference—stepped into a doorway to get out of the rain and ran into a former English professor of mine from college."

"Knowing you, I expect the 'running into' part was literal."

They were still teasing about running into people a short time later as they walked along Fleet Street toward the Aldwych bus stop. A few steps along Richard pointed to a fine, Georgian building, its tall, arched windows filled with planters over-flowing with pink petunias. "That's Child & Co., likely the oldest bank in London."

"Interesting. And Bramwell Child was having lunch only a few doors down."

"No reason why he shouldn't—" Richard began, then stopped abruptly when Child himself emerged from the bank with a deep scowl on his usually cheerful face and walked swiftly away from them up the street.

All the way back to their room in College Hall, Elizabeth kept telling herself there was absolutely nothing ominous about that. There was any number of reasons Child could have been there. She had herself almost convinced not to worry, when they got back to their room and found a message from Andrew. He was ready to place his bid. The money would be deposited with Chestermere Bank first thing Monday morning.

Now Elizabeth allowed herself to worry.

Chapter 7

THE NEXT MORNING ELIZABETH and Richard were crossing Russell Square on their way to collect Andrew for church when the bells began. Bells from a single church across the way rang out first, then it seemed that every other church within hearing chimed in, filling the air with their bright changes. "Oh, Richard! What could be lovelier on a Sunday morning?" Elizabeth held out her hands as if to catch the silver sound mingled with golden sunshine.

And bells were still ringing a short time later when they emerged from the Covent Garden tube station. "How wonderful! All we have to do is follow the sound of the bells." As near as they must be to St. Paul's, those had to be the bells of the church they were looking for. Elizabeth set off, following her ears, the brothers Spencer walking obediently behind. After a few minutes the bells stopped. She paused and looked around. It should only have been a few steps from the station to Covent Garden, but there was no sign of the broad piazza that was certain to be filled with buskers and sightseers even first thing on a Sunday morning. Then the bells started again, and she darted forward with a sense of rush. The insistence of the bells must mean the service was about to start.

Richard, who had taken out his map, caught her arm. "Wrong way." He turned her around.

The reason for the confusion soon became clear. No, she hadn't been following the bells of another church, but rather an echo of St. Paul's. As the bells pulled them forward across the broad courtyard, Elizabeth thought about misdirection. Was that what she was doing in worrying about the sale of the Austen first editions—following an echo? An echo of other times she and Richard had been involved in criminal plots that could have no bearing on the present situation? Or was someone purposefully directing people to look the wrong way?

"Here we are." Richard could be forgiven for sounding just the least bit smug.

Elizabeth looked at the massive stone-faced portico, its projecting pediment supported by a march of four monumental columns. She was taken with a desire to look around for Eliza Doolittle selling her flowers to the after-opera crowd sheltering from the rain in "My Fair Lady," but Richard ushered her on into the lovely, eighteenth century interior where ivory walls surrounded the dark oak pews. A red-carpeted aisle led to the altar, framed with a pediment and four columns echoing the exterior. At least, it looked lovely to Elizabeth, but she recalled reading that even its architect Inigo Jones, described it as a barn, although "the handsomest barn in London." The open sanctuary, with no rood screen separating people and clergy and no side chapels, was revolutionary in the eighteenth century. How would the very traditional Jane Austen have felt worshipping in such radical architecture?

Elizabeth herself settled in to worship and was quickly comfortable with the Prayer Book liturgy. The welcoming words of the sermon caught her attention: "God is bigger than we think. The church is about belonging to the human race—coming together—linked to each other and to all creation." The preacher expanded his theme that we need to recover our sense of awe and the wonder of creation through

the Sacrament, which is symbolic of something far, far greater. Then he ended expeditiously, "For now and always, even
to the end of time. Amen."

After the service the rector announced that, as yesterday
had been their annual strawberry festival, everyone was invited to partake of leftover strawberries and cream with tea
and cakes. While Richard and Andrew enjoyed their refresh-
ments, Elizabeth walked around, snapping a few pictures she
might use to accompany her article on Austen's London and
making note of the memorials. Because of its long association with the theatre community, St. Paul's was known as
"The Actor's Church," and each wooden panel of the back
wall, beneath the organ loft, was inscribed in gold leaf to
the memory of a great theatrical personage. Margaret Ruth-
erfurd, Dame May Witty, Sir Michael Redgrave ... Alan Jay
Lerner's bore the touching inscription: "One brief shining
moment."

Elizabeth had to clear her throat before she could respond to Drew's query about Jane Austen worshipping there.
"It isn't recorded for certain, but it's very likely since it's prac-
tically across the street from where she stayed with Henry.
Her only reference to it is in a letter to Cassandra where Jane
said she and Edward 'settled that you went to St. Paul's Covent Garden on Sunday.'

"I just reread those letters last night as prep for today's
visit. Since that letter was written to Cassandra when she was
staying with Henry in Henrietta Street, it seems safe to assume that was standard practice for the family.

"In another letter, Jane mentioned attending Belgrave
Chapel and possibly St. James Piccadilly when she was staying in Sloane Street, and later going to Belgrave Chapel when
Henry lived in Hans Place." She sighed. "The hints in the letters, and the questions they raise, are so frustratingly tantalizing."

His tea and cake finished, Richard joined them. "Where
to next?"

"Number 10 Henrietta Street. Finally, a place we know

in detail from her letters. We know Jane was actually there, what she did and what room she did it in, with whom, and what they ate." At Andrew's quizzical look, Elizabeth explained about the article she was writing for *Regency Realm* and her goal to give her readers a real sense of what Jane's times in London were like.

She led the way around to the back of the church, to a pleasant garden filled with roses and ornamental trees. Benches lining the broad path were filled with Londoners and tourists enjoying the Sunday afternoon sunshine.

A passage took them to Henrietta Street with Number 10 directly across from them, looking perhaps not drastically different from how it looked when Henry Austen established his bank offices there sometime between 1803 and 1804. The ground floor exterior was painted black, with three arched windows next to a bright yellow door, undoubtedly not Henry Austen's décor. But the three stories of white façade above that, each floor with three windows, decreasing in size and ornamentation as one looked upward, and the parapet rail edging the roof could easily have been there in Jane's day.

"So?" Andrew prompted, and Elizabeth gave him the highlights: Austen, Maunde and Tilson of Covent Garden flourished, and Henry and his wife Eliza moved from their crowded quarters in Brompton, where Jane had visited them once, to a grand home in Sloane Square. Jane knew the property well as a bank because she mentions calling for Henry in Henrietta Street frequently in her letters.

"Then tragedy struck in 1813, and Eliza died after a painful fight with breast cancer. Henry moved to the rooms above the bank," she pointed to the upper windows. "He stayed there for almost a year and a half before moving to more genteel quarters in Hans Place, near where he had lived in Sloane Square."

"Do we get a look-in?" Andrew asked.

Elizabeth shook her head. "I'm afraid that blue plaque between the first floor windows will have to satisfy us." She snapped a picture. "My trusty guide to Austen's London informs us that the interior was virtually stripped out when it served as a nurses' home in the 1950s."

"What a pity."

Elizabeth considered. "Perhaps, but maybe it's best to see it through Jane's words." She burrowed in the bag she always kept slung over her shoulder and disinterred her dog-eared edition of the letters. "When Jane first visited Henry here in April, shortly after he moved in, she wrote to Cassandra that it was 'all dust and confusion, but in a very promising way.' Henry would have only been in residence for a few weeks at best, so it could hardly have been anything but confusion—especially located as it was only a few steps from the bustling and raucous Covent Garden Market.

"The confusion likely didn't bother Henry much since he spent most of that summer traveling and visiting family—as Jane said, he didn't 'come to bide' there until that fall."

Elizabeth looked at her notes to be sure of the date before continuing, "Jane came back for a very comfortable visit in September with her brother Edward, his daughter Fanny and two of Fanny's sisters. Here, I have her words exactly, in a letter she wrote to Francis."

Her voice took on a precise, 'reading' tone. "'We were accommodated in Henrietta Street—Henry was so good as to find rooms for his three nieces and myself in his house. Edward slept at an hotel in the next street. No. 10 is made very comfortable with cleaning and painting and the Sloane Street furniture. The front room upstairs is an excellent dining and common sitting parlour—'" Elizabeth paused and pointed to the first floor windows, each provided with a classical entablature, then returned to her reading, "'and the smaller one behind will sufficiently answer his purpose as a drawing room. He has no intention of giving large parties of any kind. His plans are all for the comfort of his friends and himself.'"

Elizabeth turned a page in her notes, then noticed a young couple standing a few feet away, gazing at the same building. The woman turned to her. "Sorry. Is this a private tour? Only, it's so interesting. I'm afraid I'm a rather fanatic Janeite."

Elizabeth smiled. "No, no—not a tour. We're just tourists ourselves—of a sort. You're welcome to listen."

"Thank you." The woman grabbed her partner's arm and pulled him a step closer.

Elizabeth continued her reading, made only slightly self-conscious by the knowledge that she looked like a tour guide. "Jane wrote to her sister about that same visit, 'Here I am, my dearest Cassandra, seated in the Breakfast, Dining, sitting room, beginning with all my might. Fanny will join me as soon as she is dressed and begin her letter.'"

Elizabeth smiled at her enlarged audience. "I love that— such an intimate detail, and it shows what a major part of their lives letter writing was. And how thankful we are. We wouldn't have these wonderful glimpses of everyday Regency life without such detailed letters, which must have taken hours and hours to write."

After pausing a moment to gaze at the blank window, her imagination filling it with a lively scene behind, Elizabeth looked down again. "She goes on to record that Henry's cook/housekeeper Madame de Bigeon who had been Eliza's devoted servant, 'was below dressing us a most comfortable dinner of Soup, Fish, *Bouillee*, Partridges & an apple tart'— with all the ingredients probably freshly acquired from the market across the way— 'which we sat down to soon after five, after cleaning and dressing ourselves and feeling that we were most commodiously disposed of. The little adjoining dressing-room to our apartment,'" Elizabeth paused and pointed to the second floor windows, these with smaller, unbracketed cornices, "'makes Fanny and myself very well off indeed and as we have poor Eliza's bed our space is ample every way.'"

Elizabeth looked around, wondering if she should quit and allow her listeners to move on, but they appeared to be engrossed, so she continued. "Jane was writing that at half past eight in the morning. She planned to go shopping before breakfast—at nearby Layton & Shears—which she later reported that she did. They saw some very pretty English poplins and very beautiful, but expensive, Irish fabric. While she wrote that report to Cassandra, Fanny and her sisters went off to buy theatre tickets.

"At four o'clock Jane was writing again, after another round of shopping, 'We are just come back from doing Mrs. Tickars, Miss Hare, and Mr. Spence.' The hairdresser Mr. Hall was there 'and while Fanny is under his hands I will try to write a little more.'"

Elizabeth smiled. "One gets the impression that Jane was as addicted to incessant letter writing as people today are to texting. Here she says she ordered a gown to be trimmed with white ribbons and a white satin cap trimmed with lace 'and a little white flower perking out of the left ear.'"

Elizabeth scanned the rather detailed fashion news, aware that she was likely to bore her male listeners. "She reports that 'they trim with white very much.'"

She decided to spare her male companions the advice on stays gained at Mrs. Tickars. "It seems that Mr. Spence was a dentist, which was apparently a very painful visit for one of her young nieces."

Elizabeth was turning the page in her book when two middle-aged ladies approached them from the direction of Covent Garden. They paused a few paces back, looking from number 10 Henrietta Street to the speaker and back again, as if wondering whether or not to approach the group.

The young woman who had inserted herself and her companion into the assemblage earlier spoke to the newcomers. "Are you interested in Jane Austen? It's all right, this lady knows everything."

"Oh, that's very kind. If you're certain." The women approached hesitantly.

Elizabeth felt herself blush, but offered a smile. "Jane is reporting to her sister about a hairdresser who attended her nieces when they visited their uncle Henry Austen at the time he was living above his bank." Elizabeth hoped that was enough to bring the newcomers up to speed. They nodded, so she continued. "Jane had her turn at the hands of the hairdresser who 'curled me out at a great rate.' Jane thought she looked hideous and longed for a cap, but her nieces silenced her by their admiration. All that was preparation for the Covent Garden theatre that night, where they had 'good places in the box next the stage box.' They saw 'Clandestine Marriage' and 'Midas.' Which Jane later reported very much delighted her nieces, but she preferred 'Don Juan' which they had seen the night before because, 'I have seen nobody on the stage who has been a more interesting character than that compound of cruelty and lust.'

"The next morning she was up and dressed, downstairs and writing again at half past seven, so she could set off for shopping at Grafton House at nine to 'get that over before breakfast.' Apparently they didn't breakfast until mid-morning. Anyway, Jane liked to shop early because they got immediate attendance. She reported a very successful shopping trip and after dinner 'We are now all four of us young ladies sitting around the circular table in the inner room writing our letters, while the two brothers are having a comfortable coze in the room adjoining.'"

Andrew laughed and shook his head. "Imagine such bustle going on behind those very restrained windows."

One of the newly arrived ladies replied. "How wonderful to be able to stand here and picture it all in our minds. Thank you so much."

Elizabeth smiled. "You're very welcome. Thank you for being such good listeners." To her relief, they all expressed their thanks and moved off. She returned her book to her bag.

Richard looked at his watch. "How about joining us for lunch, Drew?"

Andrew looked down and shuffled his feet. "Er—thanks, but I've got other plans. Matter of fact, I need to be getting back rather sharpish."

Richard gave his brother a quizzical look, but didn't probe further.

"It's, um, business."

Later, when Elizabeth and Richard were enjoying their own Sunday dinner of traditional roast beef with Yorkshire pudding, roast potatoes and veg at Brown's, Elizabeth returned to the puzzling incident. "What do you suppose Andrew's business appointment was? On a Sunday afternoon?"

Richard shook his head. "That was odd. He seemed so nervous. Besides, I thought his business was already settled—signed, sealed and ready to be delivered."

"Could it be something about his bid? He doesn't need to be convincing stockholders or raising money or anything like that, does he?"

"He's left it rather late if he does. I don't think I've seen my little brother blush since he was a teenager."

Elizabeth groaned inwardly. Something else for her to worry about. And to think that before all this came up, if anyone had asked her she would have declared that she wasn't a worrier. Oh well, tomorrow the Queens of Crime course began, and she would get down to serious research. That would be more than enough to take her mind off imaginary troubles.

Chapter 8

RICHARD GAZED UP AT the gleaming, white stone tower of the University of London's Senate House. Its clean, art deco lines made it seem like a little brother to the Empire State Building or Rockefeller Plaza which were built at about the same time. Indeed, he had read that the university structure had been built with a donation from the Rockefeller Foundation. Richard had read some of the history of the building and learned that the university's chancellor in charge of selecting the architect for the building had declared that it was to be: "a great architectural feature ... an academic island in swirling tide of traffic, a world of learning in a world of affairs." It must "not look like an imitation of any other Universities, it must not be a replica from the Middle Ages." Clearly, the chancellor had succeeded with his vision.

"I'm really looking forward to your lecture." Elizabeth took his arm as they entered the building. Inside the double doors they came to a stop, gazing at the pristine pale marble hall with its ceiling rising high over their head. Art nouveau *torchère* lamps bracketed the walls, and ahead of them a wide, sleek staircase, with a black runner accenting the pearly alabaster of the marble, marched upward to the balcony running around three sides of the hall.

Richard and Elizabeth ascended the grand stairway to the room where welcoming tea and biscuits were being served. After a quick refreshing they went into the lecture hall for the opening session. The organizers of the course welcomed their group of international students, introduced the lecturers and gave a brief overview of the structure for the three weeks, explaining how the days would alternate between lectures and reading and writing in the Senate House Library. Then everyone was dismissed to their first class. Those sitting in the back of the hall were almost to the door when the sound of a jackhammer made Richard look around to see if the marble floor was being dismantled beneath his feet.

"Don't be alarmed." The director returned to the microphone and held up a hand. "The north block of this building is being completely redeveloped. It will be a wonderful addition to the university's facilities, with lecture theatres, office spaces and the courtyard designed for student use. Until then, however, I'm afraid we'll just have to put up with the noise." With that assurance everyone continued toward their chosen classrooms.

Richard gulped when he saw that, although those attending the course were offered a choice of four lectures, more than a quarter of the students were following him down the marble hall to the imposing wood-panelled room that was to be his lair for the coming weeks. It rather felt like an English court of law and, as he observed the eager students filing into the elevated rows of seats before him, he had an inkling what a witness must feel in a legal proceeding. Especially when his eyes met those of Babs Ellington and she waved a copy of his book as a greeting.

Jeremy Turner, his movements made slow and awkward by crutches and a heavy cast, was the last to enter. Elizabeth motioned for him to take the empty seat by her near the door. Richard cleared his throat as he looked at the avid faces and poised pens. "Right. Good morning. And welcome." He gave a brief overview of what he planned to cover in their three weeks together before launching into the day's lecture. "Jane Austen shows up everywhere these days, but a Queens of Crime course might not be the first place you would expect to find her."

Richard was amused to see that the three girls from Japan on the front row wrote down even his mild opening remarks. "This week we will be analyzing *Emma*, which many believe to be Austen's finest novel. Certainly unimpeachable as a comedy of manners, but does it deserve a place in the history of mystery novels a generation before Wilkie Collins' *Woman in White*, which is widely considered to be the first mystery novel?

"I would contend that, indeed, this is the case and would cite no less an authority than that Queen of Crime P. D. James, whom we will be studying later in our course. James says that, at its heart, a mystery novel 'is a puzzle. It does not require murder. What it does require is a mystery, facts which are hidden from the reader but which he or she should be able to discover by logical deduction from clues inserted in the novel with deceptive cunning but essential fairness.'" He paused for his intrepid note-takers to catch up, the scratching of pens and rustling of paper drowned by the sounds of construction, seemingly just on the other side of the wall.

"It's all about misdirection and cover-up. Frank Churchill and Jane Fairfax couldn't have been more sly if covering up a dead body—but in their day a secret engagement was almost as bad. And, importantly, all this in the closed society beloved of the classic Golden Age mystery writers."

"So this week as you re-read *Emma* through the particular lens of a fan of crime fiction—which I assume you all are or you wouldn't have chosen to take this course—I want you to look for the elements necessary to a good murder mystery: A strong story question with the answer hidden in red herrings, carefully planted clues, foreshadowings and misdirections; characters perfectly suited to the genre—a confident heroine who tells all exactly as she sees it, and an anti-hero perfectly situated to be a successful villain with motive, opportunity and means to commit mayhem."

Again Richard paused, worried that he was going too far too fast. This was not an upper division university course as he might be accustomed to teaching at home. From the looks on some of the faces before him, he feared that for many this might not be a case of re-reading the novel, but rather, their first time coming to it. Apart from the movies and television adaptations they were certain all to have seen, of course.

He considered. Was he asking too much of them? Should he back off? Water down the lesson? Then he looked at Jeremy, a university student who had made the effort to get there on a broken ankle. No, he would do his best to give the serious students their money's worth. The tourists were most welcome, but they would have to swim at their own level.

He gave a nod and plunged. "Today we are going to look at one of the hallmarks of Austen's style and one of the surest examples of her genius—her use of Free Indirect Speech. Jane Austen and the German writer Goethe are literature's first practitioners of this technique, which means it arose from Austen's own genius. She didn't have any college course or handbook on writing to tell her how to do this."

Perhaps half the pens in the room stilled, while the faces above them stared at Richard with blank looks.

He smiled and dictated slowly as the pens began moving again. "Free Indirect Speech is third-person narration that gives us the essence of first person direct speech. We get a character's exact words without such introductory phrases as 'she said' or 'he thought' because it is being heard in the mind of the narrator—filtered through his or her consciousness.

"You can see how this is such a useful technique when developing a mystery, because it allows the author to plant clues and explain motives in the context of the characters' thoughts. Austen takes us directly into the minds of her characters—in this case Emma Woodhouse.

"The fact that most of the novel is written from Emma's viewpoint—and that she is wrong about almost everything she views—gives the novel the ironic humor that we love. It's also what requires sharp detective skills on the part of the reader. Because Emma is that most fiendish of devices—an unreliable narrator."

They spent the rest of the hour finding examples of Free Indirect Speech in the novel, and Richard was certain his students were as relieved to be set free as he was to set them free, when he dismissed them with the assignment to return on Wednesday prepared to define the story question—the central mystery—in *Emma*.

Babs approached him before he had his papers gathered. "Oh, that was just great! I only understood about half of it, but that's okay. After all, we're here to learn. I can't wait to get started reading. Of course, I absolutely love the movies. Gwyneth Paltrow is just so cute. Don't you think she's an absolutely wonderful Emma?"

Without waiting for an answer, Babs turned to summon Jeremy, who was maneuvering out of his seat with a book bag slung over his shoulder to free his hands for his crutches. "Jeremy, I'm so glad to see you here! How are you? I can't believe how painful that must be."

"Mostly just awkward—" Jeremy tried to reply, but Babs wasn't listening.

"And your head." She raised her hand as if to touch the white bandage above his left eyebrow. "Ooooh, I'll never forget the sight of all that blood. Are you sure you should be up and around? Here, let me carry that for you." She reached for his book bag.

Jeremy pulled away quicker than one would expect of a man on crutches. "No, no. Thank you, but I'm fine."

Jeremy clumped his way to the lectern. Richard looked up from gathering his notes, expecting a query about the day's lecture, but instead, Jeremy wanted to know about the Austen first editions. "Did you learn anything unexpected?"

"We learned lot about analyzing old documents, but I'm not sure you'd call that surprising. One thing I noted, though ..." and he told him about the misprint in the catchwords.

Before Jeremy could ask more, Elizabeth joined the group

in front of the lecture desk, and Babs pounced on her. "Oh, wasn't that simply wonderful? You must be so proud of your husband." Her pause allowed for no more than a quick nod from Elizabeth. "Well, isn't this nice? I feel like I have friends here already. Let's all go to lunch together, shall we? I noticed a little Italian place—"

It was obvious there would be no escaping. Richard took Elizabeth's arm and moved toward the hall. A burst of noise from the construction outside made him lean closer to hear Elizabeth. "I got a text from Drew. He said he'll meet us by the back door. I think he has news."

"I expect he wants to tell us about placing his bid." In deference to Jeremy who was following behind, nodding at Babs' chatter, Richard turned to the elevator.

They were barely out the door when Richard saw his brother walking across the car park. Richard blinked. He hadn't realized that his little brother had become so distinguished-looking. His open-collared, grey silk shirt perfectly set off the grey hair at his temples and his silvery glasses. Richard waved. Then saw that Andrew wasn't alone.

Sara Ashley-Herbert walked beside him in a soft, blue dress that swirled around her legs at every step. A bracelet of silver beads caught the sun as she raised her hand to brush Drew's arm. The sight made Richard realize just who Drew's "business appointment" had been with yesterday. And why he blushed. Andrew and Caroline's marriage had been rocky for at least ten years, but there had been no divorce. Was his brother falling for his new acquaintance while still a married man?

"Hi, glad this worked out. I'm taking Sara to lunch to celebrate finalizing Caudex's bid, and we thought we should make a party of it."

To Richard's relief, the clatter of construction on the roof of north block to their right delayed his reply. Richard was torn. Would it be better to accept or to make an excuse and send them off by themselves? After all Drew was a mature adult. Richard could hardly tell him how to run his life. Before he could answer, though, the others arrived, and the effervescent Babs took over.

"Oh, Ms. Ashley-Herbert, you should have been here this morning! Dr. Spencer gave the most brilliant lecture!" She launched into details of Richard's class.

"Isn't that right, Jeremy?" Babs appealed to the young man behind her, and the talk became general for a moment, with Babs doing most of the talking.

Only when Sara left the circle and started walking toward the figure standing beside the north block did Richard realize a newcomer was about to join them. He looked instantly familiar, but it took Richard a moment to identify the bushy, black hair and eyebrows and the stiff bearing. Clive Kentworth. Had Drew invited the Legacy House representative to join them, too?

Kentworth raised his hand to greet Sara, when Babs Ellington swooped to retrieve a shiny object on the pavement. "Ms. Ashley-Herbert! Sara!" Babs waved the object aloft and started forward. "Your bracelet. You dropped—"

A grating of metal on stone followed by the sharp crack of shattering masonry overhead made Richard look up, just in time to see a large, blue bin break through the barrier edging the roof and hurtle toward the ground.

Richard stood transfixed as rock, mortar and rubble sprayed out as if spewed from a volcano, with the rectangular blue meteoroid in the center.

Richard's own cries were lost in the general mayhem as the dumpster crashed to the pavement, spilling building debris in every direction.

A shriek made him rush to Babs' side, but he quickly saw that the graze on her cheek was only superficial. Then he realized that the cry had not come from Babs, but rather from Sara.

He leapt over the scattered broken stones, wood scraps and roofing tiles. "Sara, are you hurt?"

She was shaking so hard she couldn't answer. Just before Andrew reached her and engulfed her in his arms Sara managed to point.

Richard saw. Legs protruded from below the skip.

Chapter 9

"THAT COULD HAVE BEEN me!" Sara's words were barely distinguishable, muffled by Drew's shoulder.

He attempted to calm her sobs with murmurs in her ear, but her hysterical cry continued. "I was there seconds ago. Just seconds. I was there." A shiver seized her body so violently it stifled her sobs.

For the second time in as many days Elizabeth punched 999 on her cell phone. The next minutes—or hours—were a blur. She was aware of Richard pulling her aside and leading her to a stone bench. Someone from the Senate House—or was it someone from the emergency services?—put a cup of hot, sweet tea in her hands. She shook so hard she slopped the tea into her lap. Someone wrapped a blanket around her shoulders. A policeman took statements from each person who, a short time ago, had been standing in the sunshine on a June afternoon, discussing Jane Austen and where to go to lunch.

Was it possible for disaster to fall from the sky in the midst of such civility?

Elizabeth could only shake her head at the officer's questions. Richard's class. Drew's text. Drew brought Sara. She had seen that fact worried Richard. Babs joined them with her incessant chatter. And Jeremy. She remembered worrying about making him stand about on his crutches. Then that man came. What was his name? She couldn't think. But she was certain she had seen him before. Then Babs dashed forward waving Sara's bracelet like a trophy. Sara turned back.

Then … Elizabeth spread her hands and shook her head. She could see it all in her head. Over and over like a video loop. But she couldn't put it into words.

As if from a great distance she heard Richard give the policeman their room number in College Hall. She felt Richard's arms lift her to her feet and propel her steps forward.

When they got back to their room she discovered that Drew and Sara had followed them. "I'll put the kettle on." That was Sara's voice. How odd. She was the one that had escaped death by a few inches, yet she was much calmer now than Elizabeth who had only watched the whole thing.

"I'm cold," was all she could say. Richard led her to the bed and wrapped her in the duvet.

When Elizabeth was warm, she felt as if she could breathe again. "Who was that poor man?" How odd, her mind had taken a snapshot of the scene. The sun gleaming off the toe of his London tan oxford. An odd choice to wear with grey trousers, surely. Or was it dust from the debris that made his legs look grey? What difference could it possibly make? And yet, the question ran around and around in her mind.

"Clive Kentworth." It was Andrew who spoke.

She frowned. The name seemed familiar.

"With Legacy House Auctions. He was handling the Austen first editions."

Yes. Elizabeth remembered now. Bramwell Child had introduced him to them when they met in that pub. Funny how something that seemed of such all-encompassing importance as the auction of the Austen first editions could mean nothing in the face of instant death.

"What was he doing at the Senate House?" Richard asked.

"I talked to him on the telephone this morning about

a manuscript Legacy House was handling." Sara shook her head. "Just informal, not a real consultation, but I used to do that sort of thing before I went to Hatchard's. I had known him a bit then. We were colleagues. Almost friends." Her brittle composure cracked and a sob escaped.

After a deep drink from her teacup she continued. "I suppose he had another question he wanted to ask me." She shook her head. "We'll never know."

"How did he know where to find you?" Drew asked.

Again, she shook her head. "I have no idea." She drew a wavery breath after a long pause. "I wish I knew. It would make it all seem less—" She sought for the word. "Random. It would seem less random."

Elizabeth pulled the duvet tighter under her chin. She agreed. That was a big part of the awfulness of it all. That death could be so capricious. She believed in order in the universe. But something so senseless struck at the very heart of her belief system.

Except for a dull ache at the back of her eyes that made her want to put sunglasses on even in a north-facing room, Elizabeth felt much better the next morning. "Did you sleep, my love?" Richard bent over to kiss her.

"Yes, I did. I didn't think I'd sleep a wink, but I did. I don't even remember Drew and Sara leaving."

"You haven't eaten anything since breakfast yesterday. Can you face the dining hall, do you think?"

"Actually, that sounds good. Toast and bacon, for some reason."

"Comfort food." Richard nodded.

A short time later, licking the butter and bacon grease off her fingers, Elizabeth asked, "Have you heard from Andrew today?"

"He rang before you woke up. I know it's crass to be thinking about business at a time like this, but he said Legacy House had contacted everyone who had expressed an interest in placing a bid to assure them that the auction would go ahead as announced. They are assigning a new person to handle it."

"Yes. I suppose there's no reason not to. How many bidders are there?"

Richard finished his bite of egg. "I don't think anyone knows. Client confidentiality, I suppose."

Elizabeth shook her head. "Well, I'll have to admit I hope Caudex doesn't win. I wish Andrew had never got mixed up in this."

"Yes, I do, too."

Elizabeth looked at him in surprise. "Really?"

"Yes, but it's not what you're thinking. I'm afraid he's falling for Sara Ashley-Herbert."

"Well, she is quite lovely."

"But he's a married man."

"Technically, yes. I suppose he has trouble thinking of himself in those terms. It's been so long since Caroline left." The silence seemed to indicate that there was no more to be said on the topic.

"What do you want to do today? Do you feel like working?" Richard broke the silence.

"Of course. After all, we didn't know him. It was just such an awful shock." And yet a man had died before her very eyes. Was it right just to go about one's schedule? A vital human being—in shoes that didn't match his suit—catapulted into eternity in the space of a heartbeat. She gave herself a shake. "Yes, I need to get on with finding the places Jane stayed in London. I thought Cork Street and maybe Sloane Street today. I'm not sure how much I can cover in one day. Are you free to go with me?"

"Yes, I only lecture Mondays, Wednesdays and Fridays. I gave my class more than enough to keep them busy at the library today."

Less than half an hour of walking and a bus ride took them to Cork Street in the heart of Mayfair. Elizabeth stood to the side of the pavement with her back to a wall, looking up and down the busy street lined with shiny, new buildings, a majority of them sporting signs of restrained good taste identifying various modern art galleries. "Jane stayed here?" Richard asked.

"Well, somewhere in Cork Street. We aren't sure exactly where. There was a well-known hotel here called The Bristol, so that's a likely guess. In the Regency this was the heart of the tailoring trade. Schweitzer and Davidson, Beau Brummel's tailor, was in Cork Street."

Elizabeth consulted her notes to be able to answer Richard's question better. "Jane was just twenty when she visited here in August of 1796 with her brothers Edward and Frank. It was probably her second visit to London, although likely her first as an adult. She wrote to Cassandra, 'Here I am once more in this Scene of Dissipation & vice, and I begin already to find my Morals corrupted.' Apparently the corrupting element was to be a visit to Astley's Circus that evening.

"The thing that makes the Cork Street visit so endlessly interesting is the possible connection with Jane's brief romance with Tom Lefroy. Tom's uncle Benjamin Langlois—the uncle for whom he was named and who apparently controlled the purse strings in the family—was believed to have lived nearby. The idea that Jane's brothers accompanied her to London for the purpose of her being vetted by the head of the Lefroy family—and of being subsequently turned down for having too little dowry—can't be substantiated, but Jon Spence makes an interesting case for it in his book *Becoming Jane*."

"Do you have a theory on the subject of Jane's romance?"

Elizabeth was more than happy to hold forth on the subject, but, before she could answer Richard's question, he held up a hand. "Wait. This is a topic that calls for an elegant accompaniment." He thought for a moment. Elizabeth had mentioned a desire to have tea at the Ritz, but he hadn't booked that yet. "How about some macaroons from Ladurée in the Burlington Arcade?"

A few minutes later they were walking into a golden cave, the walls, ceiling and arches around the displays all covered in crinkled gold foil. Elizabeth looked at the assortment of delicate macaroons in the display case before them. She pointed to the ones she wanted—well, she wanted one of each, but that was hardly realistic. Richard added his order and paid the attendant.

They took their purchases to a tiny, round table near the window. "Jane would have loved this. It's just the sort of place Eliza would have brought her." Elizabeth referred to Henry's wife whose first husband, the Comte de Feuillide, was executed in the French Revolution.

"If it had existed then."

Elizabeth smiled. "I said sort of place. Actually, there were similar shops." She paused to consult her guidebook. "It's likely that Eliza ordered from Parmentier's, confectioner to high society and royalty, which wasn't too far from here. They even sold macaroons."

"Then you should take a picture of your macaroons for your article."

Elizabeth obediently pulled out her phone and snapped. "Now, about Jane and Tom Lefroy. I suppose it could be significant that the first of Jane's letters Cassandra saved were ones about Tom Lefroy. It was January of 1796, just nine months before her visit to Cork Street. Jane was home at Steventon, Cassandra at the home of her fiancé Thomas Fowle." Elizabeth lowered her notes. "But then, I suppose that might have been the reason for keeping the letter. Every memento of him must have been precious to Cassandra after he died on the voyage he undertook to get enough money so they could get married."

Elizabeth paused, pondering that melancholy event before moving on to her chocolate macaroon. "Whatever the reason, thank goodness Cassandra kept those letters." She returned to her notes. "Jane begins by telling her sister that the day before was Mr. Tom Lefroy's birthday—just one day before Cassandra's, although Lefroy was three years older.

"After that 'necessary preamble' she says that they had 'an exceeding good ball last night.' Jane gently mocked one couple, however, because 'they do not know how to be particular.'" Elizabeth's voice took on a note of irony undoubtedly reflecting Jane's tone perfectly.

"'I flatter myself, however, that they will profit by the three successive lessons which I have given them. You scold me so much in the nice long letter which I have this moment received from you, that I am almost afraid to tell you how my Irish friend and I behaved. Imagine to yourself everything most profligate and shocking in the way of dancing and sitting down together. I can expose myself, however, only once more, because he leaves the country soon after next Friday, on which day we are to have a dance at Ashe after all.'"

Elizabeth held the book out to Richard so he could see the text. "Interesting, the words she underlines. Hearing her inflections would be such a help in interpreting her meaning."

After a moment she pulled the book back and continued reading. "'He is a very gentlemanlike, good-looking, pleasant young man, I assure you. But as to our having ever met, except at the three last balls, I cannot say much; for he is so excessively laughed at about me at Ashe, that he is ashamed of coming to Steventon, and ran away when we called on Mrs. Lefroy a few days ago.'"

Richard nodded. "'Gentlemanlike, good-looking, pleasant.' Which you'll note she does not underline. Tom LeFroy must have made a perfect candidate for a flirtation, but it hardly sounds as if she were head-over-heels in love."

"I agree. Jane was wrong about not seeing him at Steventon, however. Later in the letter she writes: 'After I had written the above, we received a visit from Mr. Tom Lefroy and his cousin George. The latter is really well-behaved now; and as for the other, he has but one fault, which time will, I trust, entirely remove— it is that his morning coat is a great deal too light. He is a very great admirer of Tom Jones, and therefore wears the same coloured clothes, I imagine.'"

Richard smiled. "That makes me think of the speculation about Tom Lefroy serving as a model for Mr. Darcy—could this visit have served as a model for Colonel Fitzwilliam and Darcy's call on Elizabeth at the Collins' home?"

Elizabeth nodded. "Very possible. I was thinking more about that coat, though. It really does seem to have offended her sense of style because four days later she wrote that she was looking forward with great impatience to the ball because, 'I rather expect to receive an offer from my friend in the course of the evening. I shall refuse him, however, unless he promises to give away his white Coat.'"

Richard wrinkled his brow in thought. "The trouble is that, with Jane, it's impossible to tell how much might be serious under the ironic joking."

"Absolutely. And it gets worse." Elizabeth turned a page in her notes. "Later in the same letter she said she was giving up all her other admirers. 'I mean to confine myself in future to Mr. Tom Lefroy, for whom I donot care sixpence.'"

"Does the lady too much protest?"

"Aye, that's the question. There's no telling. Certainly, Jane wasn't telling. The next day she wrote, 'At length the Day is come on which I am to flirt my last with Tom Lefroy, & when you receive this it will be over— — my tears flow as I write, at the melancholy idea.'

"Cassandra would have known how to separate the joke from the truth, but I can't help thinking those letters likely would not have survived Cassandra's fiery editing had she thought her sister truly heart-broken." Elizabeth shook her head, not for the first time, at the loss of the letters Cassandra had burned.

"And years later, when James Austen-Leigh was writing his *Memoir*, his sister wrote to him, 'I think I need not warn you against raking up that old story of the still living Chief Justice. That there was something in it, is true—but nothing out of the common way (as I believe). Nothing to call ill usage, and no very serious sorrow endured.'"

"And that's the last we hear?"

"Not quite. Tom Lefroy went back to Ireland to practice law, married an heiress and had a large family. Eventually he became Chief Justice of Ireland—President of their Supreme Court. When he heard of Jane's death, Tom Lefroy travelled from Ireland to England to pay his respects to the dancing partner of his youth who had become a noted author.

"In addition, at an auction of the publisher Cadell's papers, a Tom Lefroy bought Cadell's rejection letter for an early version of *Pride and Prejudice*—which adds fuel to the fire of the idea that Tom Lefroy was the model for Mr. Darcy. The cautionary note, however, is that we don't know for sure that it's the same Tom Lefroy.

"And one final, rather poignant note. When he was ninety years old Lefroy was questioned by his nephew, and he admitted 'that he was in love with her, although he qualified his confession by saying it was a boyish love.'"

Richard shook his head as he chewed thoughtfully on his last macaroon—this one lemon. "It's rather frightening. Just think, if those who suppose the affair of the heart got so far as Jane journeying to Cork Street to be interviewed by the head of the family are correct—what if Uncle Langlois had said yes, and Jane Austen had gone off to Ireland to become the wife of the Chief Justice? Would we ever have heard of her? What would life be like without Jane Austen?"

As unanswerable as that question was, Elizabeth was about to attempt a response when Richard's phone rang. He stepped out into the arcade, rather than answer in the tiny, gilded shop.

When he returned a few minutes later Elizabeth gasped at his serious countenance. "Richard, what is it?"

"That was Andrew calling from the hotel. The police have been round to question him again. Apparently they believe Clive Kentworth was murdered."

Chapter 10

"MURDERED?" ELIZABETH CLAPPED HER hand over her mouth and looked around. The refined elegance of Ladurée was no place to be discussing such a sordid subject. She abandoned the unfinished bite of macaroon on her plate, left the arcade and headed for the bus stop. Even with the security of Richard beside her she kept looking over her shoulder. Surely Richard had heard wrong. Or Andrew had mistaken the police. How could it be possible? A terrible mishap was bad enough to cope with, but an intentional killing was impossible.

Finally in the sanctuary of their room she pulled her duvet around her for comfort. "That can't be." She shook her head stubbornly. "I saw it happen. I keep seeing it happen. Over and over. Every time I close my eyes. I couldn't believe how much willpower it took me this morning just to walk down the sidewalk beside a tall building without constantly looking up."

"Elizabeth, why didn't you say?"

"No, I'll get over it. Sorry, that's not the point. My point is that it had to be an accident. The workmen have been up there for weeks. Surely it's standard practice. They have to do something with the rubble. They would put it in a bin. Those things have wheels on them. The builder was moving it, and it got away from him. It has to be."

She closed her eyes. Now it was an advantage to be able to see it all replay. "I looked up—after ... I can still see the row of white hard hats leaning over the side. Those men were yelling and gesturing. I'm sure they were as horrified as we were on the ground. Why don't the police ask them?"

"Well, that's the thing." Richard sat on the bed next to her. "They can't seem to locate the workman who was moving the skip."

Elizabeth frowned. "What do you mean?"

"Exactly that. Apparently they have questioned every man the company had on the roof at that time. The construction company seems to keep very precise records. Anyway, everyone is accounted for and no one admits to being near the bin. They were taking off for their lunch hour, so headed for the stairs until they heard the commotion. When everyone ran back they saw the gaping hole in the barrier and spotted the shambles below."

"Maybe it was someone from city sanitation or whoever collects the rubbish?"

Richard shook his head. "No, apparently Andrew suggested that to the police. There was no work order for the dumpster to be collected. No reason to be moving it."

Elizabeth thought through the scene again. "So the police believe someone dressed like a construction worker snuck onto the roof when everyone was looking the other way, pushed the dumpster over the edge, then left with the others without being noticed?"

"That's about it."

"But is that possible?" She considered her own question. The matter of timing. And knowing Kentworth would be there at that time ... Still, that didn't answer the more pertinent question. "But why?"

Richard just shook his head again.

Elizabeth's mind buzzed with questions: What kind of

madman would do such a thing? Someone who wanted to stop the redevelopment program? Had there been any protests? A disgruntled student—someone with a grudge against the university?

And Clive Kentworth—it had to be incalculable fate that he should stand at that spot at that moment. Could the phrase 'death by misadventure' ever have been more apropos? Manslaughter, maybe. But not murder. Before she could voice any of that, there was a knock at their door.

Richard opened the door to a haggard-looking Andrew who slumped into a chair by the desk. "How did I ever get tangled up in such a mess? This was supposed to be a fun holiday—merrie olde England and all that. Visit Shakespeare's and Dickens' homes—that sort of thing.

"Instead I've been grilled by a detective who all but accused me of murder."

"You?" Elizabeth was thunderstruck. "Why on earth would they think that?"

"It seems that someone giving the name Andrew Spencer rang Kentworth's office and left a message for Kentworth to meet him at the Malet Street entrance to the Senate House at half twelve."

Elizabeth sank back into her corner. So it must have been set up. Unless some secretary made a dreadful mistake, someone had arranged for Kentworth to be at that place at that time. But certainly not Andrew. "Did you mention that an American would have said twelve-thirty, not half twelve? That should prove it wasn't you."

"I didn't think. I will certainly point that out if they show up again." Andrew shook his head. "I wish I'd never got mixed up in the whole thing. As soon as the police left I decided I'd had enough, so I went to the bank to withdraw my bid. Now Bramwell Child informs me that the small print on the agreement I signed states that the bid is irrevocable. I'll just have to wait it out and hope I don't win."

Elizabeth struggled to sort it all out. "So someone— whom they believe was Andrew—left a fake message for

Kentworth. Then, what? The villain rushed up to the roof of the Senate House and pushed a bin off on Kentworth's head?" The implausibility was evident in the question itself.

"Do they really think you would have been stupid enough to give your own name if you were planning to kill someone?" She looked from Andrew to Richard. "Besides, Andrew was on the ground with us." Then back to Drew. "Surely you told them that?"

"They know I didn't push the bin. They figure I sent a signal on my phone to an accomplice. At least, that must be what they are thinking because they took my phone, too."

Richard nodded slowly. "Yes, if it is murder, there has to have been more than one person. You would need someone on the ground giving instructions to an accomplice on the roof—maybe to one of the workers who denies it?" Richard shook his head. "It still sounds far-fetched."

Andrew sat up a bit straighter in his chair. "Unlikely, I agree. But the thing is, it's happened before."

"What?" Elizabeth and Richard spoke at the same time.

"That seems to be one of the things that concerns the police—the unlikelihood of lightning striking twice in one place, so to speak. The detective who questioned me this morning told me that in 1936, when the Senate House tower was being built, a group of University officials, led by the Principal, Sir Edwin Deller, went out to inspect the work in progress. Suddenly, without any warning, a skip being pushed by a workman overhead accidentally fell down and hit them. All the dignitaries were rushed to University College Hospital. Two days later, Deller died of his injuries."

"How horrible!" Now the scene played in Elizabeth's mind, but with the bin crashing down where they were standing by the Senate House. "But that wasn't murder?"

"No, although the building of the tower had stirred up controversy within the university. I suppose the police are thinking of the possibility of a copycat," Andrew said.

"Sounds like a lot of work just to reconstruct history," Richard said.

"Okay, improbability aside, consider for a minute—why might someone want to kill Kentworth?" Elizabeth asked.

"He ran off with someone's wife? Or their inheritance? He got in someone's way? He knew something he shouldn't? He was a spy?" Andrew threw up his hands. "Silly speculation. We don't know a thing about the man."

"No, we don't," Richard agreed. "But someone will, and I'm sure the police will find out."

"There's one thing that worries me more," Andrew said. "If it was intentional, can we be certain Clive Kentworth was the intended victim?"

"If not, who else?" Elizabeth hoped he wasn't going to say it could be one of them.

"Sara. If Babs hadn't shouted at her at that exact moment, Sara would have been under the bin."

"With Kentworth. A double killing?" Elizabeth shivered at the idea of the scene getting even bloodier.

"Maybe not. He could have jumped back if he hadn't been distracted by Babs."

"You aren't saying you think Clive Kentworth was the murderer himself?" Richard asked.

"Of course I don't think it. But if we're going to believe six impossible things before breakfast this might as well be on the list."

Elizabeth thought. "Hm. Well, they had talked earlier in the morning. He might have known where she was going. But the idea of him having a henchman standing by waiting for an opportune moment ... Why not just make an appointment on some excuse and push her off a balcony or something? I mean, there have to be so many easier ways." She paused. "And we have the same problem—why should he want to kill her? Have you talked to her this morning?"

"Yes, I rang her—before the police took my phone. She said the police had talked to her again, but she didn't seem the least bit worried. She was going to work." He looked at Richard. "It seems her intern needed to spend the day working on a tough assignment some lecturer gave him, so she needed to set up their next event herself."

"It wasn't all that onerous," Richard said. "But did you ask her about her relationship with Kentworth?"

"I did a little, but I didn't want to say anything to worry her. It was bad enough for her, thinking she could have been an accidental victim. She said what she had already told us—she had known him a little when she worked for a rare book dealer in Charing Cross a few years ago. She had the idea he was a good family man—with two children, she thought. Always a perfect gentleman, she said.

"Then he called her a couple of days ago about the sale of a medieval manuscript in her field of expertise—Legacy House was going to be handling it." He paused. "It hardly sounds like any reason he—or anyone else—would concoct a convoluted plan to get rid of her. Or of him."

The brothers turned to talking about business matters for Caudex House, but Elizabeth couldn't get the questions out of her head. Nor could she find any answers. If there was anything at all to the murder theory, the police would find the answer. But what concerned her was any possible bearing all this might have on Caudex.

If—granting the long shot—Kentworth had been murdered, could it be for his involvement in the Austen first editions auction? If so, did that mean Kentworth was mixed up in something under-handed? Or that someone else was, and he was killed to keep him quiet? What if Andrew's was the winning bid—would the danger then pass to him?

Surely, it couldn't be the even more unlikely scenario that Sara Ashley-Herbert was the intended victim? If so, would that mean that she was involved in something illegal? Or was trying to stop something illicit? But if it was the latter, wouldn't she have told Andrew?

In either case, what could possibly be wrong with the deal? It worried Elizabeth that Andrew was worried. Worried enough to try to pull his bid. And he had not been allowed to do so. Still, she couldn't see where the fiddle could be. The manuscripts were authentic. The bids were deposited in a secure bank. It was all being handled by an established, reputable auction house. Whose representative had just been murdered... No. Killed in a dreadful accident. Leaving a widow and two young children.

Still, Elizabeth was determined to keep her eyes and ears open.

Chapter 11

"WHAT IS THE CENTRAL story question in *Emma*?" Richard surveyed his class.

"What's going on between Frank Churchill and Jane Fairfax?" Babs was the first to reply.

A young woman with long blond hair, whose name tag proclaimed her to be Susan, spoke without raising her hand. "That only works for readers who are savvy enough to realize something is going on."

Pleased that his students were so quick to respond today, Richard nodded to another woman, this one with a mane of curly red hair, in the second row. "That depends on whether you're reading the novel as a mystery or as a romance. The story question is, 'who will Emma marry?' if you're reading a romance."

"Or, more generally, as Mr. Knightly muses early on, 'I wonder what will become of her,'" another student, a mature woman who hadn't contributed before, added.

"Or who will Harriet marry?" an older man beside her suggested.

"No, Harriet is a sub-question to Emma's destiny. Just as 'Who gave Jane the piano?' is a sub-question to the Churchill-Fairfax relationship," Jeremy said.

"Quite right," Richard agreed. "Of course, for the purposes of this course I have asked you to read it as a mystery, but the complexity of questions again shows Austen's mastery of her craft.

"For this discussion, though, we will take the Churchill-Fairfax relationship, all of which is complicated, as I said Monday, by Emma's unreliability as a narrator. She tells us early on that she has an 'instinctive knowledge' of Frank Churchill—just as she claims instinctive knowledge of everyone, including herself. And she is reliably wrong about them all. Hence the fun.

"Again, it is Mr. Knightly who speaks true wisdom. 'Better be without sense than misapply it as you do,' he tells Emma."

Richard paused to pour a drink of water from the carafe beside the lectern. Blessedly, the construction noise from north tower had quieted today. Possibly because the police were still investigating there. No time to think about that now, however. He picked up the reins of the class discussion. "And what is the central misdirection that keeps us looking everywhere but at the truth to this relationship?"

Babs spoke without waiting to be acknowledged. "Frank's flirtation with Emma."

Richard nodded, but, before he could comment, the red-haired woman raised her hand. "Yes, Wanda, is it?"

She nodded. "Tha's right." Her soft burr indicated Scottish roots. "The red herring is Mr. Dixon."

"Precisely—which Frank Churchill serves up on a plate poached, fried, grilled, pickled, soused, marinated, salted and smoked." Richard was gratified that his class smiled appreciatively at his mild humor. "And, to extend the metaphor, one could say that herring was Emma's favorite dish. In chapter 2 of volume II Emma sees that Jane Fairfax, indeed, had 'something more to conceal' for which Emma supplies the answer Frank has planted—Mr. Dixon. Even though she mentions in the same paragraph that Frank himself had been in Weymouth at the same time.

"Later she asks Frank if he saw Jane often at Weymouth. Frank changes the subject. Emma returns to it. He hedges. 'It is the lady's right to decide the degree of acquaintance.'"

Richard smiled. "Slippery devil, isn't he? Emma and Frank then talk of Jane's piano playing—at Frank's instigation. The fact that he can't resist talking about her is another clue, but he uses the topic to implicate Mr. Dixon.

"At the end of that conversation Emma perfectly analyzes Jane's behavior—'such extreme and perpetual cautiousness of word and manner … suggest suspicions of there being something to conceal.' Indeed, there is, but then, true to form, Emma jumps to the wrong conclusion.

"Then we have the brilliant device of the Bates. Miss Bates, who is such a boring chatterbox that no one listens to her, actually sees—and tells—the truth of all. But no one pays any attention—not even Miss Bates herself.

"And, of course, Frank uses his misdirection technique in insisting on showing respect to Mrs. Bates as an excuse for repeated and early calls at the home where Jane is staying."

Richard directed his class to turn to Chapter 10 of volume III. "Emma walks in unexpectedly and finds Mrs. Bates dozing, Frank 'most decidedly occupied' with the old woman's spectacles, and Jane standing with her back to the room. Frank shows 'a most happy countenance.' Wanda, you were interested in reading this as a romance. Decipher the clues and tell me what just might have been going on here."

Wanda and the rest of the class bowed their heads over their books. "Oh!" Wanda looked up, a smile spreading over her face. "I thought Jane Austen never wrote a kiss."

"She didn't, did she?" Richard agreed. "But isn't this more fun than the most erotic description? And it continues. Under the guise of talking about music and supposedly referencing Mr. Dixon, Frank talks of the happiness of hearing a waltz again that had been danced at Weymouth—perhaps the moment he and Jane fell in love?

"But Jane 'coloured deeply and played something else.' You can just feel these two young people tingling for each other. Talk about sexual tension." Richard paused a moment for the full effect of the scene to sink in.

"Frank then alludes to the music Colonel Campbell sent as being 'so thoroughly from the heart ... true affection only could have prompted it.'

"Jane gave a smile of 'secret delight' which Emma saw. 'Jane Fairfax was apparently cherishing very reprehensible feelings,' Emma concludes quite correctly, but again, credits the vilely slandered Mr. Dixon."

Wanda's hand shot up. "And Frank had told her on page 173—oh, well, in my edition—that the piano was an offering of love."

"That's exactly right. By misdirecting Emma, Frank can say what he truly means, and Emma—and the casual reader—are both fooled. When Emma cautions Frank he replies, 'I would have her understand me. I am not the least ashamed of my meaning.'

"Emma is so completely taken in, due largely to her over-confidence in her own powers of deduction, that she doesn't tumble even when she raises one of the central questions regarding Jane. 'She is a riddle, quite a riddle.' Why does she 'choose to remain here month after month under privations of every sort'?

"And, according to Miss Bates, Mrs. Dixon had written with a warm, pressing invitation for Jane to join them in Ireland. 'She must have some motive more powerful than appears for refusing this invitation,' Emma says. Indeed, she did.

"But only the clear-sighted Mr. Knightly suspects Frank Churchill of 'some inclination to trifle with Jane Fairfax.' He had seen the symptoms. Perhaps because Mr. Knightly was so attuned to matters affecting Emma, and Frank professed to admire her. In Mr. Knightley's case love was not blind."

The class continued with examples of Frank's wiles and Emma's wrong-headedness until Richard closed his book.

"All right, for Friday I want you to undertake a close reading of volume III and prepare an essay." He gathered his papers and walked to the door. Before exiting he turned back and announced the topic of the essay, then left the room with a smile on his face.

Elizabeth hurried down the hall to catch him up. "You're having them on. You don't think that?"

Richard raised an eyebrow. "Close reading, I said. We'll see what they come up with."

Chapter 12

"IT'S SO HARD TO focus with everything that's going on." Elizabeth looked up from the outline of her article that she had been struggling with for at least an hour since breakfast. She sighed and closed the lid on her laptop.

"Can I help?" Richard set his own book aside.

"I don't know. It seemed so easy when I started—places she stayed, places she shopped, museums she visited, theatres she attended, churches where she worshipped—a few hundred words on each, a few photos, and there you have an overview of Jane Austen's London."

"And the problem is?"

"Focus, like I said. Just the little bit of research I've done and I've already got enough for three articles. And when I try to cut it, my mind goes back to trying to see a connection between Andrew's business and that awful occurrence at the Senate House, and even Jeremy at St. Paul's and the police…" She turned from her desk.

"Richard, am I completely bonkers to wonder if it's suspicious that Babs Ellington shows up in her assertive way every time something goes wrong?"

"The bubbly Babs being under-handed?" Richard paused

to think. "I can't see it."

"Nor can I," Elizabeth admitted. "But she is something of a puzzle. How old do you think she is?"

Richard shook his head. "Don't ask me! I'm hopeless with women's ages. She acts like she's in her twenties, but I suppose the truth is that she could be forty." His voice implied a question mark.

"Mid-forties even, perhaps." Elizabeth paused. "Or mid-thirties. Everyone seems young to me these days." She sighed.

"I don't suppose it makes any difference anyway. If anything untoward is going on, she's not likely to be involved, but people we know must be, and I can't help worrying that Andrew's deal is at the heart of it. Do you know how much money he deposited with Chestermere as his bid?"

"He decided to keep it simple. On the advice of his expert he went with one million pounds."

"How much is that in dollars?"

"Not sure of the exchange rate at the moment, but it's something around a dollar and a half to a pound."

"So if there are, say, between five and ten bidders, that could be something like ten million dollars. I suppose someone could think that was worth killing for."

"Yes, but the seller will only accept one bid. The rest of the money will be returned."

Elizabeth nodded. "But even one bid—we are talking about a lot of money."

"Maybe it isn't a matter of wanting to get their hands on the money. Maybe it's the books."

Elizabeth's eyes grew wide and her mouth fell open. "Richard! Do you mean another bidder bumping off the competition? You mean maybe *Andrew* was the intended victim?" She thought for a moment. "And at St. Paul's—maybe someone heard Jeremy's American voice and thought he was Andrew?"

Richard stood up. "And maybe both events were accidents. And maybe we're getting carried away. Where are we going today?"

"Well, I was going to go on with looking at places Jane stayed, but I do rather have banks on my mind, and the British Museum has an exhibit on money and banking. Plus, I want to see their Georgian and Regency collection, of course."

"Great. That's only a five minute walk from here."

A few minutes later they entered the open gate of the tall, black and gold railing, enclosing what was once the world's largest building site in Europe. They crossed the forecourt to the vast, classical Greek Revival building, surrounded by its march of Doric columns. "Did Jane come here?" Richard asked.

"If she did, it's not recorded. The museum was established a quarter of a century before her birth to house the collection of Sir Hans Sloane—for whom two of the streets Henry Austen lived in were named—so she could have come, but the building then was quite different." She showed him a sketch in her guidebook of a building vaguely resembling an Oriental fantasy.

They went first to the banking exhibit which Elizabeth studied with considerable attention: 1720, the world's first banking crisis. The Scottish economist John Law established a bank in France where he led the development of paper money. He pursued merging trading companies into a monopoly known as the Mississippi Company, then overstated their assets which created a bubble when more and more people bought the over-valued shares.

Until the investors demanded cash payment for their shares, leading to a run on the bank and financial chaos in France and London.

Elizabeth considered. Over-valued assets, more assets than the bank could afford to pay off. Bank collapsed. Investors ruined. What if the Austen books were over-valued? Or somehow the bank couldn't deliver? Would Chestermere be ruined? Could the bank be the target rather than individual bidders? She shook her head. Over-reaching again.

She moved on to the exhibit recounting the 1720 South

Sea Bubble, which she had already read about at the Bank of England. A similar story: over-valued shares, over-investment, collapse, ruin. 1720 was certainly a bad year for investors.

She turned to Richard who was likewise studying the exhibit with a frown on his face. "Do you see anything we can learn here?" she asked.

"Anything applicable to Andrew's venture, you mean?" He shook his head. "Nothing beyond a general caution to be careful about one's investments."

Elizabeth noted that the South Sea Company, however, continued to trade after the bubble until the middle of the next century. Her recent research had brought back to her mind that Jane's mother Cassandra had inherited more than three thousand pounds from her mother in 1769, with which she purchased South Sea Securities that served to supplement the family income.

Richard moved on to a more light-hearted exhibit in the center of the room—a plexiglass case filled with bank notes bearing a familiar image. "Dr. Who!" Elizabeth bent closer to the case. "'I promise to pay the bearer upon demand the sum of ten satsumas.'" She giggled, then read that these were developed for a Christmas special where a cashpoint spit out banknotes because The Bank of England strictly forbids the production of prop banknotes that look realistic.

That turned Elizabeth's mind to the subject of counterfeiting and forgery, but, again, she could see nothing applicable to Andrew's situation since the books had been so carefully authenticated. And Andrew certainly had not deposited counterfeit money with the bank. One of the other bidders perhaps? But surely that wouldn't affect Caudex.

They moved on to the rooms containing Georgian and Regency objects. Elizabeth pulled out her notebook, jotting a few words here and there about items that especially seemed to epitomize Jane's world. She had just finished describing a particularly lovely Wedgewood vase when Richard joined her, holding out his phone to display a text. "Drew is taking Sara to lunch at Fortnum and Mason's and wants us to join them. What do you think?"

"It sounds lovely, but why does he want us along? Surely he doesn't need a chaperone?"

"Perhaps his conscience does. He can tell himself it's not a date—simply being with family and friends, or friend, as long as we're there."

"So are we abetting something you disapprove of by going?"

"I think it's pretty clear he'll go anyway."

"Fine. I'll chaperone anyone who wants to buy me lunch at Fortnum's."

A short time later Elizabeth quickened her pace along Piccadilly Street, as the ornate, pale aqua façade and sunburst windows filled with tantalizing displays came into view. The liveried doorman ushered them into the red-carpeted hall filled with luscious provisions. At the back, a brass-railed stairway led to the Gallery restaurant where sun shining through the windows set the glass and silver on golden oak tables agleam.

Andrew beckoned them to the table already set for four. The others turned to their menus, but Elizabeth pulled out her notebook and jotted a few reminders. Once again, not a place Jane had mentioned but, since they were suppliers to Wellington's army, she would have been acquainted with them. Perhaps another place Eliza would have ordered from?

Elizabeth stuffed her papers in her bag and joined the conversation around the table in time to hear Richard ask whether Andrew had heard anything more from the police. "They returned my phone—thank goodness. I was lost without it."

"Oh, I should have realized that, when Richard showed me your text," Elizabeth said. "Did they say they had eliminated you from their enquiries?"

"They didn't say much of anything, really. And I was so glad to get my phone back I didn't ask."

"Surely they've moved on from the ludicrous idea that poor Clive Kentworth was killed on purpose." Sara shivered. "I certainly want to put it behind me."

"I wish I could put the whole auction thing behind me," Drew said. Then added almost under his voice, "Except for one thing." The look he and Sara exchanged was worthy of Frank Churchill and Jane Fairfax.

"Have you learned anything more?" Richard asked.

"As soon as I got my phone back I tried ringing Child, but the bank's receptionist told me he was out. Then I tried Legacy House. They've assigned a Melinda Morse to replace Kentworth, and the Austen first edition auction is proceeding on schedule. Bidding closes the end of next week, and the winner will be announced the week after that."

"Well, that's fine then, isn't it?" Sara was obviously trying to encourage him. "You really don't have anything to worry about, you know. If you win, you can go ahead with the publishing and promotion plans you've made. If you lose—" She shrugged. "You get your money back and you can invest in something else."

"You're saying it's a win-win?"

Elizabeth couldn't help feeling that Andrew's light reply sounded forced, but her smoked salmon and *crème fraîche* blinis were far too delicious to spoil with worry. She followed that with a pot of Queen Mary tea and was ready to order a lemon bar when Richard looked at his watch.

"Oh, I am sorry. I promised some of my students I'd meet them at the library to discuss their essays." He looked at Elizabeth. "You don't have to come. Enjoy your tea and I'll meet you back at the room."

Tempting as it was, she chose to go with Richard, thinking she might work on her article while Richard met with his students. As it turned out, though, she found the lively conversation with Babs, Jeremy, Wanda and Susan to be more interesting than her own work. "But doesn't Emma do that with everything—sees the facts, but jumps to the wrong conclusion?" Wanda opened her paperback copy of the novel to an early page. "'She was quite convinced of Mr. Elton's being in the fairest way of falling in love if not in love already.' He was in love. Not with Harriet, but with her."

"So you're saying we can trust Emma's observations, but not her conclusions?" Jeremy asked.

Babs cut in with another thought. "What I like about Emma is that for all her being so sure of herself she isn't conceited. Like here, 'She was not much deceived as to her own skill either as an artist or a musician, but she was not unwilling to have others deceived.'"

Susan continued, "And in the end we forgive Emma because she is repentant. Like when she cried to Harriet, 'My sins! My sins! ... I deserve to be under a continual blush all the rest of my life.'"

"Yes, but you can't help wondering how long that lasted. Undoubtedly as long as her repeated determinations not to dabble in match-making."

Elizabeth smiled as the lively exchange continued. She had missed this. As much as she loved being housemother to her young boys at Headington School, she realized now she had missed the stimulation of more rarefied academics.

She was still thinking about that later, when she and Richard were back in their room. Now that there was nothing to distract her, she really did need to get to work. She opened her laptop and pulled out her notes.

That is, she opened her bag to get her notes, but they weren't there. "Richard, have you seen my notebook? I was sure I put it in my bag, but it isn't here."

"Are you certain you had it with you?"

"Yes, I wrote in it at Fortnum's."

"Maybe you left it there. We could ring them."

She shook her head. She clearly remembered putting it away. And she hadn't taken it out in the library. So where was it? She looked through her bag. Nothing else had been disturbed. Her wallet and money were still there, so not a pickpocket, surely.

She must be mistaken. No one would take her notebook on purpose, so she must have dropped it somewhere. But that was little comfort. She would far rather have lost her money than her notes. Thank goodness she had transferred a lot of her research to her computer, but still…

She sat looking at the empty space in her bag. Something didn't feel right. She was certain she remembered doing the zipper after putting her notes away at Fortnum's. They couldn't have fallen out. They must have been taken. But by whom? And why?

Chapter 13

ELIZABETH WAS STILL THINKING about her lost note-book the next morning as she sat in the back of the lecture room watching the students enter. Susan and Wanda came in together, chatting. Elizabeth knew nothing about them beyond their names. She had sat near them in the library with her bag hanging carelessly on the back of a chair. Still, she couldn't imagine any possible reason for one of them to rifle her bag.

She heard Jeremy before she saw him, the clunk of his crutches on the marble floor. Could he be thinking his fall was less accidental than it first looked? Surely he couldn't suspect her enough to want to check up on her by reading her daily scribblings? But he had been sitting next to her. Could she say for certain that he didn't at any point reach behind her chair?

With the flurry that seemed always to surround her, Babs rushed in, almost running over the two Japanese girls in front of her. Babs made a beeline to Jeremy, plopped into the seat behind him and leaned forward to chatter in his ear. Babs. Always on the scene. Always busy about something. Could it be something devious?

Before Elizabeth could reach any conclusions or imagine any more exotic scenarios, Richard stood and surveyed his roomful of students. "All right, the jury is out." He emphasized his metaphor by gazing around the very judicial-looking room.

"Did Frank murder Mrs. Churchill?"

The buzz of anticipation filling the Senate Room indicated that the students had come well-prepared on the topic assigned to them.

"First, let's examine the matter of motive." Hands shot up around the room.

"She runs his life."

"She controls the purse strings."

"She keeps him on a lead."

Richard nodded at Jeremy who held his book open to the appropriate page, "Frank believed she might have 'many years of existence before her.'"

Babs, glancing at the book open in front of her, added, "'While Mrs. Churchill lived there could not have been a hope, a chance, a possibility' of consent for Frank to marry Jane."

Richard smiled and nodded. "Excellent. So we have the three classic motives for murder: love, money and power."

Jeremy raised his hand. "And resentment. Mrs. Churchill had caused Frank's mother to be slighted."

Again Babs chimed in, "And there's the matter of Mrs. Churchill's pride which was 'arrogance and insolence.' She was a 'high and mighty upstart.'"

"In other words, a thoroughly unlikeable person. Might not be a reason to murder her, but it indicates that she wouldn't be long mourned," Richard agreed. "Now, let's move on to opportunity."

Again, hands shot up around the room. Richard called on a man with a grey mustache who hadn't spoken out before. He pushed his glasses back up on his nose and cleared his throat before reading in a soft voice. "'Though her nephew had had no particular reason to hasten back on her account,'" he looked up, "which means she wasn't ill when he arrived ... 'she had not lived above six-and-thirty hours after his return. A sudden seizure, of a different nature from anything foreboded by her general state, had carried her off after a short struggle.'"

Richard opened his mouth to comment, but the speaker continued, "And we later learn that Frank was desperate because Jane had just ended their engagement. Which I suppose is more motive than opportunity."

"Yes, can you find the reference, Al?"

The man turned pages in his book. "Yes, here it is. Mrs. Weston tells Emma 'There were misunderstandings between them .... The present crisis, indeed, seemed to be brought on by them; and those misunderstandings might very possibly arise from the impropriety of his conduct.'"

Richard gave a single, sharp nod and his student looked pleased. "Exactly the passage I had in mind. Of course, the conversation is about the secret engagement, but is it too far a stretch to think that possibly 'present crisis' and 'impropriety of conduct' could have a double meaning—as most things Jane wrote have?"

Al thought for a moment. "Are you suggesting that Jane Fairfax might have suspected Frank of having a hand in his aunt's so opportune death?"

"I shouldn't go so far as to say I'm suggesting—just questioning, really," Richard hedged. The discussion had momentarily become a dialogue between the two men. Richard read snatches. "'Miss Fairfax was not well enough to write!' Note that Austen goes so far as to use an exclamation mark here. 'She was suffering under severe headaches and a nervous fever.' 'Her health seemed for the moment completely deranged—appetite quite gone.' 'Mr. Perry was uneasy about her.'"

He looked up at his class. "A broken engagement? Or suspicion of her beloved's guilt?"

Leaving the question unanswered, he moved on. "All right, I think we're agreed that Frank Churchill had opportunity—at least to the extent that he was on the scene when the death occurred. So now, what did you find about the third necessary element—means? Did you find anything in the text that would indicate Frank had anything to hand with which to do the old lady in?"

A student in the far back spoke for the first time. "Well, we're told she died of a sudden seizure. Doesn't that suggest poison?"

Hands rose more slowly this time. Now it was one of the Japanese girls. "This, perhaps, is more opportunity than means, but Mrs. Churchill did take medicine. One could imagine her nephew..." Her voice trailed off, leaving each one to form a picture of the subtle Frank removing the cork from a small brown bottle by his aunt's bed and solicitously pouring the liquid into a spoon...

"Fine, Noboko. Thank you." No one seemed to have anything to add, so Richard moved on. "Now, one more classic question—who benefits from the death?"

"Frank," was the general acclamation.

Susan offered to enlarge on the unanimous vote. "Emma reflects on 'how Frank might be affected by the event, how benefited, how freed.'"

"And again, Emma is entirely right—and entirely wrong. Because she calculates how Frank's freedom will benefit his supposed attachment to Harriet Smith."

Richard glanced at his notes on the lectern in front of him. "Which brings us, in the perfect style of a Golden Age mystery, to the final revelatory scene where all the loose ends are tied up—Frank's letter in Chapter 14 of Volume III."

A rustle of turning pages followed his direction, and Richard waited for the bustle to subside. "Here we learn that Jane's letter breaking the engagement reached Frank the very morning of his aunt's death. Does that pinpoint the motive?"

"And what do we learn from Frank's own words of his emotions at the time?"

Answers sprang from around the room: "Bewildered, mad." "Insane from happiness or misery." "Joy and anger."

Richard nodded. "In other words, he was in a state. Hardly knowing what he did. Is he trying here to justify himself? I think, definitely, yes. The question is for what?"

Jeremy raised his hand. "Mr. Knightly says Frank played 'a most dangerous game' and says Frank's mind was full of intrigue, mystery and finesse."

Richard smiled. "Perhaps our hero, who always has the right of it, speaks truer here than even he realizes.

"Of course, in the end we are left to make up our own minds. Was Frank Churchill the Child of Fortune as he claims? Or was he a murderer?" Richard returned his notes to his briefcase and snapped it shut.

Babs jerked forward, almost coming to her feet. "But wait. What's the answer? What do you think?"

Richard grinned and surveyed the room before answering. "I have to admit that I think Frank was most likely a Child of Fortune. One thing to consider is the fact that people were more accustomed to popping off unexpectedly from undiagnosed diseases, or poorly treated diagnosed ones, in Jane Austen's day.

"I am convinced, though, that Jane—who never wasted a word, knew exactly what she was doing. In essence, she was playing with her reader. Those clues were cleverly planted on purpose. I think Jane is smiling right now because we are asking this very question.

"And the fact that preparation for the entire event was so carefully and subtly built up that it could have been a successful murder is yet another evidence of Austen's genius."

"And a deuced clever way to get us to do a close reading," Jeremy added.

Richard smiled and bowed. Babs applauded and a few others joined in. "All right, everyone have a good weekend. I'll see you Monday morning, where we'll jump into the Golden Age of mystery writing. If anyone wants to get a head start on the reading, get going on Sayers' *Gaudy Night* which many consider her best novel." He dismissed them with a wave of his hand.

Elizabeth linked her arm through Richard's as they went down the hall. "You are fiendish. Will you stop at nothing to get your students' attention?"

Richard grinned. "Okay, I admit I was pushing the envelope, but it worked."

"Brilliantly. If that class had been a jury they would have convicted. You almost had me convinced. And I still wonder what might have been in Austen's mind. There is certainly no shortage of violent death in her juvenilia.

"We even have a serial killer in *A Letter from a Young Lady* where Anna Parker confesses—or perhaps boasts—'I murdered my father at a very early period of my Life, I have since murdered my Mother, and I am now going to murder my Sister.'" Elizabeth continued. "Jane definitely didn't shy from the subject."

She paused, then added, "And in *Sir William Montague* Sir William shoots his rival for Miss Arundel's hand—who then has no reason to refuse him."

"But, unlike Sir William who gained the object of his passion, the mature Jane couldn't have let Frank go unpunished. It would certainly have spoiled the romantic comedy effect of *Emma* had it ended like her very early *Jack and Alice*, where Sukey Simpson is consigned to the gallows for poisoning her sister," Richard argued.

"Yes, that would have been hard on Jane Fairfax," Elizabeth agreed.

Richard continued her theme. "Still, the villainous Lady Susan's thoughts always turn to murder when someone annoys her, so she has no scruples against suggesting that her friend Alicia should kill off Mrs. Manwaring by worrying her to death. You've got to admit that would be a unique means."

"And certainly the mature novels are full of wishes for convenient death, especially *Mansfield Park*." Elizabeth counted them off on her fingers. "Mary Crawford when Tom Bertram falls ill; William Price thinking of his own promotion should his first lieutenant die; Tom Bertram coveting Dr. Grant's living for Edward as a sop to Tom's conscience for wasting his own inheritance. And, in *Sense and Sensibility*, Willoughby's alluding to the 'blessed chance' should he be at liberty to marry Marianne.

"It rather makes one wonder if Jane just might have considered the idea." Elizabeth thought for a moment. "Maybe it wasn't Frank. Mrs. Churchill must have treated everyone as badly as she did him. Perhaps her hen-pecked husband..."

Richard shook his head. "You still don't see it, do you?"

Elizabeth frowned. "What?"

"Who killed Mrs. Churchill and why." Richard didn't wait for her to ask. "Jane Austen herself killed off Mrs. Churchill for the purpose of her plot. Mrs. Churchill had to die. And so she did."

Elizabeth laughed but, as they descended the grand staircase to the marble foyer, she continued to think about how it was possible to read so much into events that, at the end of the day, were quite innocent. Was that what they had been doing about Clive Kentworth's death? Would Andrew's venture prove her brother-in-law to be a Child of Fortune after all? She could only hope.

Chapter 14

"AH, SATURDAY MORNING." ELIZABETH stretched luxuriously before reaching to her bedside table and pouring herself a second cup of tea. "I think I could laze around all day."

"No reason you shouldn't. I'll run over to Leicester Square and see about getting some bargain theatre tickets for tonight and then join you in an afternoon of complete sloth."

"That sounds delicious. In spite of the guilt."

"Guilt?"

"Well, we're in London. We should be off to a museum or gallery or tourist site. I still have so much research to do."

"The theatre tonight will count as research. I'll get tickets for one of the theatres we know Jane attended. Remind me which ones."

"Of the ones still standing, Drury Lane, The Lyceum and Covent Garden. Covent Garden burnt down and was rebuilt, though, so it's not the building Jane would have known."

"Right." Richard slipped his wallet into the inside pocket of his jacket. "I'll try for Drury Lane or The Lyceum." He pulled out his phone. "I'll just see if Andrew wants to go with us."

The scheme met with success. "He'd love to. He's spending the day reading a manuscript Caudex emailed him—a new analytical study of the poetry of Robert Frost. He'll be ready for a break this evening and will be happy for the company. Seems Sara's mother is sick, and she had to go to Surrey to see her."

Elizabeth settled back against her pillows and picked up the new biography of Jane Austen she hoped would add some useful information on Jane's time in London.

Elizabeth was engrossed in her reading some time later when a knock on the door brought her back to the present day. "Richard?" She padded across the floor in her bare feet.

"Did you forget your key?" She pulled the door open, then stepped back with a gasp at the sight of the woebegone figure in front of her.

"Jack! What are you doing here? How did you find our address?"

Jack entered without waiting for a more affirmative invitation and slumped onto a chair. "Springs told me. I said I needed to return a book." He looked at the floor.

"Oh, well, thank you." She held out her hand, expecting him to unzip the carry-all he still had slung over his shoulder and produce the tome.

"No book. I lied." The carry-all slid to the floor with a plop.

"But why? What do you want?"

"To stay with you."

Elizabeth took a deep breath and sat on the end of her bed. "Jack, you aren't making any sense. Tell me what's wrong. You're supposed to be spending the summer with your mother."

He shook his head. The bouncing blond curls never failed to pull at Elizabeth's heart. This was not a good thing when she needed to be calm and stern, she reminded herself.

"Mum doesn't want me."

"Oh, you've had an argument? Well, I'm sure when you have time to cool down and—"

"No. We didn't argue. She's never around to argue with.

She doesn't want me." His skin seemed to pale, making his freckles stand out more.

Elizabeth resisted the impulse to take the little bundle of slumped misery into her arms. Jack had always been the sturdy, lively one. Ringleader of most of the schoolboy japes their house got up to. This didn't seem like the same person.

"She has a new boyfriend. Maurice." He almost spit the word, giving it its French pronunciation. "She spends all her time with him. I never see her. They've gone to Paris this weekend."

"And left you alone?" Elizabeth was horrified. Child Services would take over if they knew.

Jack shrugged. "There's Annie, the maid. She's useless. Just paints her nails black and texts her boyfriend."

Leaving Jack to spend his days alone in his mother's Chelsea flat. Elizabeth recalled seeing the list of the boys' summer addresses and thinking at the time what a nice part of London that was. But not for an eleven-year-old boy on his own all day. And all night? Did Annie slip out with her boyfriend? Or have him in her room? What was that mother thinking? "What about your dad? Have you rung him? Can't you go to him in Belfast?"

Jack slumped further down in his chair. "Da's in Dubai for his company. I rang his office. They said they'd give him a message." Jack emitted a muffled sniff which Elizabeth was certain she wasn't supposed to hear. She got up and filled the kettle with water in order to give her visitor time to compose himself.

A few minutes later she stuck a mug of very sweet, very milky tea in his hands, wishing she had some chocolate biscuits to give him as well. He looked starved. Had he been left to cook for himself as well? "Jack, we can't just keep you, you know. Not without your parents' consent." But neither could she send him back to spend the rest of his summer in such dire circumstances.

She was still wondering what on earth they would do when the door opened. "Success! 'Charlie and the Chocolate

Factory' at the Royal Theatre Drury Lane." Richard started to wave a small envelope of tickets, but stopped mid-gesture when he saw Jack.

Elizabeth explained in a few succinct sentences. Her words were a neutral statement of the facts as she knew them, but she knew her eyes spoke her desire to help the child that had been such an important part of their lives over the past three years.

Richard sat at his desk and took a directory bearing the Headington School logo from the top drawer. "You do understand that Mrs. Spencer is right, don't you Jack? You can't stay here without permission."

Jack shrugged. "Mum'll be glad to be shut of me."

A short time later, when Richard rang the emergency contact number for Jack O'Brien provided by the school, it seemed that Jack's assessment of the situation was accurate. His mother gave an off-handed assent to releasing him to the care of those who looked after him at the school. Elizabeth sat with her hands held tightly together. She could imagine hearing indifference, if not actual relief, in the woman's voice. How could someone possibly be so cavalier about turning their child over to someone else? Elizabeth couldn't fathom.

"We'll need written consent. Some sort of power of attorney—or whatever it is here—to deal on Jack's behalf in case he needs medical care or anything." Richard had barely written down the name and number of Mrs. O'Brien's solicitor when she rang off.

The look Richard gave to Elizabeth said *Jack was right.* "Well, that's all right, then." Elizabeth jumped to her feet, seeing the cautious hope on Jack's face. "I suppose we should take you back to get your things."

"I brought them." He nodded at the satchel by his feet.

"Oh." Elizabeth gulped. That was it? For the rest of the summer?

Then she looked around the spare dorm room. Barely adequate for herself and Richard. It would certainly not accommodate another for their remaining time in London.

Richard followed her gaze. "I'll ring the university housing office. Hopefully there'll be a single room available near us."

And Elizabeth was back to her role of housemother again. And for the first time she realized the parallel to Jane's own mother. That was exactly what Cassandra Austen had done for years—served as surrogate mother to the pupils that George Austen took into their home to educate in order to supplement his income—as well as raising her own family. And Cassandra had found time to write her own amusing poetry and carry on the lively correspondence that was so much a part of life in those days.

Richard had no more than returned from arranging for a room for Jack than his phone rang. Andrew was bogged down in his editing. He would have to beg off the theatre for the evening. "What luck!" Elizabeth laughed. She hadn't even had time to worry about their evening plans yet. "Have we got a treat for you, Jack!"

Evening shadows were lengthening as the three of them walked down Russell Street and turned into Drury Lane. Well, Elizabeth and Richard walked, Jack more skipped. Elizabeth was amazed at the change that had come over the child in the space of a few hours. She was certain that the three hamburgers and enormous pile of chips he had consumed had a great deal to do with this happy state of affairs.

When they rounded the corner and saw the colonnaded portico of the large, pale ivory building, Elizabeth stopped and pulled out a spiral bound notebook she purchased at a WHSmith to replace her lost one. In response to Jack's quizzical look she explained that, besides being a fun outing, the evening was also research for her, since Jane Austen had attended several performances here when she was staying with her brother in Henrietta street and had written detailed accounts to her sister.

Her young companion nodded. "Yeah, like in Dr. Spencer's book." Elizabeth had been surprised how well Jack seemed to understand her project, then she realized he had read Richard's fictionalized account of their visits to Jane Austen's homes.

"Well, not exactly like that because this is just a magazine article, but you've got the right idea." Inside the theatre Elizabeth looked around the elegant, circular lobby, recalling that this was the setting Jane Austen had chosen for Sir John Middleton to inform Willoughby that Marianne was dying, sending him flying off to confess his villainy and regret to Elinor.

Jack interrupted her contemplation by pointing to the marble statue of a commanding, robed figure holding a skull. "Who's that?"

Richard answered. "That's Edmund Keane, the greatest actor of his day. He gave his first London performance in this theatre when it was newly rebuilt after a fire."

"Why's he holding a skull?"

"He's playing Hamlet."

Jack nodded. He seemed satisfied with the answer. "Can we get some chocolate?"

Richard smiled and reached for his wallet. As they stood in line to buy Wonka Bars he asked Elizabeth. "What role did Jane see Keane in?"

"'Merchant of Venice'—Shylock. This was in March after the opening in January of that year. Keane had taken the town by storm, and Jane complained that there were no good seats available for the next two weeks. Since the theatre seats more than three thousand people, he must have been a huge success."

"Did Jane like him?"

"Oh, yes. I read the letter to check just before we came. She wrote to Cassandra that she could not imagine better acting. Her only complaint was that the part was too short. She was looking forward to seeing him again when Cassandra came to town in a fortnight. She said it appeared to her 'as if there were no fault in him anywhere.' One scene especially she thought was 'exquisite acting.'"

Wonka bars in hand, they sank into their red plush seats

in the stalls. Elizabeth savored a bite of chocolate and observed the three ornate tiers of box seats curving around the sides of the theatre. This was essentially the theatre as Jane would have seen it. Except, of course, the chandeliers adorning the front of each box wouldn't have been electric. The Theatre Royal Drury Lane was the first London theatre to have been completely gas lit. Elizabeth made a note to check the date. The gas lighting might not have been installed until after Jane's death.

The overture began, and the curtain rose, creating spine-tingling expectation. Charlie ran through the street singing "Almost Nearly Perfect" and Elizabeth felt that was exactly what this evening was, as a treat for a boy who had been having such a miserable time of it. She looked beside her, and the dim light falling on Jack's wide eyes made her smile even more than any of the magic unfolding onstage. Like Jane, Elizabeth could find no fault with the evening.

After the final curtain call they made their way back to the red and gold Rococo lobby, where their progress was slowed by people coming down the grand staircase from the dress circle. Inching forward, Elizabeth was about to ask Jack what he thought of the performance when she realized he had come to a full stop and was gazing at a striking couple descending the stairs. The man was tall with thick, silvery hair, wearing a black suit and a ruby red shirt. The woman wore a pale blue dress that set off her sleek, blond hair.

Elizabeth gasped, but Jack made the identification before she did. "That's the lady from the bookstore, innit?"

What was Sara Ashley-Herbert doing at the theatre when she was supposed to be in Surrey tending a sick mother? And who was the man she was leaning against so possessively?

Chapter 15

"YES, OF COURSE WE must tell Andrew," Richard agreed the next morning as he played with his second piece of toast while Jack wolfed his third or fourth sausage. "I'll try to find an appropriate opening after church."

Elizabeth shook her head. "If he's as enamored with her as he appears, there's no such thing as an appropriate moment for information like that."

Richard mulled over the truth of Elizabeth's words. He had resisted the idea of his little brother being romantically interested in the polished Ms. Ashley-Herbert—well, interested in anyone until his divorce from Caroline was final—but he could hardly fault Drew's taste. Her style, manners and learning were definitely top drawer. A bit old world, even. Sara Ashley-Herbert was someone their adored grandmother would have loved.

At least, that is what he would have said before last night. But Grams was above all honest. In spite of her soft-spoken charm, Alexandra Spencer saw with a clear-eyed New England straightforwardness and spoke as she saw. No nonsense. That was Alexandra.

And telling a man who is obviously falling for you that

you are tending your sick mother when you are actually going to the theatre with another man is hardly straight shooting.

Of course, there could be a plausible excuse. Just maybe. Richard considered. The Adonis on the stairway could have been a client. Didn't Sara say she occasionally did a bit of freelance consulting on rare manuscripts? Yes, that seemed a possibility. Sara's escort certainly looked like someone who might collect incunabula as Lord Peter Wimsey did.

The comforting thought lasted less than ten seconds, as Richard saw again in his mind the scene of Sara leaning into her escort's arm and looking up at him with an expression that could only be described as adoring.

He sighed. Yes, Andrew must be told.

"Church?" Jack's question, mumbled through a mouthful of baked beans, brought Richard back to the present. "But it's summer hols."

Richard smiled. "True enough, no school chapel requirements. Would you believe we go even when we're on holiday?"

"Even when it's not Christmas or Easter," Elizabeth added with a twinkle in her eye.

Jack looked thunderstruck.

"Will it soften the blow if we promise to take you out for a good Sunday lunch afterward?" Jack relaxed into a smile, and Richard turned to Elizabeth. "Where to today?"

"St. James, Piccadilly. Henry seems to have attended quite regularly as Jane mentions his meeting a cousin there, apparently unexpectedly, one Sunday morning. Henry probably got acquainted with it when he had his bank at The Albany nearby, but apparently he continued to worship there after he moved to different premises, because several years later she wrote that they went to Belgrave Chapel in the morning and were prevented by rain from going to evening service at St. James."

Andrew accepted Jack's presence without question when they met up a short time later. "Oh, yes, one of the choirboys. I heard you sing at St. Paul's. Very good."

Jack acknowledged the compliment with a nod and took the lead to the tube station. Only a short distance after exiting at Piccadilly Circus, the characteristic white spire of the Wren church came into view. Inside the red brick building Richard picked up a leaflet with black and white sketches of the church as it was in Regency times and handed it to Elizabeth. She pointed to one drawing with some excitement. "Look, 1815. The very year Jane wrote to Cassandra that they were prevented from coming here because of bad weather."

She held out the representation of the interior and seemed highly gratified that so little had changed since Jane's day. Long, dark wooden galleries extended down both sides of the nave, with high arched windows rising two stories to the white and gold, barrel vaulted ceiling. Above the altar, surrounded by ornate, Grinling Gibbons garlands, rose two levels of stained glass windows, the crucified Christ surmounted by the Ascended Christ.

Elizabeth pointed to the nineteenth century print. In Jane's day the windows were plain squares of leaded lights and the seating was in box pews. There was something comforting in the fact that other than those items, so little had changed. Jane could have felt at home here.

Although, Richard thought, perhaps not at the Taize service another leaflet advertised for that evening. Certainly not what Jane would have encountered had rain not kept her back from what would have been a very proper Prayer Book service of Evening Prayers. Richard smiled, wondering what she would have thought of the icons and row upon row of candles pictured in the leaflet and the soft, repetitive singing to the strains of a guitar that would comprise much of the service this evening.

For the moment, however, the very traditional Richard could take comfort in the familiar rhythms of morning Holy Communion. In spite of the unpleasant task he knew he faced later.

After the service they strolled around the charming, secluded garden beside the church that provided a tiny haven of tranquility off the bustle of Piccadilly. They paused to smile at the fountain with its playful cupids and the more serious Peace statue. Then, in response to Jack's plea to be fed, Elizabeth suggested they walk down Piccadilly to Fortnum and Mason to buy food for a picnic in Hyde Park. Jack enthusiastically endorsed the idea, and Richard had to admit to himself that he welcomed the activity which would postpone undertaking a sensitive conversation with his brother.

Considerably later, after consuming a selection of Scotch eggs, meat pies, cheeses, fresh fruit and cakes, Richard wanted to do nothing but curl up for a Sunday afternoon nap— no matter how impractical the desire at the moment. But his brother had more energetic ideas. "How about a row on the Serpentine?" Drew suggested to Jack, when it was obvious that even the youngster could eat no more.

"That'd be champion!" Jack jumped to his feet with Drew after him.

"Go on, lazy," Elizabeth nudged Richard.

He grinned, knowing she had guessed that he was considering letting Drew and Jack go alone. "Are you coming?" he asked.

She rolled her eyes at him. "I have to clean up here."

At least Drew, who had done crew at Harvard, took command of the oars so Richard wasn't required to wrestle with propelling the boat. And, he had to admit, the sun on the water, the antics of the bobbing ducks and the voices of happy children made for a jolly afternoon. Besides, he couldn't talk to Drew here, so he didn't even have to feel guilty about relaxing and enjoying the outing.

Andrew did a fine job of bringing Jack out of any melancholy he might have been feeling about his family situation. Drew engaged the boy in chatting about school, his friends, his choir. Being a father himself, it all seemed to come naturally to Drew. And Richard realized for the first time, Jack was perhaps not the only one in danger of depression about his family situation. Even though Andrew seemed resigned to the divorce, and it could have come as no surprise after living apart for so long, the legal proceeding he faced had to be unpleasant. Rather like the death of a loved one that had been sick for many years. The finality of the end always came as a blow—often all the more severe because the emotion was so unexpected. One thought one was prepared, but some things can't be prepared for.

Had the shock of Caroline's demand pushed Andrew into irrational behavior? Was that what was behind his desire to launch into a risky relationship as well as a risky business venture?

Richard's thoughts were interrupted as Jack playfully flicked Andrew—hair, glasses and shirt—with water, making him look as if he had been in a rain shower. Drew aimed an oar with precision to splash him back. Andrew's laugh sounded almost as light as the boy's.

Richard was well on his way to convincing himself that it would be unkind to crush Drew's spirits at such a time when his brother's phone rang. Andrew shipped the oars and let the boat drift as he looked at the display then pushed the key. "Sara, hello. How nice of you to ring. I bet you'll never guess where I am at the moment."

He told her about their outing, then asked, "And how is your mother?"

Her answer seemed to Richard to be an overly long one. Was she embroidering her story in an attempt to make it more believable?

"That's great. So when will we see you back in London?"

He smiled and nodded at her answer. "That's great. Sure, I'll give everyone your greetings. I look forward to seeing you at the end of the week."

Richard felt it was likely Andrew would have said more—something more personal—had he not had an audience. When Drew put his phone back in his pocket and picked up the oars, Richard took a deep breath. No better time than the present. Surely Sara's call provided a perfect segue. And if Drew doubted him, Jack was here to corroborate the story. After all, the boy had been the first to spot the couple.

"Sara sends her love," Drew began before Richard could speak. "But I guess you heard that. Her mum's doing a lot better. So well, in fact, she let her brother take her out last night." Drew looked amazed. "They came all the way back into London to go to the theatre."

Richard shook his head to be certain he had heard correctly. "Her brother?"

"Oh, was that the geezer?" Jack asked. "He had a wicked shirt. For an old guy."

"What? You saw them?"

While Jack recounted the scene in his open, energetic way, Richard wondered. Could the explanation be so simple? So innocent?

Or had Sara Ashley-Herbert spotted them from her elevated position on the stairs and suspected she, likewise, had been seen? Had that whole call been calculated to take the sting from anything Richard might report to Andrew?

Surely he was being far too suspicious. But if he was right, wasn't the cover-up, if that was what it was, worse than the act?

Did women really lean on their brothers in such an intimate way in public?

Chapter 16

"DOROTHY L. SAYERS EARNED her status as literary royalty for many of the same reasons as Jane Austen, primarily her inimitable style which encompasses her wit, her literary innovation and her strong heroine."

Richard surveyed the faces before him. Perhaps a bit less eager and considerably less nervous than the same countenances had been a week ago. More comfortable, settled into the routine of the course. That was certainly how Richard felt. Noboko, with her friends beside her, sat in the same front row seats they had occupied every day with their heads bent studiously over their notes. Jeremy, now with his head unbandaged, had taken his usual outside seat to accommodate his cast and crutches, and Babs, who had gone considerably out of her way to get to the seat next to him, leant over to whisper something in his ear. Wanda, Susan and Al sat scattered among students whose names he could only recall by looking at their name tags. Elizabeth winked at him from her place in the back. He gave in to the urge to return the wink and they shared a brief smile.

The shuffle of books and papers stilled in the room, signaling that his students were settled. And, blessedly, only the most muffled construction noises assaulted them. The course director had given them the good news that work for the next week or so would concentrate on the inside structure, so would be less disruptive to the classes. And less of a reminder of the unfortunate event brought about by the construction.

He cleared his throat. "Sayers reigns specifically as Queen of Golden Age Crime. Although Agatha Christie is undoubtedly the best known of the Golden Age writers, Sayers achieved a far higher literary standard. No less a Queen of Crime than P. D. James, whom we shall cover next week, has said," he read from his notes, "Sayers 'brought to the detective novel originality, intelligence and wit. She gave it a new style and a new direction, and she did more than almost any other writer of her age to make the [crime] genre intellectually respectable.' Sayers really wrote mainstream novels that happened to have a murder in them."

Several of the faces before him bore quizzical looks. Babs raised her hand with a jangle of the gold bands she was wearing. "Um, Golden Age?"

Richard nodded. It was easy to forget that this was a summer course for general interest students from all backgrounds, not an advanced seminar he might have taught at Rocky Mountain. "Yes, thank you for asking, Babs. I should have given you more orientation here.

"Let me back up for a moment to put this in historical perspective." Heads bent again over their notes as he began. "*Emma* was published in 1816, although it didn't reach the booksellers until 1817. In spite of the murders and violent and unexplained deaths in Jane Austen's work, readers had to wait a quarter of a century for a real piece of detective fiction. That was Edgar Allen Poe's short story 'Murder in the Rue Morgue,' written in 1841.

"Eighteen years later in 1859 (the year Conan Doyle was born) Wilkie Collins wrote what I, and many others, consider to be the first mystery novel *The Woman in White*—we'll be talking more about that Wednesday when we look at heroines."

Richard waited for the scribbling pens to still before he went on. The course included no exam at the end, but most of the class couldn't have been more studious if their academic career rested on learning these facts. "Then in 1885 an obscure Scottish doctor published a short story titled 'A Study in Scarlet,' thereby giving the world Sherlock Holmes. Although we think of Holmes as quintessentially Victorian, Doyle continued his consulting detective stories until 1927, well into the twentieth century.

"Poe, Collins and Doyle—who I needn't point out are all men and therefore not part of our Queens of Crime curriculum—are sometimes referred to as the 'early school' of detective fiction. These writers laid the foundation for the Golden Age style which predominated in the 1920s and '30s. Golden Age stories are light-hearted, almost innocent whodunits. The puzzle was the thing, and the ingenuity of murderer and detective are primary. There was a strong predilection for English country house settings and upper class characters, often with amateur detectives like Lord Peter Wimsey.

"Although this was an international vogue, the main writers were British. The queens were Sayers, Agatha Christie, Margery Allingham, Josephine Tey and the New Zealander Ngaio Marsh." Richard glanced at the clock on the wall. He had spent longer on this than he intended. "If you're interested in more detail, let me refer you to the Ten Commandments of detective fiction codified by Ronald Knox, a Catholic priest and writer of Golden Age detective novels himself." Richard started to say they could Google the topic, but saw several students already reaching for their smartphones. He smiled, thinking of the hours in a library such a search would formerly have required.

Richard closed his notebook on his half-delivered lecture. "I trust you're enjoying *Gaudy Night*. Next time we'll get into an analysis of Sayers' heroine. Look for comparisons to *Emma*. If you can manage the time, it will help you to take a look at *Strong Poison* where we first meet Harriet Vane. And for contrast, look at Laura Fairlie in Collins' *Woman in*

White." There, that should keep them busy. At least he hadn't required a written paper as he would have for an academic class. He noticed copies of *Gaudy Night* with bookmarks well toward the back on several students' desks, so he had hopes for Wednesday's discussion.

The room was fairly well emptied out before Jeremy, slow on his crutches, made his way to the front. "How are you Jeremy?"

"Mustn't moan. Stiff upper lip and all that." He grinned. "Actually, not too bad. It's starting to itch like fury. They tell me that's a good sign. Doc says if I'm a good boy he may be able to put me in a walking cast next week. That will be a relief." He shifted on his crutches. "I wanted to tell you, though, your assignment is really interesting, but I won't have much time for reading. With Sara off, I have to take longer hours at Hatchard's. Even if the internship is unpaid, I do want to make a good record."

Babs, standing at his elbow, broke in. "You don't need to worry, Jeremy. You'll do fine—both here and at the bookstore. I expect you've read the books anyway. You seem to know everything."

Jeremy looked embarrassed and changed the subject. "So may I ask if there are any new developments on the Jane Austen books?"

Richard blinked, he hadn't realized Jeremy had paid much attention to Drew's enterprise, but before he could reply a curly blond head charged through the door, almost running into Elizabeth who was approaching the group gathered around the lecturer. "Oh, sorry." Jack pulled back and flashed his impishly charming smile.

"Did you enjoy the Tower of London?" Her question included Andrew, who followed at a more sedate pace.

"It was wizard."

"What was the best, the Crown Jewels or the Torture Chamber?"

"The mint." Jack's answer surprised his hearers.

Andrew, though, agreed. "Very educational."

Babs, who had turned her full attention on the young newcomer, leaned over to put her at his eye level. "Tell me what you learned."

"It was where they made the money. The workers and their families lived there—in the tower—kids, too, even went to church and were buried right there in the tower. And one woman ran off with jewels, but they caught her. And a man slept for fourteen days—even King Henry VIII came to look at him. Then he woke up and went back to work."

"Educational, indeed." Richard nodded at his brother who had been the boy's escort for the morning.

"What else did you learn?" Babs seemed to be hanging on the boy's every word.

"Well, there was this bloke who counterfeited everything. He made all kinds of coins, and hundred pound notes and lottery tickets and got really rich, even if he did go to prison several times. And he even spoke to the king's Privy Council about scams at the mint. He wanted to be put in charge of it, but then they investigated him and put him in prison instead.

"When he got out, though, he helped the Bank of England, and they thanked him and rewarded him and let him keep the profits from his counterfeiting. Then they got him later for the lottery tickets and he was hanged."

Jack looked around, seemed encouraged by his attentive audience and concluded. "But he was a really talented counterfeiter, and he could have been a really important person if he hadn't been a crook."

"A most instructive morning," Richard began, but Babs preempted him.

"That's absolutely wonderful, Jack. Come over here and tell me more. Are you hungry? I've got some sweets in my bag." She led the boy back to her seat.

Richard watched them with a furrowed brow. "Strange woman," he said almost under his breath. Then he looked at Jeremy. "Oh, sorry. I didn't mean … Um, you two aren't…?"

Jeremy raised his eyebrows. "Babs? She's old enough to be my mother. Well—my aunt at least."

Richard wanted to ask more, but Elizabeth broke in, "What's up with her?"

Jeremy watched Babs with Jack for a moment. "You know, I think she's desperately lonely. I feel sorry for her and I try to be a friend. I've asked her what she does back in Evansville but she's guardedly vague. I'm not sure she has any family. All she'll talk about are her friends Julie Ann and Martha."

Richard was uneasy. Should he take his charge away from someone they knew so little about? Or should he encourage a relationship that might fill a need for both of them?

Chapter 17

"OKAY, BACK TO WORK." Elizabeth greeted Tuesday morning with determination and just a little guilt. Instead of carrying on with her research yesterday as she had intended, she and Richard spent the afternoon following Babs and Jack around London Zoo at Regent's Park. The excursion had been Babs' suggestion, and Jack was so delighted that his guardians didn't have the heart to say no, even though they didn't feel they knew Babs well enough to send the boy off on his own with her.

The excursion was a natural successor to Jack's visit to the Tower of London, because the Tower had been the home of wild beasts in London since the thirteenth century. They had even produced a guidebook for children in the mid-eighteenth century listing the attractions. The exotic animals were sent to London Zoo when the tower zoo closed in mid-Victorian times. Elizabeth salved her conscience by reviewing her notes on the Exeter Change menagerie of Austen's day. The building on the Strand had offered small shops on the ground floor and a menagerie of exotic animals on the floors above. Since lions, tigers, an ostrich, a rhinoceros and a hippopotamus were kept there, the noise, and surely the smells, must have been considerable. Equestrians were warned that their mounts might startle and rear at the roars of lions and tigers caged there. Charles Lamb said he liked to hear the big cats as he walked home to his lodgings in Temple Lane after an evening's socializing. The bestial roaring was one of the sounds of the city in Austen's day, perhaps much as the sound of traffic is today.

Visiting the menagerie was a hands-on experience, as visitors were allowed to pick up the kangaroo or pat and stroke the rhinoceros. Chunee the elephant was the menagerie's star attraction. After arriving in England in 1809, he performed on stage, delighting audiences at the Theatre Royal, Covent-Garden. Poor Chunee, though, went on a rampage a few years later and had to be put down.

Austen was well aware of the menagerie. Although there didn't seem to be any record of her going there, she sent one of her characters there. In *Sense and Sensibility* John Dashwood used it as an excuse for not calling on his half-sisters. He said he was "obliged to take Harry to see the wild beasts at Exeter Change."

That was all very well, although Elizabeth doubted how much of that information would make it into her article. And they had all had a very nice time at the zoo, despite Elizabeth's concerns about Jack's digestion with the amount of treats Babs fed him. "Boys that age have a cast iron digestion," Babs insisted, in response to Elizabeth's frown when Babs produced an iced lolly shortly after the candy floss and Cornetto.

Babs seemed to have been right, as there were no signs of ill effects the next morning, but Elizabeth firmly purposed to do a better job of balancing Jack's diet today. And that she would restrict her touring to places Jane Austen actually visited.

"Let's start with the site of Belgrave Chapel and then Henry's banks before he moved to Henrietta Street," she replied when Richard enquired as to their route.

He looked at her finger pointing to Belgrave Square on the

map. "Right, that's essentially behind Buckingham Palace."

"Are you happy to tag along with us today, Jack?" She wasn't sure what she would do if he said no. She didn't want to leave the boy alone as his irresponsible mother had done.

Fortunately, Jack had no complaints, so a short time later they were walking around the pristine white, classical buildings fronting on one of the small, green squares that gave London so much of its charm. "Do you know exactly where the chapel was?" Richard asked.

"West side where Halkin Street comes in." A moment later Elizabeth stopped beside a black iron railing to view a building of restrained elegance. Its main architectural features were a one-story portico supported by eight Doric columns and a narrow balcony surrounding the first floor.

She drew out an engraving of the building that had occupied this spot in Jane's day. The one before them was a pale reflection of the magnificent Ionic pillars rising three stories to an imposing pediment. As Elizabeth studied the print, several cars whizzed by them and a white delivery van turned the corner, its radio booming the beat of the driver's music. Elizabeth looked at her engraving which showed a man in top hat and frock coat ascending the steps to the chapel, ladies in hats and spencers on the corner, an elegant carriage arriving to deliver its passengers for the service and a little dog frolicking in the street. She could almost hear the clop of horses' hooves, the rattle of carriage wheels and the sound of the organ drawing worshippers in to prayer. Little wonder that the civility of Jane's day had such appeal to moderns.

"Anything more to do here?" Richard asked.

Elizabeth shook her head regretfully. "No, it's all gone."

"Except in your mind." Richard gave an encouraging smile.

"Yes, and in Jane's books." She looked on down the street at the classical row, every doorway with its pillared portico and a flag flying from each small balcony. "And that block hasn't changed at all." She held up the Regency sketch to compare.

"Portugal." Jack's *non sequitur* startled Elizabeth.

"What?"

"That flag." He pointed to the flag flying from the portico of the building where the Chapel of St. John had once stood. "We had to learn the flags of all the countries in the EU."

Elizabeth beamed at him. "How very useful! So that must be the Portuguese embassy. Thank you. Here, Richard, take our picture. You'll have your photo in a magazine for that bit of detective work, young man. At least, if they print it."

Elizabeth turned her attention to the next item on her itinerary. A pleasant walk across Green Park brought them to Cleveland Court, the site of Henry's first bank in London. At the age of thirty, shortly after his marriage to his widowed cousin Eliza, Henry resigned from the Oxfordshire Militia where he had risen to the rank of captain. With two associates he opened the bank that soon became Austen, Maunde and Tilson. Maunde was a fellow officer from the militia. "Cassandra stayed with Henry and Eliza at their home in Upper Berkeley Street, near Marble Arch, when Henry had his bank here in 1801."

"You have done your homework, haven't you?" Richard said.

"Homework?" Jack asked on a note of mild alarm.

Elizabeth smiled. "He means the research for my article. It's one of my favorite things—research."

Jack looked completely bemused by the concept.

"I like to understand what things were like. I want to feel I have a grip on my subject."

Jack nodded, and Elizabeth considered her own words. Was that why she felt so uneasy with the uncertainties surrounding Andrew's business enterprise? She certainly didn't have any sort of grasp on what the niggling questions could mean. But she would love to find out.

Turning back to her research, she took a picture of the fine, white stone edifice with its gracefully arched doorway and window boxes filled with bright pink flowers. It had once been Henry Austen's bank, but it wasn't readily apparent what the building was now used for. The English were so discrete about signage; it was often difficult to find even a number on a building.

Although only a few steps from busy St. James's Street, Cleveland Court off St. James's Place was quiet with no traffic in the narrow passage. There was not a person on the pavement except for themselves and a uniformed security guard in front of a nearby doorway. Elizabeth approached him with a smile and explained that she was researching for an article on Jane Austen. "Her brother Henry had a bank in that building." She pointed. "Could you tell me what the building is used for now?" For all the activity about, one might think the buildings deserted if not for their very polished upkeep.

The guard looked confused. "That's the bank."

"Still?" Elizabeth was amazed that the building would still have the same function after so many years. Or had his vague glance identified the building next door? Still, the proximity was extraordinary. "Russian, they are." The man offered no more information beyond that cryptic reply, so Elizabeth turned back to report to Richard.

He nodded. "Yes. An investment bank, then. I've read that wealthy Russians are anxious to get money to England, where they consider it safer."

The talk of money seemed to interest Jack. "Is that illegal?"

"Not at all. It's smart." As they walked back up St. James's Street, Richard continued to inform the lad on the mechanics of international banking. It made Elizabeth think again about the Chestermere Chartered Bank, holding a large sum of Andrew's money and undoubtedly similar amounts for how many others? Perhaps many from other countries as well. Could something like this private auction be used as a means for moving money? Her mind boggled at the thought—Mafia, terrorists … She stopped herself.

No, a highly civilized man from an art auction house had died in a freak accident. That was no indication that one of his clients was mixed up in anything illegal.

At the top of St. James's, just before they entered Piccadilly, Elizabeth spotted a familiar building. "Stop," she called to Richard and Jack who were several paces ahead of her. She pulled out her guidebook to be certain. "Yes, I was sure I recognized this. Look." She pointed from the picture to the building beside her.

"Wheesh, that's posh!" Jack's voice held a note of awestruck appreciation.

"White's," Elizabeth said. "London's most exclusive gentlemen's club." She pointed to the bow window. "The 'Beau' window—because Beau Brummell sat at a table there. And it seems that Henry Austen was a member.

"In the summer of 1814 London was caught up in the Prince Regent's celebrations of peace following Napoleon's abdication. White's threw a great ball that included the Prince Regent, the Emperor of Russia, the Duke of Wellington, and apparently Henry Austen. A few days before the ball, Jane replied to Cassandra's letter from Henrietta Street which must have informed Jane of the up-coming event, 'Henry at Whites! —Oh! What a Henry.'"

Elizabeth smiled. "Jane could never help being indulgent toward her best-loved brother, even when he was improvident or behaved in a way one feels must have been rather un-Austen. He was handsome and over six foot tall, and his ebullient personality was irrepressible."

They continued along Piccadilly, Elizabeth feeling at home there as she recognized Hatchard's and other shops that had become familiar to her. As they passed the Royal Academy of Arts, decorated with banners, she looked through the grand archway of the façade. The statue of Sir Joshua Reynolds, holding the place of honour in the courtyard, was decked with a garland of fresh flowers, denoting that the Summer Exhibition was in progress. A few steps past that, they turned into Albany Courtyard.

"Oh! What a Henry, indeed!" Elizabeth said as she looked at the dark, brick mansion accented with white pillars.

"Was that your bloke's house?" Jack asked, his eyes getting big.

Elizabeth smiled. "No, that was a private mansion. About

the time Henry had his bank here, it was being converted into sets for bachelor apartments. Lots of famous people have lived here, including Lord Byron." Jack's complacent nod indicated the excellence of Headington's curriculum.

On into the courtyard, she surveyed the pair of buildings lining each side of the stone-paved area. "Henry's bank was Number 1." She spotted it immediately inside the courtyard, marked with a blue door. A less grand accommodation than the mansion itself, perhaps, but an incomparable location.

"That must 'a cost him a packet," Jack observed.

Elizabeth agreed. "Perhaps that's why Austen, Maunde and Tilson only stayed here for three years before moving to Covent Garden. And before you can ask," she turned to Richard, "we don't have an account of Jane being here, but apparently she was, because she mentions a letter from Frank which seems to have missed her and been taken to her at Godmersham by Henry and Eliza."

"What did he do to make so much money?" Jack asked.

"Henry had what you might call a chequered career," Elizabeth said. "He was a captain in the Militia, a London banker, his sister's literary agent, and he married a cousin whose first husband was guillotined in the French Revolution. Then he went bankrupt when his bank failed, and he became a country parson."

"Certainly adaptable," Richard said.

"And apparently kept a cheerful attitude through it all. Jane said he 'couldn't help being amusing' and put 'life and wit' into a party. She also reported that he wrote 'very superior sermons.'" Elizabeth smiled. Little wonder he was Jane's favorite brother.

"But what made him go broke?" Jack asked.

"Well, we don't exactly know," Elizabeth answered. "Maybe imprudence, maybe bad luck. In October of 1815 Jane was in London to negotiate the publication of *Emma*. She only meant to stay a week or two, but Henry fell will with 'something bilious, chiefly inflammatory.'" Elizabeth's voice put what Jack would have called inverted commas around the quotation.

"Jane stayed and nursed him, but he got so sick she wrote to his brothers and Cassandra, summoning them to his bedside. She even wrote to their cousins to prepare them for Henry's death.

"Then he recovered. His illness could have contributed to his business failure. Or the other way round. His financial situation could have contributed to his illness. What we would call stress today."

Elizabeth paused. *Stress, indeed,* she thought. A possible murder, the police suspecting Andrew, a million pounds at stake—yes, she could certainly relate to Henry's stress.

"A lot of Henry's problem would have been the general economic climate of the time. Banks did well during the war with France, but Napoleon's defeat at Waterloo that summer was followed by a sudden economic depression. Henry, always generous and a bit of a social climber, had made large loans to friends and to aristocrats he probably wanted to become friends with. Henry wrote to his brother Edward, who had invested in Henry's bank, about the ruin he was facing and read the letter aloud to Jane. In empathy with her stricken brother, Jane reported to Cassandra, 'alas! I wonder that with such business to worry him he can be getting better.'

"Four days after she wrote that, Henry's branch bank in Alton, a town near Chawton, collapsed. The Henrietta Street bank stayed open, but Henry left London to avoid his creditors. He was able to return to London after a short time, but the following year he was obliged to borrow ten thousand pounds from Edward in an attempt to shore up the Henrietta Street bank. As Jane said, 'Alas!' The desperate attempt to salvage his fortunes didn't work, and in March of that year the bank collapsed and Henry was declared bankrupt.

"The whole family's finances were in disarray as all the brothers had invested with Henry. Jane herself lost something like thirteen pounds, which represented a lot of money to her, and Henry was no longer able to provide the hundred pounds a year he had given for the support of his mother and sisters."

"So Henry became a vicar?" Jack was following the account with unusual attention for one his age.

"That's right, and apparently quite a good one. He continued in that profession for thirty-four years."

But Jack was clearly more interested in following the money. "So why'd the money go down after Boney was defeated? You'd think that would make things go up."

Elizabeth blinked. She'd never thought to question it. But Jack was right. A nation's economy is tied to confidence. Surely a great military victory should have promoted confidence. You'd think everyone would start building and expanding, and the economy would rise. She remembered learning that was exactly what happened in America after World War II.

"Well, I know a lot of military people were suddenly out of jobs—Francis Austin, for example, went on half pay—that would affect the economy." She looked at Richard for a more complete answer.

He shook his head. "Sorry. Econ was never my favorite subject. That was one reason I hated running Caudex. Andrew has made a much better job of the financial end of things than I ever would have."

Elizabeth hoped that would continue to be the case when Drew's current financial venture was completed. She would certainly hate to see the fortunes of the Spencer family go the way of the Austens. Even though they all recovered, 1816 was an *annus horribilis* for them.

One thing was apparent, though; Elizabeth needed to understand more about Regency banking. Perhaps she would do a sidebar for her article on the subject, since Henry's bank had played such a central part in Jane's London life. She continued to mull the question over as they headed back to College Hall. By the time they reached the Goodge Street station she knew what she would do. She would ring Bramwell Child at the Chestermere bank and ask for a crash course in English banking. Then, realizing that might be an unhappy term to use to a banker, she asked for a history lesson.

Child agreed to see her on Thursday afternoon, so Elizabeth began a list of questions about the past troubles of English banking. All two centuries ago—still, she resolved to keep her mind open to anything she might learn that could be a clue to danger in the present situation.

Chapter 18

"HEROIC HEROINES." ELIZABETH STARTLED at the emphasis with which Richard announced his topic for the day. Then she looked around and realized the reason for his ardor. The class appeared to be drooping, much in need of having their attention revived. Had they been partying or staying up late perusing Richard's rigorous reading list? Or was it merely the natural rhythm of a mid-course slump? Whatever the cause, she was glad Richard seemed to have no intention of allowing them to go to sleep on him.

"In spite of the notable exceptions, such as Boudicca and Brunhilda, that one can find in history and literature, through the ages the classic heroine was a shrinking violet in need of being rescued and propped up by the hero. Evidence again of Jane Austen's innovative skills as we saw last week when we looked at her strongest heroine Emma Woodhouse and how she, along with her creator, functions as a Queen of Crime. Emma herself, of course, would consider it quite natural that she should be queen of absolutely anything." A few smiles and nods around the room indicated that Richard was succeeding in capturing his students' attention.

"And Austen poked overt fun at the fashion for wilting violet heroines in her 'Plan of a Novel' in advising that the heroine be 'often carried away by the anti-hero' but then must be rescued by either her father or the hero—which rather puts one in mind of Lydia (who was not the heroine) in *Pride and Prejudice*.

"For today, I asked you to consider Dorothy L. Sayers' Harriet Vane—who, ironically, was anything but vain. In spite of having Emma's example, the world of literature had to wait a hundred and fifteen years for Dorothy L. Sayers' Harriet to find a heroine with equal starch."

Elizabeth doodled a question mark on the paper before her. What about the Brontes? Jane Eyre, at least? But Richard was in full steam, so she turned her attention back to him.

"We first meet Harriet in *Strong Poison* where she is charged with murder. Yes, it is Lord Peter Wimsey who proves her innocent, but Harriet does not then fall into his arms. 'I'm going to marry the prisoner,' Lord Peter tells his brother at about the same time Harriet is telling her friend, 'I won't do that.' We have to wait four more novels until Harriet, in spite of repeated refusals, accepts Lord Peter.

"In turning down a startlingly advantageous offer of marriage, Harriet is like her literary predecessors Emma, who declared she would never marry, and Elizabeth Bennett, who turned down Darcy's first proposal—and like Jane Austen herself, who rescinded her acceptance of the wealthy Harris Bigg-Wither's proposal.

"The point, of course, is not avoiding marriage. The point is that Harriet is strong enough to face life on her own terms.

"*Gaudy Night*—which I hope you're all enjoying reading—is arguably Sayers' best novel—and is, also like *Emma*, a mystery without a murder. It is far more about the women characters and a manifesto for women's education than about the mystery. And here Harriet goes it alone as a detective. Until at the end, she does what she had told her friend four novels earlier she wouldn't do—she sends for Lord Peter. And, finally, does what she had repeatedly told Peter she wouldn't do—she agrees to marry him.

"But Harriet has not succumbed to convention, to social pressure, or to a need to fall into her hero's arms. She is finally convinced that she will not lose her own integrity in doing so. Indeed, she will become more her true self."

Elizabeth didn't realize she was grinning until Richard caught her eye and returned her smile. "More her true self." That was exactly what love and marriage should do. Had done for her. And she remembered so vividly their own Harriet Vane/Lord Peter Wimsey experience almost a quarter of a century ago, when she herself had repeatedly refused Richard's proposals—until that Golden Age style mystery week high in the Rocky Mountains changed her own life view.

And then there had been all those years of growing together....

Her blissful reminiscence might have lasted through the lecture had Richard's next statement not captured her attention: "That is the core of a strong heroine: self-understanding and doing the right thing without compromise." As he continued to develop that theme, Elizabeth glanced aside and caught the conflicted look on Babs' face at the end of the row below her. Was it fear or determination? How could such diverse emotions be reflected in a single aspect?

Elizabeth would have told herself she was mistaken had not Babs dropped her head into her hands at that moment. What a contradiction that woman was. Their "bubbly Babs," ever pushy and assertive, apparently crumpling. Jeremy must be correct in his assessment of her need.

Babs raised her head at Richard's next words, and Elizabeth returned to listening to her husband with an increased awareness of how fortunate she was to share her life with this man. "Emma Woodhouse and Harriet Vane are classic examples of what is required of a truly heroic heroine—whether in the pages of a novel or in real life: Being true to oneself. That requires knowing oneself. Which in turn demands learning and changing. Then acting in accord with the knowledge one has acquired."

Elizabeth glanced again at Babs. Regret? Guilt? Resolution? Or a cry for attention? It was impossible to decipher what was written on her face. This was not the simple woman from Midwestern America on a summer holiday that she would have people believe. Elizabeth determined to learn more.

"Now, in contrast, I want to take a look at Laura Fairlie, the heroine of Wilkie Collins' *Woman in White*, written a generation after *Emma*. Did some of you get a chance to read it?"

Wanda half-raised her hand. "Wanda, you got started?" Richard asked.

"Um, not exactly. We watched the video. Some of us. All five episodes." She ducked her head in apology.

Richard smiled. "Oh, does that explain the yawns and drooping heads I see? Sorry if I kept you up past your bedtime, but the video is fine to make my point: Collins' Laura Fairlie is the quintessential Victorian maiden. As I'm sure you saw, Marian Halcombe, her devoted half-sister, is much more heroic, but is not the heroine—although she would be today. Laura, the Victorian ideal of a heroine, is trapped in an arranged marriage, easily tricked by the villainous Count Fosco and must be rescued by the hero Walter Hartright. Laura is acted upon. She does not act.

"And there-in lies the key to a strong heroine," he paused for effect, as pens scribbled around the now fully awake class. "Heroines take action. They follow their own lights. They do what they know to be the right, the courageous thing.

"True Queens of Literature like Austen and Sayers achieved this greatness because they were such careful observers of human nature. They didn't have 'How to Write a Novel' handbooks. They didn't have any women's movement to raise their consciousness. They observed what worked in real life and presented their insights through their characters."

The discussion then became general, with students sharing understandings and opinions from their reading. Only Babs did not follow her usual form by jumping in first with her ideas. She pulled the shocking pink scarf she was wearing today closer around her face and seemed shrouded in her thoughts.

Elizabeth tried to think what it could be. She tried tying together words from Richard's lecture and actions or remarks made by Babs over the past days, but she could form no clear pattern that would provide a clue to reading Babs' earlier expressions. Had Elizabeth seen regret for past actions or determination for a future act? Was Babs involved in a tangle that would require heroic action on her part? Was she heroine or victim—actor or acted upon?

Maybe some of it. Maybe none of it. Guesses were no good. Elizabeth resolved to talk to her when she could.

Richard brought the day's lecture to a close. "Friday we will explore Sayers' worldview which is a theme that will carry us over as we explore P. D. James next week. To prepare for this I would like for you to read—or watch—" he added with a smile at Wanda, "*The Nine Tailors* or *Busman's Honeymoon*. I'll let you play detective. See if you can spot the elements in these books that reflect their author's philosophy."

Elizabeth's opportunity to talk to Babs came sooner than she had expected. As soon as the lecture was over, Jeremy turned to Babs with what appeared to be a probing question. Elizabeth felt she would have liked to listen in, but Babs replied only briefly and sent Jeremy clumping away on his crutches.

Elizabeth blinked. Odd, that. She had always felt that Babs was making the running in that friendship. Was it really Jeremy trying to get close to Babs? If so, was it for anything darker than responding to her neediness?

Certainly Babs, sitting alone in the emptying room, looked needy now.

"Want to go get some lunch?" Elizabeth approached her.

Before Babs could reply, Jack hurried in with Andrew in tow. He made a beeline for the two women, babbling about his morning outing to Madame Tussauds. It seemed that the honours for top attraction had to be shared between the Chamber of Horrors and the Star Wars Experience. Shakespeare and Charles Dickens, whom Andrew insisted on viewing, had not held much appeal.

But now he was ready for lunch. Uncle Andrew—Jack had easily slipped into the English habit of assigning honorary titles to close friends—had promised him a visit to the kebab caravan in Russell Square. Elizabeth said she was taking Babs out and suggested Richard go on with Jack and Drew. Richard looked surprised, but did not demur.

There was no such thing as a quiet eatery in London at this time of day, but Elizabeth managed to secure a booth at the back of a small café, and both women ordered what was billed as an American style salad, although Elizabeth had her doubts as to how American it would be. When the waitress was gone, she turned to her companion who sat with her head down, staring at the table.

"Babs, I don't mean to pry." Elizabeth stopped herself. "Well, I suppose I do, really, but something is wrong, and I thought maybe I could help."

Babs managed the first smile Elizabeth had seen from her that day. "You already have. Inviting me to lunch was a big boost."

Elizabeth didn't think her companion looked particularly boosted. She waited. Babs sighed. "Okay." Her shoulders slumped even lower than they already were. "You're my only friend on this side of the Atlantic. I guess I would like to talk to someone." She took a drink of the tap water Elizabeth had requested for each of them. "I'm afraid you'll despise me."

Elizabeth remained silent, wondering what she could possibly say to that.

"I know I act like I don't have a care in the world, but it's all a big act. I'm a fraud." Even saying the words seemed to lighten her load. She took a deep breath and plunged. "I'm running away. From my husband. He's a brute." She rubbed her elbow, that Elizabeth now noticed bent at an odd angle. Babs nodded at it. "Yeah, he pushed me down the stairs. Long time ago."

"Babs, that's horrible." Elizabeth reached instinctively for her friend's hand.

Babs shrugged. "Old story. Black eyes recover." She gave a self-deprecating grin. "I had a whole drawer of blingy sunglasses. He wasn't usually physical, though. Too clever for that. It was the constant denigration I couldn't take.

"It was being told constantly I was worthless. I came to believe it was true. That's why the lecture this morning was so hard. All that talk about being strong and doing the right thing. I thought I was being courageous. It felt like it took a lot of courage. But now I see I was just running away, and I haven't really accomplished anything at all."

"It looks like you took a huge first step."

"Maybe. It was so odd. You see, I used to be an investigative reporter. Before I got married. I thought it would be interesting to read some of my old stories, so I was searching to see if I could find any online, and this conference on crime came up in a search. I just knew I had to do it.

"I was so frightened, but I looked at myself in the mirror and almost shouted, 'You're not worthless. You can do this.' Then I called my friends and they helped me. They don't know the whole story—not half of it—no one does, but they'd suspected a bit.

"Anyway, Martha arranged for Tommy to go to summer camp with her son—they're best friends—"

Elizabeth held up her hand. "Whoa, who?"

"Martha, my friend."

"No, who's Tommy?"

"Oh, my son. He's ten. I couldn't leave him alone. I mean, Cranston has never raised a hand to him, but I couldn't take that chance."

Elizabeth nodded. Now she understood why Babs had latched on to Jack with such alacrity.

"And Julie Ann got a ticket in her name so I could use her passport. We look so much alike people are always thinking we're sisters."

"Was all that cloak and dagger stuff necessary?"

"Oh, yes. Cranston Ellington is a very powerful man.

He'd have hired a detective—I'm sure he has—and he'd have dragged me home by now. He doesn't care about me—he only married me for the money I'd inherited when my parents died—but he won't stand for humiliation."

Elizabeth was trying to get her mind around everything Babs had poured out: The carefree, scatter-brained Babs a beaten wife, the mother of a ten-year-old son, a former investigative reporter, a scheming runaway who was in England illegally ... "Goodness, what a story," was all she could say. She couldn't help feeling this was more like hearing the plot of a novel than a true life experience.

Now Babs looked frightened. "You do believe me, don't you?"

Elizabeth nodded, but she kept thinking. It was a lot to take in, yet she knew such things did happen. "Yes, I do. Of course I do." She did; it made sense. She realized now there had always been a shadow, a desperation under Babs' frivolity. "But what are you going to do? You can't stay in London forever."

"I have a month, but it's going so fast it frightens me." She shook her head. "I can't go back. I can't face it. I just can't."

"Babs, there are all kinds of laws against battery. You need to go back, but not to Cranston. Get a divorce."

Now Babs looked truly frightened. "Cranston is the most powerful man in Vanderburgh County. He's a judge and on about twenty committees and commissions. I doubt I could even get a lawyer to represent me. And I'd never get a fair trial. He'd take Tommy and my money."

Elizabeth pushed her half-eaten salad aside and stood up. "We need advice."

Babs blinked at her. "We? You mean you'll help me?"

Elizabeth didn't bother answering. "Come on."

They found Richard back in the dorm room, reading. Jack was in his own room, most likely playing video games on the ipad Andrew had loaned him.

Richard listened to Babs' whole unhappy story with the calm Elizabeth knew he would. Only the part about Cranston pushing Babs down the stairs and telling her she was worthless made him flinch. When it was over he sat so long thinking Elizabeth began to wonder whether or not he was going to answer.

"What you need to do is retain an attorney—from outside Vanderburgh County. Better yet, from out of State. Kentucky, but licensed to practice in Indiana. The attorney can hire a private investigator to gather evidence. Are there medical records of your broken arm?"

She nodded. "And dental. He knocked a tooth out, too. But I said I fell."

"Well, tell the truth now. It's amazing what evidence they can turn up. Did anyone ever hear him belittling you?"

"The neighbors might have."

"Right. Your attorney needs to have the case built before you get back. Can you and Tommy stay with Martha?"

"Probably. I'll think about it." Babs looked about ten years younger. "How can I thank you enough—both of you? You hardly know me, yet you seem like you really care."

Elizabeth moved closer and gave her a hug.

"Thank you again so much. I'll go see what I can work out about a lawyer before I lose my nerve." Babs was halfway to the door when her cell phone rang. She pulled it from her pocket and glanced at the screen.

Her face went so white Elizabeth thought she might faint.

"It's Cranston." Babs looked around as if she expected him to stride through the door.

Chapter 19

"RIGHT, YOU THREE GO on to Apsley House." Elizabeth looked at Richard, Jack and Drew after breakfast the next morning. "Babs and I will join you after I've had a look at Sloane Street and Hans Place."

"Oh, I don't want to intrude," Babs protested. "I'll be fine here on my own."

"Don't be silly," Elizabeth put a hand on her friend's arm. "We're not leaving you on your own."

Babs looked relieved. "Oh, thank you! I know it's silly of me. Cranston couldn't know where I am just by ringing my cell phone, but I can't get over the feeling that he's following me." She gave Richard a sheepish look. "I know I should stay here and read Sayers for tomorrow's discussion."

"No you shouldn't," Elizabeth insisted. "Some things are more important than reading. Not many, but a few."

At Marble Arch the women waved the men on to the Duke of Wellington's home, then walked up Park Lane and turned toward the leafy, green oasis of Portman Square. They walked around the square to the east side to Orchard Street, then stood under the thick, green branches shading the pavement and observed the red busses, black taxis, and cars of every description filling the street in front of them. Across the street, the entire block of modern buildings was fronted with scaffolding covering the bank, shops and offices.

Elizabeth sighed. "In Regency times this was one of the most fashionable addresses in London. I suppose it still is, but hardly as a residence."

"Who lived here?"

"For my purposes, Jane's aunt Mrs. Hancock and her daughter Eliza, who later became Henry's wife. They lived here in 1788 when Jane made her first visit to London. At least, first that we know about. Mr. and Mrs. Austen stopped here to visit his sister Philadelphia Hancock with Jane and Cassandra on a trip to Kent. Jane was only thirteen years old. If this was her first time in the city, she must have been wide-eyed."

"Did the Austens stay here, then?"

"We aren't sure. The only recorded fact is that they dined here." Elizabeth snapped a photo on her phone but didn't think it likely she would use it to illustrate her article. *Regency Realm* readers would be far more interested in how things were in Jane's day than in seeing more evidence of today's bustle and clutter. Hopefully their next locations would be more evocative.

A five minute walk took them to Upper Berkeley Street. Although lined with parked cars on both sides, Elizabeth was happy that the area was, indeed, considerably quieter. She pointed to a small hotel in the middle of the block. The pristine white of the Portland stone ground floor was accented with boxes of cascading red petunias, at the windows and above the fanlight over the door, blending with the red brick of the three upper stories.

"This was Henry and Eliza's first home. We don't know that Jane ever visited them here, but Cassandra stayed here in 1801, and Jane wrote to her." Elizabeth paused and turned to read from her notes. "'I dare say you will spend a very pleasant three weeks in town. I hope you will see everything worthy notice, from the Opera House to Henry's office in

Cleveland Court; and I shall expect you to lay in a stock of intelligence that may procure me amusement for a twelve-month to come.'"

Babs regarded the first floor windows behind the red petunias. "You can just imagine Cassandra sitting up there, reading her letter and smiling, can't you? Eliza must have loved living here, since it's so close to Portman Square where she had lived with her mother."

Elizabeth led the way to the bus stop, chatting about her plan for her article. She was about to congratulate herself on the job she was doing, keeping her friend's mind off her troubles, when she saw Babs look uneasily over her shoulder as if she feared she was being followed.

"Relax, Babs, you're safe with us."

"I know. I think it's just habit. I don't know what I'd do without you."

"Don't worry, we'll get you through this. Did you get hold of an attorney in Kentucky like Richard suggested?"

"I did. I know it's the right thing, but I suppose hiring a detective myself has made me more aware that Cranston undoubtedly has one looking for me."

"But he has no reason to look in England, has he?"

Babs shivered. "I hope not."

At 64 Sloane Street, Elizabeth drew Babs' attention to the elegant, three-story, octagonal-shaped, stone building before them and launched into her explanation. "Henry and Eliza lived here from 1811 until she died in 1813. Jane stayed with them in April of 1811. She was correcting the proofs of *Sense and Sensibility* at the time. She assures her sister that she is 'never too busy to think' of it, but her letters recount a rather constant round of visits, dinners and museums. She tells of one day she visited a museum and a gallery with a friend, and then a party with Henry. Her brother, after being confined to his bank all day and 'putting life and wit into the party for a quarter of an hour, put himself and his sister into a Hackney coach.'" She paused to smile at the oh-so-Jane phrasing.

"Henry and Eliza gave a very grand party while Jane was

with them, and she recounts it all to Cassandra in great detail." As she spoke, Elizabeth dug in her bag for her annotated copy of Jane's letters and turned to the appropriate one. "'Our party went off extremely well. There were many solicitudes, alarms and vexations beforehand of course, but at last everything was quite right. The rooms were dressed up with flowers, etc. and looked very pretty.'"

Elizabeth stopped and lowered the book. "I'm sorry, Babs. I wasn't thinking—I'm probably boring you cross-eyed. I'm so used to being with Richard, and he's as avid for these details as I am."

"No, no. I'm loving it!" Babs assured her.

"But this isn't your field at all. Do you even read Austen?"

"I'm certainly going to after this! No, it's because I don't know anything about it that I'm enjoying it so much. Do go on. Her letters are wonderful—you can just see it all happening, can't you?"

Elizabeth smiled. That was exactly how she felt. "Here, let's walk around the corner. I think we can see the back of the house from Hans Street. Yes, there." A moment later she pointed, through the scrolls of an ornate iron fence, to the yellow and red brick wall mirroring the octagonal shape of the front. "The first floor, where the party was held, was a salon to the front and drawing room to the back, with a connecting passage and stairway between."

She looked at her companion. "Are you certain you want to hear all this?"

"Yes, please."

There was no doubting Babs' sincerity, so Elizabeth read, "'At half past seven arrived the musicians in two Hackney coaches and by eight the lordly company began to appear … I spent the greatest part of the evening very pleasantly … The drawing room being soon hotter than we liked, we placed ourselves in the connecting passage, which was comparatively cool and gave us all the advantage of the music at a pleasant distance, as well as that of the first view of every new comer … We were all delight and cordiality of course. —Including everybody we were 66— which was considerably more than Eliza had expected and quite enough to fill the back drawing room ... the music was extremely good.'"

Elizabeth scanned a bit. "She gives quite a list of the music. Cassandra was at Godmersham, and Jane knew Fanny would be interested. They had Glees, a harp, harp and piano duets and a female singer.

"And fashion—Jane never leaves out the sartorial details. She reported to her sister that her headdress was a bugle band, like the border to her gown, and a flower which she had borrowed from Mrs. Tilson, the wife of Henry's bank partner. The party was mentioned in the paper the next day. Even if they did spell the name Austin, it must have been a triumph for Eliza."

Babs looked thoughtful. "That was 1811?" Elizabeth nodded. "And you said Eliza died in 1813—just two years later. That's sad."

Elizabeth agreed but carried on down the street to number 23 Hans Place. A row of rather gothic-looking red brick houses faced the small, green square of Hans Place Garden, its wrought iron fence firmly gated against intruders. "The house on the corner was Henry's. Of course, it didn't look anything like this. This exterior is pure Victorian. After Eliza's death Henry moved from Sloane Street to Henrietta Street in Covent Garden to live over his bank. He only stayed there about a year before he moved back here, next door to his partner Tilson."

"And Jane visited him here?"

"Oh, yes." Elizabeth took that as an invitation to refer to her letters again. "In August of 1814 Jane took a stagecoach to Sloane Street. In spite of later referring to the journey as her 'long jumble,' she said the coach wasn't too crowded, but they arrived late. Henry himself met her and helped with her trunk and basket and took her on to Hans Place 'in the luxury of a nice large cool dirty Hackney Coach.'" Elizabeth slipped once again into her quoting voice.

"She reported to her sister that 'It is a delightful place ...

I find more space and comfort in the rooms than I had supposed and the garden is quite a love. I am in the front attic, which is the bedchamber to be preferred.' Then she later says, 'I live in his room downstairs, it is particularly pleasant, from opening upon the garden. I go and refresh myself every now and then and then come back to solitary coolness.'

"Jane was back here again in October of the next year, to negotiate the transfer of her publishing to the prestigious John Murry and Son. She hadn't planned to stay long, but Henry quite suddenly became ill. She had hoped the medicine he took, along with a good night's rest, would set him quite to rights, but the illness lingered. And Jane stayed to nurse him.

"'They say the disorder must have originated in a cold. You must fancy Henry in the back room upstairs and I am generally there also, working or writing.'" Elizabeth realized she was getting lecturely again so looked up to see if Babs was still with her.

Her companion was looking slightly puzzled. "When she says working she means needlework. A lot of the writing was letters to John Murray regarding the publication of *Emma*," Elizabeth explained. "I'm sorry if I'm running on too much."

Babs, however, insisted that she was fine, so Elizabeth continued. "In his illness Henry was attended by one of the Prince Regent's physicians who told his patient's sister that the prince was an admirer of her novels and kept a set of them in every one of his residences.

"The physician then told the prince that Miss Austen was in town. That resulted in James Stanier Clarke, the Regent's librarian, calling on Jane and showing her over Carlton House. Clarke informed Miss Austen that a dedication to HRH would be acceptable."

"How exciting—so that's the book Jane signed!" Babs said.

Elizabeth frowned. She didn't realize Babs knew about the auction. Had Jeremy been talking about their business? "No, she had the dedication copy sent straight from the publisher.

She was reluctant about the whole thing because of the prince's moral character, but a royal suggestion was a royal command, so she had no option but to dedicate *Emma* to him.

"Fortunately, though, she wasn't obliged to follow Clarke's literary advice that she 'delineate in some future work the habits of life and character and enthusiasm of a clergyman—who should pass his time between the metropolis and the country ....'

"Oh, my goodness." Elizabeth suddenly became aware of the length of time they had spent. "Richard and the others will surely have finished at Apsley House by now, and I did want you to have a chance to see it. It will probably be fastest to walk across the park. Is that all right with you?"

Babs assured her it was, so a brisk twenty minute walk found them back at the frenetically busy Hyde Park Corner, where the imposing equestrian statue of the Duke of Wellington faced Apsley House, the grand mansion of golden Bath stone that had been the Iron Duke's London base for the political career that followed his military victories.

The women made it only as far as the golden marble entrance hall. They were gazing at the grand staircase, which split in its ascent to curve upward in both directions, when a thoroughly chuffed Jack led his escorts to meet the newcomers. "I must congratulate the history master at Headington School," Richard said. "This lad knows the history of the Battle of Waterloo better than the guides."

"And there was a statue of Boney without his clothes on," Jack added.

"Do you ladies want to see the house? The art is absolutely magnificent," Andrew joined them. "Or are you ready for lunch?"

"I'm sure Babs is famished. I've walked her legs off and talked her ears off," Elizabeth said. "But I have an appointment with Mr. Child at the bank, so I'm afraid I'll have to leave her in your care."

Babs, however, didn't accept that plan. "No, no. I'm not at all hungry. I ate an enormous breakfast. Let the guys go eat.

I'll go with you."

Elizabeth started to protest.

"Don't be silly, you don't want to go all the way to the City alone. Much nicer to have company," Babs insisted.

Elizabeth admitted it would be pleasant to have company, and Richard said they would all stick together. "Well, if you're sure you all don't mind."

Richard bought their tickets, and the Central line whizzed them across London with surprising efficiency. Bramwell Child was waiting for Elizabeth in the foyer of the Chestermere Chartered Bank. Andrew said he would wait outside with Jack, while Richard went on with the ladies. Elizabeth introduced her friend, and Child ushered them into his high-ceilinged, wood-panelled office with his usual old world courtliness. "How charming to see you again, Dr. Spencer." He motioned to the leather chairs in front of his desk. "What can I do for you?"

Elizabeth explained briefly about her project researching London in the time of Jane Austen and the troubles that beset Henry Austen's bank in 1816. "Can you give me some insight into the banking crisis after the Battle of Waterloo? I know very little about Regency banking."

"Yes, of course, delighted. The thing is, there's nothing all that unique about Regency banking. It's the principles of economics—a simple matter of supply and demand."

Elizabeth took out her notebook and began writing.

"You see, the banknote was overprinted by the British government. After they declared war on revolutionary France in 1793, they had to finance it. As military expenses increased, the government printed more and more banknotes. The Bank of England was then required to exchange the notes for gold should the banknote bearer request it."

Child held up a finger. "Ah, one minute, if you will. I'm sure I have the figures here somewhere." He turned to a shelf of books behind his desk and pulled off a heavy tome. It took him only a few minutes to locate the passage he was looking for. "Yes, here it is. By the end of the war in 1814, the banknotes had a face value of 28.4 million pounds of gold, yet were backed by only 2.2 million pounds of gold, which caused the currency to depreciate by 30%."

Apparently Child caught Elizabeth's slightly dazed look. "Don't worry, it's not a mathematical formula. The value of currency is the value people place on it and the value they believe other people will place on it. Fortunately, there was sufficient confidence that the government would repay the war loans to keep the value from falling further."

Elizabeth smiled, appreciating his explanation. Yes, confidence—that was really what had to be behind any financial transaction, wasn't it? "Still, 30% was bad enough for Henry. If he had over-extended loans to friends, the money that they had to repay him was worth only a third of what he had loaned?"

"If they could repay at all," Child agreed. "Which then made it impossible for Henry to pay his creditors."

"Yes, that would explain why Henry then borrowed more money from his brothers."

Elizabeth finished her notes and stood up with a smile. "Thank you so much, Mr. Child. I think I understand now. That's very helpful."

"You're most welcome, dear lady. Any time I can help you at all, don't hesitate to ask." He came around his desk to hold the door open.

"I assume the bidding on the Austen first editions is going well? With only two more days we're all getting rather nervous." Elizabeth's comment was more in the nature of making conversation than in anticipation of information.

"Ah," Child tapped the side of his nose with his forefinger, "nothing to be nervous about, I assure you. It's all in good hands. Safe as the Bank of England, as they say." He opened his office door for them and followed them into the hall.

They were just back to the foyer when a young man, with black hair close-cropped to show the intricate tattoo at his hairline, wearing a black designer shirt and jacket over tight, ripped jeans, sailed through the front door carrying a sleek leather pouch. "Ah, Child, just the man. Still open to receive the winning bid, I assume."

Their host looked slightly embarrassed as he said a hasty good-bye to Elizabeth and turned to the newcomer.

Richard stepped on out to the street to find Andrew and Jack, but Elizabeth stood looking at the departing back of the designer-clad man. "Well, there's competition. And good luck to him." Since Babs' earlier question had indicated that she knew about the auction, Elizabeth felt free to speak her thoughts, relating Child's lecture on financial confidence to Andrew's venture. "I don't know. I suppose it's all absolutely fine, but I just don't feel good about the whole thing. How did Bramwell Child strike you? Do you think he was too helpful? Could he be covering something up?"

Babs thought for a moment. "Like what?"

Elizabeth sighed. "That's just it. I don't have any idea. Something just doesn't feel right. And there was that man that was killed at the university. Did you know he worked for the auction house that's handling the books? I can't help feeling there has to be a connection."

Babs wrinkled her forehead then smiled. "How wonderful. I used to be an investigative reporter. I've had experience digging out dirt. Let me help you. I'll see if I can find out anything. It's amazing what one can turn up online if you know where to look."

"Babs, you shouldn't get mixed up in this. You have enough worries of your own."

"No, that's fine. It'll help me take my mind off Cranston and all that. Where shall we start? Do you have any clues?"

"Well, nothing you'd call clues. We don't even know if anything is connected, but…" Elizabeth told her about seeing Sara Ashley-Herbert at the theatre. "Maybe he really was her brother, but it didn't look like it."

"That shouldn't be too hard to check. A quick Google search will make a start."

The thought of investigating a puzzle had obviously raised Babs' spirits, but Elizabeth worried. What had she done by sharing her own worries? Had she created more trouble for her friend? What if she led her into danger?

Chapter 20

"SAYERS, LIKE AUSTEN, WAS a clergyman's daughter and, like all honest artists, her worldview informed all her writing. I have always maintained that who the writer is will, ultimately, speak louder than her words. Perhaps this is more evident in Sayers than in almost any other writer." Richard took a deep breath and looked around his classroom of students from all cultures and backgrounds. In this age of multi-cultural tolerance and political correctness, the last thing he wanted to do was put his hearers off with his views. But if he hoped to give his students a valid assessment of his subject, he had to be equally honest.

"Of course, we see Sayers' worldview expressed most explicitly in works other than her novels: in her radio plays 'The Man Born to be King' in which she presents the life of Christ in the setting of a modern Englishman—which caused a scandal because she didn't present Jesus speaking in King James' English; in her translation of Dante's *Divine Comedy*, which she considered her most important work; and in my personal favorite, *The Mind of the Maker*, her theological/psychological work in which she compares the creative human mind at work in producing a novel or other work of art, to the mind of God."

Richard smiled at the glazed look on most of his students' faces, although Jeremy, at least, was intent on his note-taking. "All right, don't worry about that—it was just an introduction. For our purposes, the interesting thing is how this worldview plays out in Sayers' classic mystery novels which, as opposed to her works of serious scholarship and theology, she considered mere 'pot-boilers.' She wrote them because she was desperate for money, and mystery lovers have been grateful for her penury ever since.

"Of course, Sayers was too good an artist to write 'mere crime fiction.'" Richard indicated the quotation marks with his fingers. "She explores the plight of World War I veterans in *The Unpleasantness at the Bellona Club*, the ethics of advertising in *Murder Must Advertise*, and she advocates education for women while opposing Nazism in *Gaudy Night*." He paused to allow his more assiduous pupils to finish their writing.

"All right, let's see what your own sleuthing turned up as to Sayers' beliefs informing her mystery novels. How many of you had a chance to take a look at *The Nine Tailors*?"

Wanda's hand was first up. "We watched all four hours of the mini-series." Susan and Noboko nodded. "Just the church setting for so much of the action is a start."

"Beyond providing the setting for the bells, which are the centerpiece of the book, what does the church setting add?" Richard prodded.

Susan answered. "It shows the importance of the church to the community. Especially when everyone gathers there in the flood. It's sort of like Noah's ark."

Richard nodded. "Good. That's an excellent analogy. The church is a haven. A place of sanctuary. And incidentally, I've always thought that if Hitler had read that wonderful picture of the community keeping calm and carrying on, which is such a basic part of the English character, he wouldn't have bothered trying to break their spirit with the blitz."

Al was next. "And aren't there quite a few casual Biblical references? Like Lord Peter saying the killer was 'hanged higher than Haman.'"

"Right, Al. Which Sayers could safely take for granted that her readers would understand as well. One can't help wondering how much of that is lost on modern readers." Richard shook his head, thinking of the literary foundation that had been lost in the contemporary abandonment of Bible reading. "Anyone else?" He looked around the room. "There is one aspect of the plot—"

Jeremy raised his hand. "The death of Will Thoday. Wimsey suggests Will might not have wanted to live when he learned that his actions caused Deacon's death, but I think Sayers felt she had to kill Will because he was responsible for a man's death."

Richard nodded vigorously. "Excellent. That's exactly what I was looking for. And what does that show about the author's worldview?"

Jeremy's response was immediate. "The value she placed on human life."

"Precisely. If I had been writing that story, I don't think it would have crossed my mind to punish Thoday. I still remember how surprised I was the first time I read the book. He was a husband and a father. His family needed him. His actions were manslaughter at worst. But because he had taken a life he had to pay."

"'An eye for an eye and a tooth for a tooth.' Isn't that a bit harsh?" Wanda asked.

"I think Sayers would say there is justice in the universe," Susan said.

Richard opened this point up for a lively class discussion, then brought them back to the topic by moving on to *Busman's Honeymoon*.

This time Jeremy was first to volunteer. "It's the same thing we were saying about Sayers' respect for human life, except here Lord Peter regrets, even mourns, the death of the murderer."

Noboko added, "And Crutchley was a horrible man. He

didn't seem like a person worth mourning."

Jeremy continued. "That's a lot of the point, I think. Crutchley was an unrepentant brute, but Sayers would still say he was God's child so no one had the right to take his life. Not even the state. And Wimsey grieved being a part of that. So, really, this is a novel against capital punishment?"

The last had been said with a note of questioning, so Richard encouraged him. "That's right. It is. Sayers would definitely say that life belongs to the Creator and no one has the right to interfere."

"Oh!" Wanda's hand shot up. "So Frank Churchill couldn't have been a murderer because letting him get away with it would have been inconsistent with Austen's beliefs, too."

After another spirited exchange Richard was able to dismiss his class for the weekend with a glow of satisfaction. There was nothing he enjoyed more as a teacher than guiding his students to new understandings and seeing them apply things that had been learned in earlier classes. He had noticed, though, how unaccountably quiet Babs had been. She sat in her usual seat next to Jeremy, but hardly spoke to him, even when he tried to engage her with questions after class.

Apparently Elizabeth had noticed too, because she hurried to her friend as the others left the room. "Are you all right, Babs? You're so quiet."

Babs' smile looked forced, but she insisted that she was absolutely fine. "You didn't get any more phone calls, did you?"

"No. Well, I don't think so. It did ring once last night. Unknown caller. So I didn't answer."

"Babs. Switch your phone off and put it in a drawer or something until this is settled. Go to a Carphone Warehouse and get a pay-as-you-go with a new number."

Richard seconded Elizabeth's advice. He was surprised Babs hadn't thought of that herself already.

"Thanks. I definitely will," she agreed readily. "But mostly I just had my mind on our investigation."

"Our investigation?" Richard frowned.

Elizabeth hastily explained about Babs' investigative reporter background and that had she offered to see what she could learn.

"And have you learned anything?" He wasn't entirely happy with involving an outsider in their suspicions, but he would take that up with Elizabeth later.

"Yes, it seems pretty likely that man you saw was Sara's brother. At least she does have one. I found a Julian C. Herbert who is an art dealer. He has galleries in London, Paris and Rome. His bio mentioned he has a younger sister Sara. Unfortunately, I didn't find any pictures of him on the web, but I'll show you the information I found when we get back to the dorm."

They were entering College Hall when Andrew and Jack returned from riding the London Eye. Andrew seemed as pleased with their outing as Jack was. "To tell the truth, I didn't expect much of it," Drew said. "It just seemed like a good way to keep my squirrely friend entertained, but the views of London were stunning. London through the eyes of a child can be a very refreshing perspective."

"Uncle Drew said we could go for a boat ride, too. And see a fencing exhibition."

Drew nodded. "Yes, I've promised the Tate-to-Tate and a rehearsal at The Globe. But you all look very intent. Have we interrupted something?"

Richard was trying to work out how to tell his brother they were investigating the friend he suspected Andrew of becoming fond of, but before he could say anything Babs jumped in. "I've been looking up that Sara Ashley-Herbert. It seems that she does have a brother."

Andrew stiffened. "What do you mean—investigating? I told you she had a brother." He looked from one to the other of them. "What's going on?"

"Nothing's 'going on.'" Richard tried to sound reassuring. "We just wanted to be sure—"

"Be sure the little brother didn't make a mess of things again this time? I think I can make my own decisions in that department, thank you."

Richard wished he could feel as confident as Andrew sounded.

"You might be interested to know that Sara and I are meeting for dinner at Rule's tonight—her invitation, as a matter of fact. And I'll have to say she sounded as anxious to see me as I'll admit I am to see her. She even said she has learned something interesting about the auction, so you could call it a business appointment if that would make you feel better."

Richard wasn't certain he felt the least bit better, but he did know when to keep quiet.

"And we're going to 'Lion King' tonight," Jack was telling Babs.

"On stage, you mean? I saw the movie. I can't imagine how they'll do all that live. You must tell me all about it."

"Oh, Babs, I'm so sorry. I didn't think—we got the tickets a week ago. Maybe you can still get one, too," Elizabeth said.

"Oh, no. Don't worry. I have plenty to do. I still have to finish *Death in Holy Orders*, and I haven't even started *Death Comes to Pemberley*. I was also wondering if there are any more people I could do any snooping on for you. How about the companies involved in the auction? Of course the bank and auction house are well established, but is anyone else concerned?"

Richard glanced uneasily at his brother who was fortunately occupied by Jack. Richard wasn't completely at ease with Babs looking into this affair. He couldn't imagine what his brother would say if he knew they were investigating his business deal as well as the woman he was dating—er—having a business dinner with, Richard amended his thought.

Richard almost sighed with relief when Babs, with a reminder from Elizabeth to lock her door, turned to her own room.

A while later in their room, with Elizabeth typing rhythmically on her laptop, Richard kept going over in his own mind the idea of investigating the auction. Where could there possibly be a fiddle? Could the books be a fake? Not unless Gerard Asquith was terribly mistaken. Or had been bribed. The likelihood of either, for one with his qualifications, seemed nearly impossible. As much as he disliked the idea of Babs' investigation, he supposed she might be able to look into that.

Could the books be authentic, but their anonymous seller be corrupt? A member of the mafia or something? Asquith said the provenance was sound. And surely an auction house with the reputation of Legacy House would have checked very carefully on the legitimacy of their client. But if Clive Kentworth's death wasn't accidental, did that indicate he might have been involved in a scam? Or maybe he wasn't involved but discovered someone else was. That could have been a motive for murder. If that was the case, what about Melinda Fulsom who replaced Kentworth? Or had he fulfilled his job and was therefore expendable?

What did that leave? The bank? Richard recalled the brass plate by the door: Chestermere Chartered Bank, est. 1837. If he wasn't very much mistaken, that was the year Queen Victoria ascended the throne. It seemed impossible that a bank that had weathered close to two hundred years of financial disasters, wars and political storms would be likely to succumb to any under-handed dealings now. And wouldn't Bramwell Child and all their officers be bonded or whatever they called it in England?

They had seen, though, that being with an established financial institution didn't preclude criminal activity—even in the Bank of England itself. The brother of "The Old Lady of Threadneedle Street" had been a forger. And there was the man at the mint in the Tower of London who had counterfeited hundred pound notes and lottery tickets. What if one of the bidders deposited counterfeited money? Richard mulled that over in his mind, but couldn't see how that unlikely event would affect Caudex. Could the bank substitute counterfeit money when they returned the unsuccessful bidders' deposits? No, surely all that would simply be done by electronic bank deposit. No actual currency would exchange hands, would it?

Richard became aware that Elizabeth's typing had stopped. "How's the writing coming?"

"Fine, but much too long. I'm just putting everything in and then I'll cut it when I'm done."

"What are you working on now?"

"Since our visit to The Lyceum tonight will finish my research on theatres Austen visited, I thought I'd give some background on ones she attended that are no longer here."

"Like Covent Garden?"

Elizabeth sighed. "It's such a shame there's nothing left of the theatre Jane knew except the location. She would have attended the second theatre built on that site, but that theatre burnt in 1856. The current building retains that façade, but the interior is from the 1990s, so I'm afraid there's very little left of Jane there.

"When she and her nieces were staying in Henrietta Street in September of 1813 they went to the theatre twice." Elizabeth picked up her spiral bound notebook, momentarily missing the feel of her lost leather book. "Jane reported, 'Of our three evenings in Town one was spent at The Lyceum and another at Covent Garden;— The Clandestine Marriage was the most respectable of the performances, the rest were Sing-song and trumpery, but did very well for Lizzy and Marianne, who were indeed delighted;— but I wanted better acting.—There was no actor worthy naming.—I believe the theatres are thought at a low ebb at present.'

"That was unlucky for Jane because, a year before, Edward and Fanny were staying in Sloane Street and they got to see Mrs. Siddons perform. Jane would have loved that."

"She was a severe critic, wasn't she?" Richard observed.

Elizabeth smiled and turned a page in her notes. "And she was well aware of that fact. She wrote to her niece Anna, 'We were all at the play last night, to see Miss O'neal in Isabella. I do not think she was quite equal to my expectation. I fancy I want something more than can be. Acting seldom satisfies me. I took two pocket handkerchiefs, but had very little occasion for either. She is an elegant creature however and hugs Mr. Younge delightfully.'

"You can always trust Jane to speak as she sees. I do wonder, though, if the laws governing the theatres at that time didn't promote 'sing-song and trumpery.' Only Drury Lane and Covent Garden were licensed to perform plays. All the other theatres had to get around the law by putting on puppet shows, burlesques, pantomimes and the like.

"That probably explains why, when they went to The Lyceum on the Saturday after the great Sloane Street party, they saw a play called 'The Hypocrite' which was taken from 'Tartuffe,' rather than seeing the Moliere itself. Jane was lukewarm on her opinion of the actors. She wanted to see Mrs. Siddons at Covent Garden, but Henry had been told by the boxkeeper that he didn't think she would be performing, so they gave up the idea. Then Siddons did act, and Jane wrote that she 'could swear at her with little effort for disappointing me.'"

"And we're going to the original Lyceum tonight?"

Elizabeth sighed. "Sadly, there was a fire—the usual story. The original entrance was on the Strand just down from the Exeter Change. It's now the Lyceum Tavern." She brightened. "We could go there for dinner before the show; it's only around the corner from the theatre."

Elizabeth's idea turned out to be a good one. A few hours later Richard and Jack waited patiently on the pavement while Elizabeth took pictures. "The upper floors are very much what Jane would have known." She pointed to the four-story, stone front with the peaked roof suggesting the classical pediment that had capped the rows of windows in former times. The dark wood ground floor, however was nothing like. "In Jane's day the entrance was a pillared portico."

She continued as they crossed the Strand. "They did all kinds of shows here, including the first exhibition of Madame Tussaud's waxworks." That caught the attention of the youngster who had enjoyed that exhibit only two days ago. "They had boxing, fencing, concerts," she continued. "Astley's circus even performed here, although when Jane went to Astley's, on her Cork Street visit, that was probably to 'Astley's Amphitheatre of Equestrian Arts' on the south side of Westminster Bridge."

As they went into the welcoming, dark wood tavern Elizabeth tucked her phone and notebook away. She was no longer in research mode. Now she could enjoy the evening. They went through the cozy interior to the garden behind, where children could be accommodated, and made quick work of their dinners. Richard and Jack went for the traditional bangers and mash, but Elizabeth chose mushroom, cranberry and brie Wellington with the lovely surprise of hazelnuts.

The evening was warm, and strings of lights in the tiny garden behind the tavern added a glow to the diners gathered around wooden tables. They didn't linger, though, because they were anxious to get on to the theatre. A few doors down the Strand they turned into the cul-de-sac at the bottom of Wellington Street to be greeted by the grand, colonnaded entrance of the two thousand seat theatre.

They were riveted from the moment the curtain went up. Elizabeth couldn't have said which one of them was the most delighted and amazed at the production. The skill of the dancers, the artistry of the costumes and masks that turned the actors into a fantasy of creatures, and the ingenuity of the articulated animals, especially the giraffes and the panther that moved with such sinuous grace, held them spellbound.

Afterwards they chose to walk back through the still-busy streets in the warm evening, with Jack dancing before them singing, "Hakuna Matata."

They saw their young charge to his room then closed the door on their own. "What a perfectly magical evening!" Elizabeth put her arms around Richard and snuggled against his chest. She felt so secure, so happy. It was a moment she wanted to hold on to forever—complete and all-encompassing as if nothing sordid or distressing could ever enter the circle around them.

It was only the tiniest niggling of superstition that held her back from voicing her bliss.

Chapter 21

SUCH EUPHORIA COULD ONLY be followed by a night of deep, uninterrupted sleep. Elizabeth closed her eyes with thoughts of being wakened by the dawn chorus.

The frantic pounding on their door that penetrated her consciousness a few hours later, however, couldn't have been further removed from that paradise. "What?" Elizabeth sat upright and shook her sleeping husband. "Richard, something's wrong!"

"All right, all right. Just a minute," Richard called as they both scrambled for dressing gowns. Sleep-dazed, he fumbled with the latch then yanked the door open.

"Andrew! What is it?" Elizabeth stared at the disheveled state of the man that entered: glasses askew, hair uncombed, shirttail hanging half out, feet jammed into shoes with no socks.

Richard pulled him into the room and all but pushed him into a chair.

Elizabeth looked at the bedside clock. Just after four. What had Drew been doing? Dinner at Rule's with Sara, she recalled. But something had gone very, very wrong.

"Sara. She's dead." Andrew dropped his head into his hands.

Elizabeth was too shocked to reply. No. She must have heard wrong. Andrew must be mistaken.

"The police. Got me out of bed." He blinked at the two speechless faces in front of him. "Oh, sorry. Like I did you. I didn't think..."

Richard waved his apology aside. "Start over. Tell us everything."

Elizabeth scrambled off the bed and put the kettle on.

"From the first," Richard prompted a few minutes later, after Elizabeth had administered strong, sweet tea to them all. "You had dinner..."

"Yes. That's right." Andrew seemed to be coming out of his stupor. "Excellent dinner. Such fun. Lamb, we both had lamb. And A Kiss for Lillie—champagne cocktail for Lillie Langtree—she used to dine there with Edward the something. He was king." He shook his head. "Oh, I don't know. What does it matter? I'm rambling." He took a deep breath. "But she was so alive. Like she loved every minute." He choked. "Like she loved me."

"It's all right. Take your time," Richard encouraged his brother.

"Then we walked along the river to St. James's Park. Sara had her bread roll. She ordered it special—the waiter put it in a bag for her. She wanted to feed the ducks in the moonlight. Silly. They were mostly asleep. But the flowers." He looked around the room as if trying to locate them. "They smelled so sweet on the night air."

His breath came in shuddering gasps in the silence. "Then we walked across Westminster Bridge. Only partway across, so we could look back at the Houses of Parliament—all lighted. It was unbelievable. Like a fairy tale."

Andrew closed his eyes, and Elizabeth knew he was seeing it all again. His voice was soft, as if recalling a dream only for himself. "I kissed her and she was so warm. So soft. So alive. Her hair smelled like apricots.

"I'd never known anything like it. 'I love you.' 'I love you, too.'" His voice seemed to dissolve into the memory. "I don't know which one of us spoke first. We could have stood there all night. Just like that."

A sob shook his whole body. "Oh, dear God, I wish we had. If only we had. She invited me to stay the night. Why didn't I?"

"You've lost me, Drew." Richard refilled Andrew's tea cup. "You were on the bridge. Then what?"

"I walked her home. She lives in Marsham Street, near St. James's Park." He paused. "Lived."

"And?"

"I walked home."

"Walked? Wasn't that a long way?" For the first time Elizabeth asked a question.

"I don't know." He looked puzzled. "It didn't seem like it. I was so happy."

Elizabeth nodded. She had felt the same a few hours earlier.

"I was asleep. Not long, I think, but it felt like hours. The police came. They told me—" He shook his head violently as if trying to clear out the image. "She—Sara—" He choked on the words.

Richard crossed the room and put his hands on his brother's shoulders. "Steady. Take a breath."

"She fell under a train at St. James's station."

Elizabeth's gasp of horror rang in her own ears. "But how is that possible? Are they sure it's Sara? You left her at her flat?"

"In the lobby. I didn't go up ... I think we were both afraid of what might happen if I did. I know I was."

"But surely there's a doorman or guard or something—"

Andrew shook his head. "He wasn't there. We were glad at the time because we could..."

The image of them locked in an embrace gave her a new idea. "CCTV. There must be footage of you entering together, then you leaving alone. Apparently she went out alone later. It should show that, too. And you walking home. And Sara going to the tube ... London is covered with cameras, isn't it?" Did she go alone, or was she with someone who pushed her? It hardly sounded like she would have been in a frame of mind to commit suicide. And they hadn't had enough to drink to make it accidental. Assuming Andrew was telling the truth. Elizabeth stopped herself. Of course he was. Andrew would never hurt anybody—especially a woman he was in love with.

"But how did the police find you? How did they know to look for you, even?" Richard got the questioning back on track.

"Her phone. It wasn't smashed. All our texts..."

"And the police think you..." Elizabeth couldn't bring herself to say it. "Did they accuse you?"

"Same as. They took my passport."

The three continued to talk, Elizabeth and Richard asking questions and Andrew repeating what he had already said, in an endless loop that might have gone on and on had not a knock at the door, followed by Jack's entrance, reminded them that it was breakfast time.

Jack stood in the middle of the room, regarding them with a perplexed look. "You been up all night? You look awful."

Elizabeth told him in as straightforward a manner as she could manage. He thought for a moment. "The one that looked like an old film star?"

Elizabeth nodded. "Grace Kelly. Yes. How clever of you."

He shrugged. "Sahil wants to make movies. He's mad about Hitchock. We watched them on his ipad after lights out." Then he ducked his head. He had apparently forgotten he was talking to his housemaster. When no reprimand followed he continued. "And they think Uncle Andrew did it? That's a load of old cobblers."

Elizabeth nodded. Indeed, it was. But how could Andrew prove it? Surely the police would come up with surveillance footage that would prove Andrew innocent. Failing that, she hated to think how bad it looked for him. Andrew had spent the evening with Sara. He was undeniably captivated by her. Elizabeth could easily imagine the scenario a suspicious detective could come up with. A lovers' tiff. Sara turned him down. He pushed her in frustration. Surely an accident, but fatal. As Jack said, codswollop. But how did one prove it?

And all this brought back again Clive Kentworth's death. They had questioned at the time whether or not Kentworth was the intended victim. Elizabeth saw it all again: Kentworth hailing Sara, Sara hurrying to meet him. Then Babs calling her back, waving Sara's bracelet just as the skip went off the building.

If the murderer had been aiming for Sara, he didn't miss his target this time.

"It's more likely the bloke she pushed down the stairs."

Elizabeth turned open-mouthed to Jack. "What did you say?"

He repeated it.

"What bloke? You don't mean Jeremy, do you?"

Jack shrugged. "That his name? Him with the cast."

"What do you mean, she pushed him down the stairs?" Elizabeth had forgotten that Jack was even there when Jeremy fell, but now she remembered the Headington choirboys running up to them just before Jeremy plunged down the steps. They had been part of the confusion that contributed to no one having a clear picture of what happened.

Jack shrugged again. "That was what it looked like."

"No, you're mistaken." Andrew seemed to waken from the trance he was in. "Sara told me about that. She felt so guilty. She saw him start to go and tried to reach him, but her fingers only grazed his arm. She said several times, 'If only I'd been quicker.'"

"I need some air." Elizabeth grabbed the notebook off her desk and went out to the small private garden behind the dorm. She struggled to think back in detail through the past two weeks. So much had happened, it seemed more like two months. She opened her spiral notebook, which was becoming dog-eared with her constant use, and made a list of events, putting a check by those when Sara had been present, starting with Richard's book signing at Hatchard's.

And Sara had come on to St. Paul's with Jeremy after

Richard had invited him. If Elizabeth recalled correctly, that was where Sara met Andrew and he told her about the book auction.

Then at the bank for the book evaluation—to which Sara had inveigled an invitation—no, that wasn't fair, Sara had expressed an interest in the proceedings and offered her services as someone with some background in the field.

But she had been more than on the scene when Clive Kentworth was killed. She had been a few feet away and was sprayed with rubble. After that Sara had gone back to their room with them—to rehash the event or to find out what they knew?

Then there was the matter of the mystery man at the theatre. Brother? Lover? Client? Could Sara have been blackmailing someone? Over a rare manuscript, perhaps? The one she was advising Kentworth on? Perhaps they had misinterpreted the appearance of intimacy between Sara and the mystery man. Elizabeth started to line through that flight of fancy, then decided to leave it.

Nearer to home, was Sara truly fond of Andrew; or was she staying close to him to cover something up or to learn what he knew? About what?

Elizabeth drew herself up short and all but ripped the pages from her pad. Sara wasn't a suspect. She was the victim.

Chapter 22

ELIZABETH ROSE TO GO back to her room but, before she could take a step, Babs rushed into the garden. "Oh, my goodness! I've just heard! Whatever next?" She looked over her shoulder as if fearing being followed, then looked up, surveying the rows of staring dorm windows facing on the garden. "I'm terrified."

Elizabeth couldn't help thinking the woman looked more exhilarated than frightened. But then, oddly enough, murder did take some people that way. Still, Elizabeth was baffled. "Terrified? Why?"

"I think it's Cranston."

"Your husband?" Elizabeth pulled Babs over to the bench and they both sat.

"Oh, not him himself. He'd never deign to get his hands dirty. I think he's hired a hit man. I think I was the intended victim both times."

Elizabeth bit her lip. Laughing would not be the right reaction. Still—"But you weren't anywhere near St. James's station when Sara died."

"I did go out last night. I was going to read and have an early night, but it was so stuffy in my room I needed some fresh air."

"You went all the way to St. James's for fresh air?"

"I'm not sure where I went. I just went out and wandered around a bit. But we are both blond, and in the dark someone could make a mistake."

Only if Babs' husband had hired a blind man. Was the woman unhinged or simply a drama queen? Of course, she had been under a lot of stress.

"Did you know that the police suspect Andrew?" Maybe that would get Babs' mind off herself.

Babs looked thunderstruck. "Andrew? Why would they suspect him?"

Elizabeth told her the story of Sara and Andrew's evening.

Now Babs was thoughtful. "Do you know what time Sara died?"

"No, not exactly. Why?"

"I might be able to help. I saw Drew come back at midnight. If she died after that..."

Elizabeth was baffled. "You saw Drew last night?"

"Yes, I was sitting in Russell Square, looking at the hotel—the way they light up all that Victorian Gothic at night and the flags flying—"

"And you know it was midnight?"

"I heard a clock chime. I don't know—is there one in the square or something? Anyway, you know how automatic it is to count the strikes of a clock."

Elizabeth sighed. "You should definitely tell the police, but they'll probably just say he could have gone back out again."

"I kept sitting there for a long time, and I didn't see him leave."

"Right. You ring the police. They probably left their number with Andrew. We can hope that will help." Elizabeth stood again. "Now, I need to think of Jack. We don't want him upset by this." She thought fast. Where did she need to go for research that could also entertain her two charges?

"Why don't you come with me to, um, the park? Kensington Gardens." Hopefully that would offer some relief for Babs' anxieties, too.

At Jack's request they took a double decker bus. The tube would have been much faster but, Elizabeth reminded herself, the main purpose of the outing was to entertain Jack and, if he found looking at the London traffic creeping along Oxford Street entertaining, that was all to the good.

Babs looked down on the tops of the cars and assorted vehicles crowding next to the bus and sighed. "We could have walked faster. No wonder you enjoy studying the Regency so much."

Elizabeth considered. "I'm not sure it would have been much better in those days, but one has a feeling the vehicles were more elegant. Parading about in a carriage did amuse Jane. She wrote to Cassandra about going to an exhibition— where she was disappointed because she couldn't find a picture of Mrs. Darcy and could 'only imagine that Mr. D. prizes any picture of her too much to like it should be exposed to the public eye.'"

"Oh, I do love *Pride and Prejudice*. I've seen all the films. How wonderful that she kept Elizabeth and Darcy in her mind just like real people." Babs rooted in her bag to unearth a notebook. "Say that again, I want to make a note."

"Yes, it is fun, isn't it?" Elizabeth took out her copy of the letters and opened to the appropriate one. "Earlier in the day Jane and Henry had gone to an exhibition in Spring Gardens. She says, 'It is not thought a good collection, but I was very well pleased—particularly (pray tell Fanny) with a small portrait of Mrs. Bingley, excessively like her. I went in hopes of seeing one of her sister, but there was no Mrs. Darcy ... Mrs. Bingley's is exactly herself, size, shaped face, features and sweetness; there never was a greater likeness. She is dressed in a white gown, with green ornaments.' This convinced Jane that, as she had supposed, green was Mrs. Bingley's favorite color. She expected Mrs. Darcy to be in yellow."

"Did she find her later?"

"No, Jane and Henry were quite indefatigable in visiting galleries. They went to that one in Spring Gardens, then to see Sir Joshua Reynolds' paintings in Pall Mall later in the day. They had planned to go to Somerset House where the Royal Academy exhibited, although their plan was interrupted by business at Henry's bank." Elizabeth made a mental note that the sites of those galleries were locations she still needed to visit.

Their bus left Oxford Street to travel along the equally busy, but slightly wider, Bayswater Road, and Elizabeth remembered that it was actually the traffic she had meant to allude to when Babs' interest took her down the art exhibit rabbit trail. "What I was going to say, though, was that Jane loved driving about London, especially in an open carriage which she said she found very pleasant."

Elizabeth picked up the book still resting in her lap and leafed through a few pages. "Here it is," as always, her voice took on a slightly ironic tone when she read Jane's words, "'—I liked my solitary elegance very much and was ready to laugh all the time, at my being where I was.—I could not but feel that I had naturally small right to be parading about London in a Barouche.'"

"Oh, I love that. I must read her letters."

"Yes, I'm sure you would enjoy them. Get this edition, it's the best." She held out her copy of Deidre Le Faye's collection.

Babs was making note of the reference when the bus lurched, narrowly missing a motorcyclist who pulled in front, barely fitting in the space between two taxi cabs. Babs' pen and notepad flew to the floor, the pad lodging under the seat behind them and the pen rolling all the way to the back. Jack jumped to his feet and scrabbled under the seats to retrieve Babs' belongings, just in time for them to scramble off the bus at their stop.

Elizabeth found walking across the fresh green park in the summer air to be a relief after the stuffy bus. No wonder Jane Austen enjoyed going about in an open carriage so much. Then she saw Babs turn back to view those exiting the bus, as if she feared being followed. Not only that, Jack observed it. She certainly didn't want him to pick up on Babs' fears. "Are you all right, Babs? You weren't hurt in that jolt were you?"

Babs turned back to her. "No, no. I'm fine."

"Good. You know, even in Jane Austen's time, carriage accidents were a danger. Jane herself was involved in one very near here— on the other side of the garden." Elizabeth pointed in what she hoped was the direction of Hyde Park Gate. Jack, always interested in vehicles, gave her his attention as well.

"One Sunday evening, Jane and Eliza and Henry were on their way to pay a visit to a family of French aristocrats— probably some Eliza knew from her time living in France— when the horses gibbed near Hyde Park Gate. A load of fresh gravel had been dumped on the road and made it a formidable hill for the horses. One of them had a sore shoulder anyway, and they refused to pull. Eliza was frightened, so she and Jane got out. They had to stand about in the evening air for several minutes. Jane blamed the event for the cold in the chest her sister-in-law caught."

Her hearers seemed to be enjoying her story, so Elizabeth continued. Since she had just reviewed this section of the letters, she had the details in mind. "They went on with their visit, though, and Eliza enjoyed it very much. Jane said her cousin meant to cultivate the acquaintance of the aristocrats, and Jane couldn't see anything to dislike in them except that they took large quantities of snuff. She said the old Count was a very fine looking man with quiet manners 'good enough for an Englishman.' Jane said she would take to him if only he spoke English. She especially admired his taste in paintings, and his son was a fine musician, which pleased Eliza.

"Things weren't at all what they appeared, however. What Jane didn't know was that the Comte d'Antraigues was a spy, in the pay of both the Russian and the English governments. Add to that, his wife, the Countess, was a retired opera singer and Jane's 'old Count'—who was all of fifty-eight years old— wanted a divorce."

Elizabeth's story took them beside the Long Water to the statue of Peter Pan. Elizabeth was looking at the delightful statue of the "Boy Who Wouldn't Grow Up" standing on his plinth of carved squirrels, rabbits, mice and fairies, when Jack noticed the sign attached to an iron railing: Talking Statue / Hear Peter Pan Here. "Hey, can we do that?" he asked.

"Oh, that's fun! You swipe the QR code with your smartphone and Peter Pan will call you. Here, give it a try." Elizabeth dug in her bag. When a moment of scrounging was unproductive she realized she had left her phone on her desk. Little wonder after the upsets of the morning.

"I'm sorry, I don't have my phone. Babs, do you have yours?"

Babs pulled out her phone and held it up to the code. In a moment there was a tinkling sound, and the screen pictured Peter Pan calling from Neverland.

They followed that triumph of modern technology with their own visit to Neverland in the Princess Diana Memorial Playground. Jack, as carefree as any of the Lost Boys, joined a group of children playing Captain Hook on the pirate ship and doing Indian dances around the teepees. While Elizabeth and Babs sat in the shade on a comfortable bench.

Jack called to them from the crow's nest below the flapping skull and crossbones flag. Elizabeth waved back. "Oh, I wish I had my phone. Babs, can you get some pictures?"

Babs hurried off to capture Jack's antics.

Then it struck Elizabeth. Babs had her smartphone with her. She said she had replaced it with a pay-as-you-go, so she wouldn't be harassed by her abusive husband. Well, she said she would do so—had seemed very relieved at the idea.

So why had she changed her mind? Had she just been too busy? Or had their befriending Babs made her feel sufficiently safe she didn't think she needed to take that precaution? No, Babs had been almost hysterical this morning when she heard about Sara. Strange. It didn't add up.

Then Elizabeth glanced at Babs' bag laying on the bench beside her. Elizabeth blinked at the red cover of Babs' notebook sticking out. It couldn't be. But that looked suspiciously like her own notebook that had disappeared so mysteriously. She looked around to spot her companions. Jack was doing a war dance in front of a teepee for the benefit of Babs' camera. Elizabeth pulled the notebook from the bag.

A ragged edge at the binding showed where several front pages had been removed. About as many as Elizabeth had filled with her notes. She thought back. She had last written in it when they had lunch at Fortnum and Mason with Andrew and Sara. Afterwards she had gone with Richard to meet his students at the library. She closed her eyes to recall who had been sitting around the table: Wanda, Susan, Jeremy and Babs—with Elizabeth's bag slung casually on the back of her chair. Later that evening she had discovered the loss.

"What fun that was! Princess Di would be so pleased if she could see how much pleasure this gives children. It's a perfect memorial to her." Babs flopped down on the bench beside Elizabeth.

Elizabeth held out the notebook. "Babs, where did you get this?" She tried to keep any accusatory note out of her voice. There must be a logical explanation.

Babs blinked as if trying to recall. "Oh, Jeremy gave it to me."

"Jeremy?"

"Yeah, last week in class. I forgot mine and needed something to take notes on."

"Did he say where he got it?"

"I think he said he found it somewhere. Anyway, he didn't need it, so he said I could keep it. I like it because it's just the right size to fit in my bag."

Babs chattered on, but Elizabeth didn't follow her. She was too caught up trying to sort out the questions whirling through her mind. Did Jeremy steal her notebook? Or did one of the other students, then leave it around for someone to find? It seemed clear, though, that it had been taken on purpose and her notes removed. But who? Why? And what could that have to do with the problems that seemed to be plaguing them?

Chapter 23

IN SPITE OF THE fact that he and Elizabeth had sat up late into the night examining the mounting questions from every angle and seemingly ending up only with more questions, Richard woke the next morning in a hopeful frame of mind. At least Babs reported that the police seemed to accept her evidence of Andrew's whereabouts at the time of Sara's death, and that should help them pinpoint CCTV corroboration. They could look forward to a quiet Sunday today.

Beginning with sung Eucharist at Westminster Abbey. Andrew, Babs and Jack all seemed more than pleased to accompany Elizabeth and Richard to the comfortingly traditional service. Such order and beauty were definitely what they needed in their lives at the moment, and Richard felt himself relax as he joined his own voice in singing "Praise to the Lord, the Almighty" along with the choir processing to their stalls. He smiled, noting the careful attention Jack paid to the choirboys, undoubtedly knowing exactly how it felt to be in their position.

Elizabeth helped Babs find her place in the prayer book, but Richard preferred to do the service from memory, letting the rhythm of the ancient words still his mind and his soul.

He noticed Andrew gazing upward at the long, fan-vaulted ceiling rising more than a hundred feet above their heads. Richard hoped his brother might be drawing assurance from the stability of the heritage this great abbey represented—the faith of its founders and nearly a thousand years of royalty, builders, monks and common people. A faith built on principles of justice and mercy.

They remained in their seats until the last echoes of the Bach toccata and fugue faded, before making their way up the black and white marble aisle to Poet's Corner in the south transept. A confusion of statues, tombs and memorials made it difficult to know where to look first. But Jack homed in on his favorite, guided to the grey marble plaque in the floor by a spray of fresh white roses above it. C. S. Lewis/1898-1963. "I believe in Christianity as I believe that the sun has risen. Not only because I see it, but because by it I see everything else," Jack read from the inscription running around the edge of the memorial.

He gave a satisfied nod. "He's buried in Headington, though," he informed Babs and Andrew and went on to explain how his school was organized into houses honouring Headington's most famous resident. "We're Perelandra. Stav, Nilay and me. Well, him, too." He pointed to Richard, their housemaster.

"And me, too," Elizabeth reminded him.

They moved on to another tomb with a dark, carved stone canopy. "Chaucer," Richard pointed out. "He was the first person to be interred here. More because he was Clerk of Works of Westminster Palace, though, than for his poetry. But then, all the rest of this just grew up around him. Most appropriate for 'the Father of English Poetry.'"

Babs noted Charlotte Bronte, and Andrew mentioned two of his favorites, Dickens and T. S. Eliot, but it was Elizabeth who spotted the simple, pale stone table engraved Jane Austen/ 1775/1817. She stood some time regarding it with a small smile playing around her lips. At last she nodded. "I'm sure she would approve. Once she got over the shock of being included here. Of course, it's nothing like all the hoopla around her grave in Winchester Cathedral, but I'm sure she would feel that the fact they put her next to Shakespeare said it all."

Indeed, the life-sized, white marble statue of England's— indeed, the world's—greatest playwright stood in full Elizabethan regalia, leaning on books atop a pedestal adorned with the heads of Elizabeth I, Henry V, and Richard III. Jack leaned in to read Prospero's speech from "The Tempest" engraved on the scroll under its author's hand. "'The cloud-capp'd towers, the gorgeous palaces,/ The solemn temples, the great globe itself,/ Ye all which it inherit, shall dissolve/ And, like this insubstantial pageant faded,/ Leave not a rack behind.'"

Richard placed a hand on his shoulder. "Well done. That's probably my favorite quotation from Shakespeare."

"And certainly appropriate in the present circumstances." Richard hoped Andrew was referring not to his own situation, but rather to the general transience of life, standing, as they were, in the presence of so many departed greats.

But Babs brought them back to the current unpleasantness they had managed to escape for a space of time. "I think it's morbid. It's far better to get what you can from living for the moment than to worry about it all fading away. Look at Sara and that Kentworth fellow. I mean, any of us could fall under a bus at any time, and what would any of it have mattered?"

"All the more reason to do it right while we have the chance, I should have thought." Richard would have liked to say more, but this was not a line of philosophy he wanted to subject his brother and Jack to at the moment, so instead he took Babs' arm and turned toward the exit. "Time and past for lunch, I think."

Fortunately the prospect of food was more than adequate to distract Jack from any gloomy thoughts. They chose a nearby Italian restaurant, and a few minutes later the energy with which the boy attacked his plate of Spaghetti Bolognese evidenced the success of the plan.

When they had finished, Andrew suggested they walk along the Victoria Embankment. "Have you seen the Statue of Boudicca?" he asked Jack, rather as if offering an excuse for the excursion. Richard wondered whether it was in truth, though, reluctance on his brother's part to return to a lonely hotel room. Or was it a desire to stroll again near Westminster Bridge where only a few hours before he had been so happy with Sara?

Richard immediately dismissed the darker possibility that it could be a desire to steer them away from the nearby St. James's Station. He assured himself that, if there were any element of that, of course it would be because of the unpleasant association with Sara's accident and not from any guilty conscience on his brother's part.

Jack gave the statue of the Celtic Queen, who defeated the Romans for a time, his full approval. "The horses are wizard." Then he frowned. "The harnesses should be poles, not leather, though. Did you know the Celtic warriors ran along the traces of their chariots when they charged into battle? They were amazing. If the Romans hadn't brought in elephants they would never have beaten them." The pride in his own Celtic blood gave a touching emphasis to his words. "It was the smell of the elephants. Not their size. The smell spooked the horses."

Having impressed his hearers with that historic footnote, the schoolboy was more than happy to pose for pictures with the warrior queen. While Elizabeth snapped away, Richard allowed his thoughts to turn to the subject he had been so studiously avoiding.

If Kentworth's and Sara's deaths were connected—and the coincidence was too great to believe otherwise—the obvious connection was the auction.

He wasn't sure how much the police knew about that, but if they came poking around again Richard would take care to put them in the picture. Other than that, he considered what they might do to uncover the facts. After all, his telling the police was no assurance they would choose to follow that line of investigation. Elizabeth had been the one that, from the first, worried most about the legitimacy of Andrew's business venture. Richard himself had been more concerned about the plan paying off for Caudex than suspecting any malfeasance. But now he wondered if he had been too sanguine.

He let his own pace lag, as they moved on along the river toward Westminster Pier. What was the most obvious possibility for a fiddle? Faked or stolen books. That had to be it. The bank was legitimate. The auction house was legitimate. There didn't seem to be any other possibility.

"A penny for them." Babs dropped back from the others and fell into step with him.

Richard gave a sardonic smile. "My thoughts? Wouldn't be worth your money."

"Try me."

Richard hesitated. He was the one who had objected—strongly—to the idea of involving Babs in their family business. But Babs had involved them in her family business by telling them about Cranston. It seemed that she was involved, whatever he did.

He sighed and told her his thoughts about the authenticity of the Jane Austen first editions Andrew had bid on.

She nodded. "Yeah, I'd heard bits and pieces about that." She thought for a minute. "So you're wondering if the books are genuine?"

He told her about the intensive examination Andrew's expert had conducted.

"So either the books are authentic—but maybe stolen—or your expert was incompetent or a fraud." The three ahead of them stopped at the pier. Richard and Babs leaned against the low cement wall lining the river side of the walk and watched tourists departing from a recently docked tour boat, while another queue inched down the pier for their turn on the Thames.

"Want me to see what I can find out?"

"You?" Richard was afraid his incredulity showed in his voice.

Babs seemed unfazed by his skepticism. "Elizabeth told you I used to be an investigative reporter. I worked pretty closely with the police in Evansville. Of course, that was a long time ago, but I still have a few friends with connections. They wouldn't tell me anything about an on-going investigation, but—Frank's probably the one I would ring—he could see if there's anything on Interpol about stolen rare books or an investigation of fraudulent assessors—anything like that."

Richard considered. He still didn't like it. But he didn't have a good alternative idea. "Sure. If your friend's happy to help, why not? That could be very useful information."

Babs almost skipped ahead to join the others. Richard wished he felt like skipping. He wasn't sure whether he was more afraid of learning that, indeed, the deal was fraudulent, or that there was nothing wrong with it and Sara's death was due to an altogether more personal reason.

Considerably later, after agreeing to allow Andrew to treat Jack and Babs to an early supper at the Russell, but declining the offer for themselves, Elizabeth and Richard were finally alone together in their room. Richard cleared his throat. It was never an easy thing to admit you just might have been wrong. Elizabeth looked at him quizzically. "Confession time. Good for the soul and all that."

"Goodness, this sounds serious." Elizabeth sat down.

"Not too serious, I hope, but I need to admit that I've done an about-face and asked Babs to do a spot of investigating. She says she has a contact in the police that might be able to get some information for us."

"Oh, that's great. So you don't disapprove of my bringing her into it all?"

Richard shrugged. "No more than I disapprove of my own action. The whole thing makes me uneasy, but overall it seemed like a good idea to see what we could find out. It might help Andrew—although I'm hopeful he won't need help. Surely the police will catch the real criminal soon, and we can all breathe easy again."

"Amen to that." Elizabeth kissed him. "And thank you for telling me."

With that off his chest Richard suggested they take their books to the common room, where they could snuggle into easy chairs and spend a quiet evening reading. He wanted to re-read P.D. James' *Talking about Detective Fiction* before tomorrow's lecture.

The room was quiet and the comfy chairs welcomed them. Richard was well into James' chapter on the Golden Age when two frantic figures burst through the double doors at the end of the room, both issuing high-pitched sentences at break-neck speed.

"Whoa, whoa!" Richard held up a hand. "What is it? I can't make out a word."

Elizabeth had done somewhat better at deciphering. "Andrew? What's happened to him? Police, you say?"

Jack reached them first, bobbing his head up and down and gasping for breath. He and Babs had apparently run all the way from the hotel. "They took him. Just like on 'Sherlock.'"

Richard's heart sank. "You mean they arrested Andrew?"

"For suspicion of the murder of Sara Ashley-Herbert. That's what they said," Babs added.

Chapter 24

BABS KNEW VERY LITTLE beyond the stark reality that, after the briefest of protests, Richard's gentle, scholarly brother had been led, shaking his head, from the Victorian elegance of the marble and crystal hotel foyer where they were enjoying coffee and chocolates after dinner.

"They read him his rights and everything." Jack was obviously still caught up in the cinematic quality of it all.

"I need to go to him." Richard pushed himself out of his chair. "Do you know where he is?"

Babs fumbled in a pocket and pulled out a small card. "I, um, sort of yelled at them, I'm afraid. They gave me this."

Richard could picture the scene, Babs demanding, "You can't do that!" at the top of her voice. It's a wonder she didn't attack an officer and get taken in, too.

Elizabeth took the card. "Holborn Police Station." She took out her phone and looked for directions. "Right. Sixteen minutes' walk. Babs, you'll take care of Jack." It wasn't a question.

"Come on, I've got a great video game on my laptop." Babs led him off over Jacks' protests that he wanted to go to the police station, too.

Richard was grateful for Elizabeth's efficiency. He knew he needed to function, but he couldn't seem to shake the unreality of it all. "We need to get him a lawyer, er … solicitor. Caudex must have used a firm here over the years," Elizabeth said.

Richard shook his head. It had been more than thirty years. He had been in London negotiating a contract for the family business when he'd received word that his first wife and his brother had been killed in a plane crash…

"Let's see about the lawyer first. That way we'll have something encouraging to offer Andrew." Elizabeth brought him back to the present and led the way to their room. In spite of his best efforts, however, Richard was able to accomplish little beyond leaving a few telephone messages. Sunday evening in London and Sunday morning in Philadelphia were not convenient hours for obtaining legal counsel.

Again, Elizabeth was the one to find the most useful information by the simple expedient of a web search. "A U.S. Consul can visit U.S. citizens arrested in a foreign country, provide a list of attorneys, provide information on the legal system, protest mistreatment, and monitor prison conditions."

"Please God it won't come to that," Richard said. But then, who would ever have thought it could have come to this?

"Family members concerned about a U.S. citizen arrested in England can call the Embassy in London during office hours," she read from her screen.

Richard groaned. "During office hours. Andrew can't sit there all night. He must be desperate."

Elizabeth continued to read. "In the case of a genuine emergency, the Duty Officer will take the call." She wrote down the number.

Richard rang the number. A young woman with a deep southern drawl answered. She identified herself as Gail Walters and became immediately attentive and efficient when Richard explained the situation. Beyond emailing him a list of solicitors, however, there wasn't a lot that could be done at this hour. "The best she can do is arrange for us to see him,"

Richard told Elizabeth when he rang off.

A few minutes after they arrived at the police station, it was apparent that Ms. Walters' undertakings had actually done quite a lot. They were shown into a quiet room by a young constable in a crisp white shirt and black skirt, and offered tea which they both accepted. A short time later Andrew was ushered in and likewise served with tea. An officer who introduced himself as Constable Lambert stayed in the room, but made himself as invisible as possible, taking a chair in the far corner.

Andrew insisted that he was all right. "They're very polite. This is my third cup of tea. It's this awful accusation. I keep telling them I loved her. I wanted her to be my wife—in time."

He shook his head. "They seem to think that's a motive."

"Do you mean they questioned you already? Without an attorney?"

Drew shrugged. "I agreed to it. They said they'd call someone for me, but I don't have anything to hide."

"What do you mean they think loving her was a motive?" Elizabeth asked.

"Wanting to marry her. They think I lost my temper when I learned she was already married."

"So that man we saw her with was her husband." Richard had to admit he hadn't fully accepted the story of a brother, even with Babs' research to back it up.

But Andrew shook his head. "Not if Babs is right that his name was Herbert. Sara's husband was Ashley."

"It's far more likely the husband found out about Andrew and killed her," Elizabeth said. "Have you thought of that?" Elizabeth's accusatory tone and scowl were directed at Constable Lambert but got no response from him.

Again, Andrew was the one who replied. "Unlikely. They were separated."

It took a moment for Andrew's information to register. "You knew?" Richard's tone was accusatory.

"Of course I knew. We talked about how we both had to

untangle things before…"

"Why didn't you tell us?"

"You would only have disapproved."

Richard dropped his head. Had his attitude been so judgmental he had pushed his brother away? Had his censoriousness contributed to landing Andrew in this predicament?

"And there's no CCTV evidence that you were where you say you were? Not even with Babs' evidence to help them pinpoint the time and place?" Elizabeth's questions brought them back to the immediate situation.

Andrew shook his head.

Constable Lambert finished his tea and sat patiently in his corner, allowing the brothers to have their visit. Richard told Andrew about contacting the American embassy and that he would have a lawyer tomorrow.

Andrew thanked him, but Richard couldn't help feeling his brother wasn't connecting with the reality of the situation. With the best words of encouragement Richard could manage and a hug and kiss from Elizabeth, they left Andrew to be taken back to his cell.

Richard felt as desolate as his brother seemed. "There must be something more we can do."

Elizabeth put her arm in his as they walked back to their room. "Pray?"

The next morning there still seemed to be little more than that. Richard got up, after very little sleep, feeling as if his head had been wrapped in burlap—an old bag that had once held onions and been stored in a dusty corner. Even the normally excellent tea in the dining hall couldn't get the sense of decay out of his mouth. He couldn't begin to think about sausage and eggs. The first bite of toast made his throat close as if he had bitten into sandpaper.

Fortunately it was raining—the first time in their just over two weeks in London. He went out into the courtyard and stood there, letting the drops fall on his head and run down his cheeks, chill his neck, and drip off his nose. At last he could breathe. He returned to the room to do what must be done. The American Embassy's list of legal counsel was in his inbox, and Richard contacted the chambers of the first name on the list, rang Caudex to fill in the details beyond the brief message he had left the day before and, as Elizabeth reminded him, prayed.

Then, giving himself an almost physical jab between the shoulders, he straightened his back and reminded himself that, no matter how worrying family and business matters were, he had a professional commitment. A few minutes later, staunchly forcing all personal matters to the back of his mind, Richard faced his classroom. There was comfort in being required to do something that took one beyond one's immediate concerns. Focusing on purely academic questions and following an established routine could be good medicine. Even if the routine had only been established for two weeks.

Noboko and her Japanese friends sat on the front row, pencils poised, as they had every day; Wanda's cloud of red hair and Susan's blond bob bent together as the women chatted; Al sat in the exact middle of the top row, looking deeply thoughtful as always; and Babs did her mother hen routine with Jeremy, offering help he didn't need with his crutches and book bag.

Elizabeth's absence was the only break in the pattern. Concerned that Jack would be missing his usual guide about town, she volunteered to oversee the planned outing, knowing how especially Jack had been looking forward to this one. They would see the classical paintings at Tate Britain, then take the Tate-to-Tate water taxi across the Thames to Tate Modern. "Don't look for us until you see us," she admonished when they set out after breakfast. "And don't worry."

Staunchly not worrying, Richard turned to his notes. "Phyllis Dorothy James, Baroness James of Holland Park, the grande dame of mystery writing in the second half of the twentieth century," he announced the day's topic. "Today we will look at James as the successor of Austen and Sayers, and

Wednesday we will consider how her worldview informed her writing.

"James was a link with the Golden Age of detective writing—the successor to Agatha Christie, Margery Allingham, Josephine Tey, and Ngaio Marsh. After Christie's death, James was called the new Queen of Crime—a title to which she never objected. Although I believe she is more clearly the successor to Sayers because of the literary quality of her writing. Kingsley Amis described her as 'Iris Murdoch with murder.'" The puzzled looks on many faces reminded Richard, once again, that he wasn't teaching an upper division college course, although he was gratified to note that Jeremy looked appreciative.

Richard's head began to pound. Thank goodness the builders on the north tower didn't seem to be working today. The thumping in his head didn't need any competition. He looked around for a drink of water and spotted the pitcher and glasses their thoughtful director had set on the side table. *You can do this,* he assured himself. *You will do this.* He took a long drink, followed by a deep breath, and turned back to his class. "How do you see James as the heir of the Golden Age?" It would have been better educational technique to ask whether or not his students, indeed, did see her as such and why or why not, but Richard was in no mood for open-ended wrangles.

Fortunately, Jeremy was the first to raise his hand. "Three things," he counted them on his long fingers as he enumerated. "First, her settings. James liked to choose isolated, enclosed settings. Her first novel, *Cover her Face*, was in a country house with a body in a locked room—pure Golden Age stuff. *The Lighthouse* is on an island off the coast of Cornwall, which seems almost a conscious reference to Christie.

"Second, her hero. Although Dalgliesh is a professional policeman, like Wimsey he is a man of education and refinement."

"Yes, he writes poetry," Babs interrupted the speaker with a wide, proud-of-herself smile.

Jeremy nodded and continued. "And Dalgliesh is a tortured hero. Having his wife and child die in childbirth was akin to Wimsey's shellshock from the Great War."

He held up a third finger. "And then, the quality of the puzzle. The puzzle was everything for a lot of Golden Age writers who invented highly contrived murders, like the rigged pulley on the pot plant in *Busman's Honeymoon*. With James it's more the layers of mystery. Like peeling an onion."

Richard nodded. Thank goodness for such an insightful student. Richard doubted that he could have done as well himself at the moment. A few more students commented, requiring only nods from their lecturer.

"Excellent. Now, moving on to James and Jane Austen." Richard picked up James' book on detective fiction and read: "'But perhaps the most interesting example of a mainstream novel which is also a detective story is the brilliantly structured *Emma* by Jane Austen.'" He looked up from the book. "Which brings us back to our first week's study. James says, 'Here the secret which is the mainspring of the action is the unrecognized relationships between the limited number of characters. The story is confined to a closed society in a rural setting ...'"

Richard looked up. "Sounds like James herself, doesn't it?" He returned to the book. "James points out this 'is to become common in detective fiction,' then she goes on, 'and Jane Austen deceives us with cleverly constructed clues ... At the end, when all becomes plain and the characters are at last united with their right partners, we wonder how we could have been so deceived.'

"And there you have a classic definition of a Golden Age mystery from the Queen of Crime of our own age. Interestingly, our study of Queens of Crime comes full circle with James' last detective novel which is a work of homage to her literary exemplar—*Death Comes to Pemberley* in which she imagines Elizabeth and Darcy six years into their marriage, and we get glimpses of James' forecasts for the lives of other Austen characters.

"There is a division of opinion among Janites as to James' wisdom in choosing not to attempt an imitation of Austen's voice, but rather tell the story in her own voice. I personally think the decision was valid as I agree with James' statement that no one else can write in Jane's voice.

"To my mind, though, the cleverest part of the novel is the fact that the vital clue to the mystery is in the title of the book." He looked out on three tiered rows of blank faces. Only Al, Jeremy, Wanda and the three Japanese students told him by their smiles and nods that they understood and agreed. "So, since apparently only six of you have read the book, I shall forebear to elucidate. I hope I have piqued your interest sufficiently that you will want to read it for yourselves."

Richard could only hope that the full extent of his relief didn't show as he closed his briefcase and strode from the room. He needed to see Andrew. He needed to follow up on his call to the chambers in Lincoln's Inn. He needed to go to bed and pull the duvet over his head.

He had made it less than halfway down the grand marble stairway, however, when Babs hailed him from the top and plunged after him at such speed he held his breath for her safety.

"Look! I have a reply from Frank!" She extended her cell phone, although he could make out nothing on the screen.

It took Richard half of the distance back to College Hall to remember that Frank was Babs' detective friend from her days as a journalist. And to realize that she had not replaced her phone so as to put her out of the reach of the nefarious Cranston. Come to that, though, Babs seemed to have forgotten the threat of her abusive husband as completely as Richard had. He supposed that was a good thing. She did need to move on.

Richard led the way to the common room and sought a quiet corner. Babs was already scrolling down her screen when he turned to her. "He doesn't have a thorough report on missing first editions of Jane Austen, although nothing obvious showed up when he searched international crime report lists. But look at this." Again she extended the phone.

Richard shook his head. "Never mind. Read it out."

"He ran the information we had on Gerard Asquith through Intelus—it's one of those background check services. Asquith came up absolutely on the level." She beamed at Richard. "Isn't that super! It means the auction is all above board, doesn't it!"

Richard nodded. He only wished he could feel half as gratified.

Chapter 25

ELIZABETH HIT THE SEND button, then threw both hands into the air. "Whew! What a great feeling!"

"You finished your article?" Richard asked. "I thought you had more research to do."

"I do, but the amount of information was getting out of hand, so I sent the first sections to my editor. I need to know how much I'm going to have to cut. It's really frustrating because today I'm likely to get enough for a whole article just on the shops Jane visited." She held out the list of locations she hoped to find. "Have you got your walking shoes on?"

"Afraid not." Richard stuck out his size ten oxfords. "Well, I do—but to walk to the police station. I'm meeting Andrew's lawyer there. You can take Jack with you, can't you?"

"He's hardly a substitute for you. I'll see if Babs can go along to keep Jack company while I'm doing the boring, historical stuff."

The idea had been a good one, but it didn't seem to be working out so well today. Babs was unaccountably quiet and withdrawn, leaving Jack his own. When Jane Austen took her nieces shopping, the morning out had included seeing Indian jugglers. Elizabeth wished there were some such entertainment for Jack now.

There didn't seem to be anything to do, however, but to get on with her work. They stood at the corner of Grafton and New Bond Streets, with Elizabeth struggling to identify which, exactly, of the buildings was the former Grafton House, home of the high-class drapers Wilding and Kent where Jane Austen was fond of shopping. Several ornately historical shop fronts offered themselves as candidates. The classical, white stone, or the red sandstone, or perhaps the red brick with a black wood ground floor offering fine jewelry and luxury items?

"So what are we doing here, then?" Jack shifted from one foot to the other.

"I'm trying to locate which store Jane Austen did her shopping in. She shopped here a lot, even though she often complained about the service. 'The miseries of Grafton House,' she called it."

"You need one of those blue signs." Elizabeth sighed at the truth of Jack's observation. At least he was trying to be helpful.

"I'm very much afraid it might have been there." She pointed to the starkly modern building on the other side of the street. "I would say that looks like Grafton House might have been the victim of a German bomb. Or modern redevelopers."

She knew her history lessons weren't likely to hold the attention of an eleven-year-old boy for long, but she took a chance and pulled out her guidebook. "Jane's niece Anna wrote to her about shopping there, and Jane's reply gives a good picture of what the shops were like then. 'I was particularly amused with your picture of Grafton House; it is just so.— How much I should like finding you there one day, seated on your high stool, with 15 rolls of persian before you and a little black woman just answering your questions in as few words as possible!'

Elizabeth smiled when she saw the shocked look on Jack's face. "Oh, dear, was that politically incorrect of me to read that bit out? My best guess is that her shop assistant would have been from India because muslin, a thin cotton fabric, which was wildly popular during the Regency, was imported from India."

Jack gave a jerky nod, and Elizabeth continued her explanation. "A typical arrangement of linen drapers—fabric stores—of the day was to have long counters down each side. The shoppers sat on one side of the counter; the clerks stood on the other and selected fabric from the shelves behind them to present to their customers. Most of the fabrics were on enormous rolls stored in pigeon holes around the ceiling. Swaths of the fabric could be pulled down like banners for ladies to examine." Another brief nod from Jack indicated that she hadn't lost him completely. Thank goodness the youngster had an appreciation for history.

"When Jane was staying with Henry in Henrietta Street, her brother 'kind, beautiful Edward' gave her five pounds. She wrote to her sister that 'Instead of saving my superfluous wealth for you to spend, I am going to treat myself with spending it myself. I hope at least that I shall find some poplin at Layton & Shears that will tempt me to buy it. If I do, it shall be sent to Chawton, as half will be for you; for I depend upon your being so kind as to accept it, being the main point. It will be a great pleasure to me. Don't say a word. I only wish you could choose too. I shall send 20 yards.'"

Jack thought for a moment, wrinkling his freckled nose, then broke into a broad smile. "So she made it sound like she was going to spend it all on herself, but she was really buying a present for her sister?"

Elizabeth laughed. "There. You've cracked the Jane Austen code. She never says directly what she means. You always have to look for the joke."

He was still thoughtful. "That was nice of her, wasn't it? To spend her money on her sister."

"Very generous, yes. They were very close."

Jack put his hand in his pocket and clinked a few coins together. "I might buy something."

"What a good idea." Elizabeth was as pleased as she was surprised. She hadn't considered the possibility that he would enter so thoroughly into the spirit of the outing. "Everything here is incredibly expensive, but we might find something somewhere else. Let's move on."

A few minutes later they emerged from the tube at Leicester Square. It took Elizabeth a moment to locate tiny, dark Cranbourne Alley off Bear Street. She was just about to apologize to her companions for bringing them to such a hole-in-the-wall passage and explain that Jane had admired "a great many pretty caps in the windows" here, when Jack gave a whoop. "Diagon Alley!"

Indeed, if no longer appropriate for Regency ladies and offering the pearl-edged, black satin ribbon Jane bought, the alley would certainly suit the witches and wizards of Harry Potter's world. "Perfect! Here, let me take your picture." Jack struck poses for her as if waving a magic wand.

They hurried on to Haymarket, with Elizabeth explaining that from Elizabethan times through most of the nineteenth century this was where one came to buy hay and straw, especially as it served to provide for the horses in the Royal Mews, Horse Guards and numerous stables in the area. As fond as she was of history, however, she refrained from mentioning that this was also the center of prostitution in Regency and Victorian times where the women were given the sobriquet "Haymarket Ware."

They stopped before a shop with bow windows filled with Union Jacks, dolls, bits of china and colorful London souvenirs. One white-framed pane still held the fading antique lettering that declared it to be Fribourg & Treyer Tobacconists to His Majesty and Purveyors of Foreign Snuffs to the Royal Family. Elizabeth extended her hand toward the door tucked between the projecting curves of the two windows. "This is one of the oldest shops in London; even some of the interior is original from 1720, too."

Although it was unlikely Jane would have shopped here, it was entirely conceivable that her brothers might have. Elizabeth's primary motivation at the moment, though, was to provide a place where Jack's allowance might cover the price of a purchase or two. Was he missing his parents? Or even hoping to gain their attention with presents? The thought made her heart cramp. He had seemed so cheerful lately, she hated to think that he might be pining for his family, although it would be understandable enough if he were. She stood back and let him have free run of the shelves filled with wares designed to catch the eyes of tourists. And from the number of shoppers in the small rooms she would say they were fulfilling their intention.

"There are some rather fun mementos here." She turned to Babs who had been unaccountably quiet all morning. "You might like to pick something up for Martha and Julie Ann."

For a moment Babs looked puzzled, then she smiled. "Oh, what a great idea. I should have thought of that. Help me find something."

"Well, what do they like to do?"

Babs thought for a moment. "Cook. They both like to cook."

"Perfect. How about a book of English recipes? Or a Union Jack apron? Or an oven mitt with London scenes on it?"

Babs made a couple of selections, and they continued to browse happily until Jack joined them clutching a bag. "Well, looks like you were successful. Only one more research stop, then we'll meet Richard for a late lunch."

Their bus rolled along the Strand at a much better pace than London busses usually managed and let them off outside the Royal Courts of Justice. Elizabeth regarded the gothic splendor of the grey, stone building that could easily have been something out of a maharaja's dream. But just now it was a reminder to her of a nightmare. The high court of England and Wales. For a moment her imagination ran away with her, and she pictured Andrew being led into that overpowering magnificence in chains.

She gave herself a shake. No, they didn't chain prisoners these days. And, if worst came to worst, he wouldn't be brought here. It would be to the Old Bailey criminal court. Not that this thought brought any more comfort. Surely by now, though, Richard would have legal counsel on the case. Most likely Andrew would already have been released—or did they grant bail for murder charges? She continued to argue with herself as she led the way across the Strand to the tiny, white shop front that looked like a toddler barely rising to its parents' knees, squeezed between two tall buildings. Thomas Twinings began selling tea on this site in 1706, and for more than three hundred years his company had supplied tea to England's most discriminating palettes. Including Jane Austen's.

"It was Jane's job to make the morning tea for her family at Chawton, and she always bought their supply of Twining's when she was in London. In March of 1814 she complained because there had been a rise in the price of tea. 'I do not mean to pay Twining till later in the day when we may order a fresh supply,' she wrote to Cassandra. The next day she reminds her sister that their mother had given her no money to pay for the tea, 'and my funds will not supply enough.'"

They paused before the Corinthian columns bracketing the doors. Above, two Chinese figures sat back to back with the royal warrant between them and a golden lion overhead. Elizabeth pointed. "In Jane's day all tea came from China. The East India Company started importing it from India a few years after her death."

They walked the length of the narrow shop, attractive tins of tea blooming like flowers on the shelves lining the walls. Elizabeth considered the array, wanting to sample them all. At last she settled on a purple and gold tin of Queen's 90th Birthday loose tea as a gift for her tea-loving husband. She could only hope it would cheer him.

She went on to the history display and made a few notes. Samuel Johnson, who lived only a few minutes' walk away, also bought his tea here. As did William Pitt, a friend of Richard Twining, Thomas's son and heir. Pitt led the fight for the reduction of the tea tax from eighty per cent to twelve per cent to make it less attractive to smugglers.

"Oh, here, this is fun." She pointed Jack's attention to a board explaining that the custom of tipping first began in London's coffee houses, such as the establishment which Thomas Twining converted into his tea shop.

"T.I.P. 'to improve promptness,'" he read.

"There, you can impress your friends." Ever polite, Jack nodded, but Elizabeth couldn't help feeling the impressive patience he had demonstrated all day was nearing its end. She glanced at the itinerary she had set for the day. Even though she knew the lofty, colonnaded showroom in York Street off St. James's Square was long vanished, she would have loved to look up the location of Wedgwood's where Jane had gone with Edward and Fanny to choose a dinner set to bear the Knight family crest.

Perhaps another day. She had to admit it wasn't just Jack's fidgets behind her decision. Her feet were aching, and she could feel a headache coming on. Elizabeth returned her notes and guidebook to her bag. "Right, who's for lunch? I told Richard we would meet him at Harrod's."

It had seemed like a good idea at the time, but now she quailed at the thought of the time and effort required to cross London on the tube in the middle of the day. She even briefly considered splashing out on a taxi, but common sense and her pocketbook prevailed, so half an hour later they emerged from the Knightsbridge station and walked down Brompton Road toward the golden brick dome of the Victorian fantasy building with rounded, green awnings lining the exotic show windows. The sight was something of a lift to Elizabeth's fatigue, but the real energy came from Jack whose attention was focused in quite a different direction.

"Whoa! Look at that! That's a Mclaren!" He stood transfixed before a gleaming red sports car that looked like it was exceeding the speed limit even while parked. "Someone drove that here. Actually drove it on the street."

Before Elizabeth could look for the golden paving under

its wheels, Jack danced on, enumerating the vehicles with an excited reverence she might feel in an art gallery or church on a feast day. "Ferrari! Maserati! Rolls!" He passed over the Merc as if it were almost commonplace, but the pair of shiny, black Porsches made him pause. The ivory Bugatti with Dubai license plate brought him to a full stop with his mouth hanging open.

And Jack wasn't the only one. A small crowd of admirers had gathered around, many of them taking photos. Even Elizabeth had to admit she was impressed. For her, a car was a means of transportation. If it got you there it was good. But these were works of art.

At the curb directly in front of the department store's main entrance, an Arab-looking man with a beautiful, dark-eyed woman in a creamy, cashmere scarf seated next to him pulled up to the pavement in a rich ivory-colored Lamborghini. Jack stood, star-struck. The man smiled at him, nodded and pushed a button. The falcon wing doors opened up and out like an exotic butterfly spreading its wings. The woman, eyes sparkling, leaned forward and offered Jack a gleaming smile. He smiled back.

A lovely moment of international connectedness, Elizabeth thought. It brought to her mind a recent article in *Regency Realm* about the Jane Austen Society of Islamabad. If only, she mused. If only. More Jane Austen, more moments of kindness and connectedness. This could be a different world.

Jack might have stood there transfixed for the rest of the afternoon, but Elizabeth took his hand and led him through the door being held for them by a green-coated doorman. Feeling overwhelmed by the opulence around her, Elizabeth smiled, thinking of Jane Austen laughing at herself driving around London in Henry's fine equippage.

Rather than take an escalator—Harrod's had installed the world's first and, in those early days, greeted shoppers at the top with a glass of brandy as a restorative after their ordeal—they mounted the dark wood stairway flanked by statues of bewigged, green-coated, eighteenth century footmen holding candelabra. And on up to the fourth floor. Richard had agreed to meet them at the Terrace, and Elizabeth hoped he wouldn't be late.

He wasn't. As soon as Elizabeth spotted him standing by the entrance to the restaurant, she felt something tight inside her relax. Everything would be all right. Richard was here.

And, indeed, things did appear to be right because Richard approached them with a broad smile. "I have a surprise for you." He led the way onto the covered balcony and pointed to their table.

"Andrew!" Elizabeth didn't dare to believe her eyes. "How wonderful! What happened?" She sat across from him at the small, marble table next to a scrolling iron railing surrounded by potted palms.

"That posh solicitor Richard hired for me convinced the police they didn't have enough evidence, although I suspect they were beginning to figure that out for themselves. Anyway, they dropped the charge." He grinned at his brother. "Not that the lawyer is likely to drop his."

"Don't worry, I'll send the bill on to Caudex. We'll find out just how much value the company puts on your services."

Elizabeth eased her feet out of her shoes under the table and let the brothers' banter float around her. The slight breeze fluttered the green branches surrounding her, and she took a deep breath of fresh air. "Do you want to celebrate with their afternoon tea?" Richard asked.

Elizabeth considered. This was certainly a moment worth celebrating. Still … "No, I think I'll save that for the Ritz. You did make reservations, didn't you?"

Richard assured her he had done so, and they turned their attention to the menus. Jack chose the burger after Babs promised to help him with the accompanying truffle chips if he didn't like them, and Elizabeth settled on a *croque-monsieur* with thoughts of Jane's French-by-marriage cousin.

She listened with half an ear to Richard and Andrew. As interested as she was in Andrew's case, the fact that the charges had been dropped and he was here was all that mattered for the moment. Although it was cause for concern that the police still held his passport. She looked around as she listened and realized that, though the greenery between tables provided a sense of privacy they were actually very close to their fellow diners. Fortunately Richard and Andrew were speaking in low tones and, since English voices were soft, no intrusive sounds jarred her relaxation.

She did become aware, though, of one somewhat more exuberant group at the table across the narrow aisle from them. A banquette against the wall served as a throne for the matriarch and patriarch whose assorted family members gathered around chatting half in English and half in another language. The bald, heavy-featured man wore a grey suit that must have been cut in Saville Row, although his massive shoulders would have been a challenge for the tailor. His open-collared silk shirt displayed numerous gold chains. His broad-faced wife wore her greying blond hair in a loose knot on the top of her head and, in spite of the fact of it being late June, had a fur jacket over the sofa behind her.

Richard noted Elizabeth observing the group. "Russian oligarchs, if I don't miss my guess." Just then, a stunning young woman with flowing black hair bustled in, laden with bulging bags bearing designer labels. Elizabeth eyed her tight designer jeans and haute couture jacket featuring dollar-size brass buttons and wide lapels in a tan that matched the gleaming leather of her boots. She could only guess at the price tags those luxury items must have carried. Two teenage girls with long, blond hair falling down their backs and over their eyes greeted the newcomer. She sat and pulled a soft cashmere sweater from a bag and held it out for their approval.

"What are oli-gacks?" Jack asked.

Richard replied in a quiet voice, although he was unlikely to be overheard by their demonstrative neighbors. "Oligarchs. Wealthy Russians who want the freedom of spending their money in the west and come here to shop, buy houses, art—whatever."

"Cars." Jack added the single word with a greedy look on

his face.

"Like those who invest in that bank next to Henry's?" Elizabeth asked. Never mind that it was two hundred years ago—in her mind the Cleveland was still Henry's bank.

"Very likely," Richard agreed.

Their food arrived and Jack fell on his burger. Elizabeth was a bit more restrained with her delicious sandwich, but not much. She hadn't realized how hungry she was. The waiter brought a tray of goodies and a fresh pot of tea to the table next to them, and Elizabeth asked for a pot for their table as well, while keeping a fascinated eye on their neighbors.

In the free-flowing style that seemed to be their pattern, the teenage girls wandered off. Their places were taken by two young men with stubbly beards. They were clad in denim and leather that made them look like they had stepped out of the pages of *Gentlemen's Quarterly*.

The tea arrived and Elizabeth poured steaming cups for everyone at their table, then asked the waiter for a tray of cake and lemon curd Madeleines. She was just savoring her first Madeleine when "The 1812 Overture" issued from a cell phone near her.

The paterfamilias on the settee answered his phone in a carrying voice. Apparently the news was highly acceptable. "*Da!*" He punched the air with an exuberant fist and, with a broad smile, spoke rapidly in Russian to those around the table.

The woman in the brass-adorned jacket reached across the table and threw her arms around him. "*Dedushka*, you won! Those lovely books are ours!"

"Shall we send Gregor to collect them?" one of the young men asked.

"*Nyet*. They deliver. Don't you listen?" his brother said.

A mother with two children joined the party, with a general scramble of adjusting seating and a waiter bringing more chairs.

"Well, that was interesting," Richard said. "Wouldn't it be a coincidence if they were bidding on the Austen books, too?"

"Surely too much of a coincidence?" Babs said shook her head emphatically.

"Well, we can hope. If they were we don't have to worry about that anymore." To Elizabeth's ears the note of relief in Richard's voice rang louder than his words.

How wonderful—Andrew out of jail. The auction over. The dark clouds of Monday's rainstorm had disappeared. Richard could finish his lectures and she her final day of research without any weight of worry hanging over them.

Chapter 26

MUCH OF ELIZABETH'S EUPHORIA accompanied Richard to the Senate Room the next morning. Andrew had proposed a trip to the Transport Museum but had been quite easily talked round to a tour of Lord's Cricket Ground when Richard explained that Jack was one of Headington's top bowlers. That left Elizabeth free to attend class today. She smiled at him from her usual top row seat.

Richard surveyed the other students, those he had come to know well and those he barely knew by name. He suddenly realized he would miss them all greatly. In spite of the stresses of the past weeks this had been an extraordinary experience. He believed that for most of his students he had opened their eyes to new perspectives on the world of literature—aspects they could apply to their own reading and thinking hereafter. No teacher could ask for more.

He hoped he wasn't being overly optimistic. He would know for certain when they wrote their essays and filled out their evaluation forms on Friday. Not an exam, because they weren't being graded, but a reflection on the course for their own elucidation and for the directors' help in planning for further courses.

"Good morning." The smiles and energetic greetings from around the room encouraged Richard to believe his summation was correct. "All right. P. D. James' worldview. She was a devout high church Anglican and a lay patron of the Prayer Book Society where she worked untiringly to maintain the beauty of the language over modernization of speech."

He paused to allow their note-taking to catch up. "A member of the Prayer Book committee once accused her of arguing to retain the phrase 'devices and desires' in the general confession for morning and evening prayers because she had used it as the title for one of her books. 'No,' she replied, 'the phrase should be maintained because nothing else so precisely describes the machinations of the human heart.'

"And who should be better acquainted with those machinations than a mystery writer? Especially a Christian mystery writer. That is very like Father Brown's statement in Chesterton's 'The Blue Cross.'" Richard picked up *The Complete Father Brown*, opened it to the page he had marked, and read:

"'How in blazes do you know all these horrors?' cried Flambeau.

"'Has it never struck you that a man who does next to nothing but hear men's real sins is not likely to be wholly unaware of human evil? But, as a matter of fact, another art of my trade, too, made me sure you weren't a priest.'

"'What?' asked the thief, almost gaping.

"'You attacked reason,' said Father Brown. 'It's bad theology.'"

Richard turned back a couple of pages. "Flambeau should have been warned. Earlier Brown had said, 'I know that people charge the Church with lowering reason, but it is just the other way. Alone on earth, the Church makes reason really supreme. Alone on earth, the Church affirms that God Himself is bound by reason.'

"James herself said in her introduction to Chesterton's *Essential Tales*, 'We read the Father Brown stories for a variety of pleasures, including their ingenuity, their wit and intelligence, and for the brilliance of the writing. But they provide more. Chesterton was concerned with the greatest of all problems, the vagaries of the human heart.' James, of course, recognized and applauded this because she, too, understood the vagaries of the human heart."

Richard noted the beginnings of restlessness in his class. "I share her comments on Chesterton because I believe they tell us as much about James herself as about her subject." He only hoped he didn't sound too defensive. Time to get to the heart of his lecture. "My favorite James, her 2001 work, *Death in Holy Orders*, displays her familiarity with the inner workings of church hierarchy, her understanding of the meaning of the sacraments and the high church traditions. Even to including the poetry of George Herbert and Pre-Raphaelite art. My particular favorite scene, with irony worthy of her idol Jane Austen, is where Sir Alred, the arrogant, high-powered, man of the world, wants to rewrite the Nicene Creed."

A few of his students snickered. Most didn't. Oh, well. It was one of those things—if you didn't understand it there wasn't much use trying to explain it. Irony was like that.

"Her books always contain at least one religious character, a sign of her devotion to Anglicanism and the central role she saw the church playing in community life—again, a given among Golden Age writers. This paved the way in her stories to much discussion about the nature of good and evil, with Dalgliesh, the son of a vicar, often taking the lead.

"I recall watching television a few years ago when the interviewer asked James why she wrote mysteries. She considered for a moment and then replied that she enjoyed 'bringing order out of chaos.'

"The most chaotic world she creates, however, is not a mystery, but her one foray into futuristic writing. In *The Children of Men* the theme, similar to one we mentioned for Sayers, is respect for life—in this case especially the unborn—by examining what happens to a society when no babies are being born."

Richard again picked up *Talking About Detective Fiction*. "James returns to Chesterton to point out that he was among the first to use detective fiction as a 'vehicle for exploring and exposing the condition of society, and for saying something true about human nature.' And, of course, as James points out, Father Brown solves his crimes, much as Miss Marple later does, solely by common sense, observation and knowledge of the human heart. Although Father Brown has the added dimension of applying his own 'immutable spirituality.'

"James gives us a summary of her own philosophy in discussing Chesterton. 'Before he even planned the Father Brown stories, Chesterton wrote that "the only thrill, even of a common thriller, is concerned somehow with the conscience and the will." Those words have been part of my credo as a writer.'

"Interestingly all three of our Queens of Crime have shared a similar worldview. But I don't believe this is mere happenstance because mysteries are, paradoxically, of all genres, the most moral. All deal with order versus chaos, good versus evil; all conclude with the triumph of good, an affirmation of the ultimate justice in the universe."

There. He had said his piece. "Your turn now." He turned it over to his students to discuss the characters: Jeremy—"James' characters almost all have dark secrets to hide, which makes them really rounded and, I suppose, true-to-life." Noboko—"I think it's significant that the priest, while having a guilty secret, is not the villain. James had respect for the clergy."

And the setting: Al—"The crumbling cliff was an important symbol. It added atmosphere, provided a ticking clock and echoed the crumbling of society and the church." Wanda—"You asked us to note high church references. Plainsong, Trollope, incense, the Oxford Movement are some that haven't been mentioned."

A plump, white-haired lady who had sat on the far end of the front row every class for three weeks, without ever once saying a word, raised her hand. Richard looked at her name tag. "Eleanor, yes."

"I like the archdeacon because he's a character you love to hate, yet James gives us reasons to sympathize with him. Also, he's such a perfect foil for dear Father Sebastian. I do love Father Sebastian's speech to the archdeacon." She opened a well highlighted and tabbed paperback. "'What is it that you want? A Church without mystery, stripped of that learning, tolerance and dignity that were the virtues of Anglicanism? A Church without humility in the face of the ineffable mystery and love of Almighty God? Services with banal hymns, a debased liturgy and the Eucharist conducted as if it were a parish bean-feast?'"

Richard smiled and nodded. "Yes, one of my favorite passages, too, and a good example of how James used character to develop her church setting—a very subtle technique."

"Excellent. Now, let's move on to plot. In *An Unsuitable Job for a Woman* James has Cordelia Gray quote John Bunyan: 'Then I saw that there was a way to Hell, even from the gate of Heaven.' James says, 'It is often these paths to hell, not the destinations, which provide for a crime novelist the most fascinating avenues to explore.'"

The ensuing discussion covered the psyche of the murderers, the circumstances that drove them to murder, and the conditions under which the act was committed. The discussion stayed with Richard for the rest of the afternoon. When Andrew and Jack returned from Lord's with Jack full of stories about famous cricketers and the Ashes, Elizabeth volunteered to take him to the Transport Museum in Covent Garden for the afternoon, but Richard begged to be let off. He needed to think.

All the analysis of avenues to murder and the criminal psyche that his students had bandied about, alongside theories he had propounded in recent days, circled in his mind like planes around a fog-bound airport, trying to make a landing. There must be a pattern. These same principles must be applicable to real life crimes. Perhaps they even held the key to understanding Sara's death. In this situation he must take on P. D. James' goal—to bring order out of chaos.

He could apply the same principles of understanding. Unless it was simply an act of insanity or random violence, the motive behind a murder like Sara's had to deal with greed, lust, envy—the darkness in the human heart.

What dark passion could have driven a killer to push Sara Ashley-Herbert under the wheels of a rushing train? Had she stood in someone's way to money, power or love? How would Father Brown, Dagleish, Wimsey or even Mr. Knightly set about solving this?

Of course, life wasn't like a book. Not nearly as tidy. Not all the players had to have a prior introduction. Someone from Sara's past, or even her present that they knew nothing about could be the villain.

But if this were a book, a closed society and not the whole of London, if not southern England, how would he apply that yardstick to the people he knew around Sara? He made a list.

Jeremy. He had met her first at Hatchard's. She would have had a large number of co-workers there, whom the police surely would have interviewed. But Jeremy was the one she worked with most closely. Richard considered. Jeremy, helpful, well-mannered, an excellent student. Could Sara have learned something about him that he wanted to keep hidden? Could someone as seemingly open and cheerful as Jeremy be harboring a dark secret? All of James' characters did, even the theological students. But sometimes in life what you saw was truly what you got. Richard had noted a sometimes puzzling inquisitiveness in Jeremy, but that hardly seemed like a quality that would be high on a list of murderers' characteristics.

Gerald Asquith. The apparently well-qualified fine arts appraiser who had certified that the books were authentic, providing the assurance Andrew needed to place his bid. Sara had worked with rare manuscripts, had consulted in the field. Did she know something about Asquith? Was his work inaccurate or fraudulent? Did he kill her to protect his reputation? Could Sara have been blackmailing him?

Clive Kentworth. Handling the auction for Legacy House who represented the unknown seller of the books. Now dead himself, Kentworth obviously couldn't have killed Sara, but their deaths must be connected. Even the manner of death seemed similar. A killer who pushed—whether the victim or the weapon. Sara said she had known Kentworth slightly when she worked for a rare book dealer in Charing Cross a few years ago, then Kentworth had contacted her a few days before his death about the sale of a medieval manuscript Legacy House was going to be handling. Was it possible that manuscript held the key—someone wanting to prevent its sale or valuation?

Richard looked back over that paragraph and underlined the words "unknown seller." Just the phrase held mystery. But a dead end. Undoubtedly the police would be able to secure the identity if they felt it pertinent. But there was nothing Richard could do in that direction.

He considered the fact that at the time of Kentworth's death they had wondered if someone might have been aiming for Sara—would have killed Sara had Babs not saved her life by calling her back. Now it did look very much as if Sara, indeed, might have been the intended victim. But that told them no more about who the perpetrator could be. Richard moved to the next on his list.

Bramwell Child. The bank's representative. The middle man who received the money from all the bidders and held it in trust until the auction ended. Then it would be Child who delivered the winning bid to the seller and returned their surety to the unsuccessful bidders. That was the plan. Of course, if Child got greedy and elected to keep some of the bid money ... was there a way he could do that? Richard didn't know enough about banking to answer his own question. But if that were the case, how could Sara possibly have known?

Richard considered. Who else should be listed here? Oh, yes. Ashley, Sarah's estranged husband. Had the police located him? Was he enough removed from Sara's life to be apathetic about their separation and her new romance? Or was he harboring passion or wounded pride? If so, wouldn't Andrew have been the more likely victim?

Or what about the brother they had seen Sara with at the theatre? The siblings had appeared to be very close. Affectionate, he would have said. He thought briefly of the incestuous brother and sister in *Death in Holy Orders*, then dismissed the thought.

Richard hesitated, but after a moment continued writing with determination. To be of any value his list needed to be as complete as possible. Andrew. By his own admission Andrew was captivated by her. Had the relationship gone much further than his brother had admitted to him? Again, the motives of passion and pride he had assigned to the husband could equally apply to the lover.

Was that the list complete? Was there anyone else Sara knew from the Queens of Crime course other than Jeremy? Oh, yes, Babs. He sat for some time, his pen hovering over the page. He could see no motive or connection to write down. And yet, could he be missing something?

Richard looked back over the page, then ripped it from his notebook, wadded it into a ball and threw it into the wastepaper basket. Fine mystery writer he was. Even allowing his imagination full play he could see no motive substantial enough to be worth killing a beautiful, charming, intelligent young woman.

Chapter 27

ELIZABETH SAT WITH NOTEBOOK, guidebook, her map of London and her volume of Jane Austen's letters spread over her desk. She sighed. This was to be her last day of London research for her article, and she wanted to make it count. Babs and Jack had expressed their willingness to accompany her, when Richard mentioned at breakfast that he would like to spend the day with his brother. Elizabeth knew they expected to receive word about the Caudex bid on the Jane Austen books soon. She supposed the brothers had business matters to discuss, and Andrew had mentioned an appointment with his solicitor that afternoon, as he was concerned because the police hadn't yet returned his passport.

Well, she was sure Richard could handle whatever needed to be done. She only wished she were as confident about her own day. Jane had been an inveterate gallery-goer, but so few of the museums she visited were still here. Elizabeth looked at her list.

Pall Mall. Sir Joshua Reynolds exhibited there. In the British Gallery or another? Wherever it was, Jane did not find the portrait of Mrs. Darcy she was looking for. Pall Mall seemed to have been a center for galleries. The Gallery of the

British Institution, usually simply called the British Gallery, was established to encourage and reward the talents of British artists. Half of the year it exhibited and sold the works of living artists, but Reynolds had been dead for a decade when Jane visited the exhibition of his paintings in 1811, so presumably it was during that half of the year when the gallery featured paintings by the most celebrated masters.

On the same day, Jane had gone to an exhibition in Spring Gardens. Elizabeth checked the guidebook. Spring Gardens was a remnant of an Elizabethan pleasure garden, which featured Wigley's Royal Promenade in Jane's day. For the price of a shilling visitors could see a mechanical orchestra. If Jane bothered about that we aren't told, but Spring Gardens also offered paintings of The Society of Painters in Watercolours. This was where Jane saw Mrs. Bingley's portrait. Elizabeth marked Spring Gardens on her map. It might be worthwhile seeing whatever was still there, although it appeared to be quite built up around it.

And she would definitely go to Somerset House—one gallery from Jane's day that was still here. Now, as then, Somerset House featured fashionable exhibitions and art shows. Jane had planned to attend the British Academy Exhibition there and hoped to find a picture of Mrs. Darcy. As it turned out, though, they had to deliver a message for Henry's bank and by the time the errand was done there was no time for the exhibit.

And there was another Austen connection. Since the Royal Navy occupied one wing of Somerset House, Francis and Charles, Jane's admiral brothers, would have been well acquainted with it.

And perhaps Elizabeth could find a remnant of the Liverpool Museum in Piccadilly. At the height of its success it offered to delight the viewer with upwards of thirty thousand articles, including animals—stuffed, she assumed—ancient weaponry, mummies, and works of art—all arranged in scientific order. And the *piece de resistance* after the Battle of Waterloo—Napoleon's famous Berlin Carriage, which he preferred to a horse for riding into battle. Elizabeth shook her head. No, Jane would not have seen Napoleon's carriage as she went to the museum in 1811—four years before the Battle of Waterloo.

Elizabeth put a line through the Liverpool Museum but, on something of a whim, added Sir John Soane's house to her list. There should be plenty of time, and it was of the Regency period. But primarily, it was simply a place she had long wanted to visit.

Elizabeth's research had taken her longer than she expected—it often did—so they were late setting off. It was already after eleven o'clock when they emerged from Green Park station and walked to Buckingham Palace. The sites that applied to Jane Austen were at the east end of the Mall, but she thought starting at the palace would help orient the other sites in her mind. As they walked across the park toward the elegant but restrained neo-classic building, Elizabeth was happy to listen to Jack explaining to Babs that this had originally been the home of the Duke of Buckingham and that Queen Victoria was the first monarch to live there. Once again, Jack's history master would be pleased that his pupil had retained so much of his lessons.

Elizabeth herself was having difficulty realizing that in Jane Austen's day this would have been the Queen's House where Queen Charlotte, wife of George III, gave birth to fourteen of her fifteen children. When the Prince Regent became King George IV three years after Jane died, he began the reconstruction that turned a house into a palace.

It took Elizabeth a minute to figure out why a large crowd was gathering outside the ornate, black and gold fence surrounding the palace. Then she realized. "Oh, it's almost time for the Changing of the Guard. Would you like to see that, Jack? You and Babs could stay and watch and we could meet up later."

The words were barely out of her mouth before he darted off, seeking the best spot for viewing the ceremony. Elizabeth laughed. "I'll take that as a 'Yes.' Do you mind, Babs?"

Babs readily agreed. "I'd like to see it myself."

"Good." Elizabeth checked her watch. "I think the ceremony takes something less than an hour. Why don't you ring me when you're ready to leave? We can probably meet at Somerset House." Elizabeth looked around at the crowd. "Don't lose the scamp."

Elizabeth walked past the Queen Victoria Memorial and on down The Mall, appreciating the cover of the leafy trees and enjoying the sight of the Union Jacks lining both sides of the ceremonial drive. How many state events had she watched on television with the royal cars or carriages driving this very route, cheering crowds lining the way? She couldn't help but feel that in a small way she was living history simply by being here.

Elizabeth was thinking of Jane coming here to see the Reynolds exhibit and the paintings in the British Gallery—the event that prompted Jane's laughing at herself, "parading about in a Barouche." as she wrote to Cassandra. Where might the galleries have been? She looked about, then realized her mistake. No, this was The Mall. The galleries had been in Pall Mall. She stepped to the side of the walk, out of the path of the busy pedestrian traffic: joggers, people pushing prams, dog-walkers, people ambling, people hurrying. She needed to reorganize her thinking and check her map. Yes, Jane had visited galleries on the street just north of here. And there were still art galleries in Pall Mall. She sighed.

She would make that detour later. For now she would enjoy her elegant venue. Besides, ahead of her was Carlton House Terrace, the site of Carlton House which had been the residence of the Prince Regent. And the purview of the Reverend James Stanier Clarke, Librarian to the Regent, who, at the Prince's direction, had reveled in the pleasure of showing Miss Jane Austen around the Prince's library at Carlton House and suggesting that she dedicate her next book to the Prince.

The same Mr. Clarke, of course, who, with no concept of its absurdity, solicited Jane to write "an historical romance illustrative of the history of the august House of Coburg," or, perhaps better yet, to depict a literary clergyman, resembling himself in history and character.

The memory brought such delight to Elizabeth she thought there could be no better place to reread those letters than on the very site where they were written. She found a bench under a tree and pulled out her volume. It took only moments of searching. Yes, here was the eccentric clergyman's advice: "Do let us have an English clergyman after your fancy—much novelty may be introduced—shew, dear Madam what good would be done if tythes were taken away entirely."

Elizabeth paused in her reading and smiled. Well, at least Jane would have agreed on that point. In her "Plan of a Novel" she had the heroine's father expire in a "fine burst of literary enthusiasm, intermingled with invectives against holders of tithes."

Still smiling, she returned to the reverend Clarke's advice, "and describe him burying his own mother— as I did— because the High Priest of the parish in which she died did not pay her remains the respect he ought to do. I have never recovered from the Shock." He went on to advise her to carry her clergyman to sea as the friend of some distinguished naval character about a court.

One can hear Jane's gurgle of laughter—after her snort of disgust. If *Pride and Prejudice* had not already been published, one would be certain James Stanier Clarke had served as a model for Mr. Collins. Again, evidence of how true to life Jane's characters were.

Elizabeth turned a few pages to Jane's reply to such nonsense. Brilliant in its self-effacing appearance while actually standing up for herself. "You are very, very kind in your hints as to the sort of composition which might recommend me at present, and I am fully sensible that an historical romance, founded on the House of Saxe Cobourg might be much more to the purpose of profit or popularity than such pictures of domestic life in country villages as I deal in— but I could no more write a romance than an epic poem. I could not sit seriously down to write a serious romance under any other motive than to save my life, and if it were indispensable for me to keep it up and never relax into laughing at myself or other people, I am sure I should be hung before I had finished the first chapter. No— I must keep to my own style and go on in my own way."

With a sigh of satisfaction, Elizabeth returned her book to her bag and continued down The Mall to Admiralty Arch on the other side of the pedestrian walkway, passing through a small arch beside the large spans under which traffic whizzed with a steady roar into and out of the ceremonial road to Buckingham Palace. She looked at busy Spring Gardens Street to her right, which was apparently all that was left of the former Elizabethan pleasure garden where Jane had gone to an art exhibit. Not the faintest echo remained of the sound of pipes and tabors which would have sounded here in Tudor times, let alone anything Regency that Jane might have encountered.

Elizabeth consulted her map and considered. Should she walk back to Pall Mall to get a feel for the art galleries Jane had visited there? And then on up to Piccadilly to locate the site of the Liverpool Museum, even though her guide book told her that the Egyptian façade of the museum that replaced the one Jane visited had been long demolished?

A ringing from her bag sent her scrambling for her phone. "Hi Babs. Is the ceremony over already?" Elizabeth had no idea she had spent so long enjoying Jane's letters. "Great, let's meet at Somerset House. Are you okay to find your way there?" Babs assured her that, with Jack's help, she wouldn't have any trouble.

Elizabeth considered her route. It would be a sixteen minute walk down the Strand or a thirteen minute bus ride— once she found the correct bus. She would walk.

Whoever had set the pace for the Transport for London maps, however, had either had much longer legs than Elizabeth's, or didn't find the heat and humidity or the crowds such a detriment as she did. She felt considerable relief when the impressive, neo-classical building filling the space between the Strand and the Embankment came into view. Elizabeth had looked at the history of the building that morning, so she knew that from the middle of the eighteenth century there had been growing concern that London had no great public buildings. The former Tudor palace which had been restored by Sir Christopher Wren was in sad decline by the time of Jane Austen's birth.

That very year Parliament passed an act for the purpose of erecting and establishing Somerset House for government departments and learned societies. Finishes to the decorative work would still have been going on when Jane failed to find a portrait of Mrs. Darcy at the British Academy Exhibition there in 1813. Perhaps just as Jane had done, Elizabeth walked through one of the open arches leading from the Strand to the grand central courtyard. As she expected, she found Babs leaning against the balustrade surrounding the courtyard, watching Jack romp with several other children among the dancing fountains that sprang to life in varying patterns from the surface of the paving stones.

Shrieks of laughter from the children mingled with the splashing of water on stone and the background chatting of adults milling around while the children played. Muted traffic noises reached them from the busy street beyond, but inside this enclosed space was another, magical world where sunlight danced on water drops. "I hope you haven't been waiting long," Elizabeth greeted her friend.

Babs assured her that they had been there only a few minutes and quite obviously Jack would be happy to stay here far longer. "If you're sure you don't mind staying with him, Babs, I'll just nip on in and take a look at the exhibition area to get a feel for what it would have been like in Jane's day, then we can go on to Sir John Soane's House together."

Again, Babs was amenable. "Thank you so much. I don't know what I'd do without you, Babs." Elizabeth gave her a quick hug and hurried back toward the main entrance.

Inside the colonnaded lobby she bought a ticket and ascended the spiral staircase, feeling like she was inside a chambered nautilus, to the Courtland Gallery. The Courtland collection was famous for its Impressionistic Art, a style which Elizabeth liked very much, but today she had come to see the space itself rather than to enjoy the works of Manet, Monet, Renoir, Degas or Cézanne.

The modern method of exhibiting paintings, with only one masterpiece holding pride of place on each section of the beautifully panelled walls, gave the viewer a chance to enjoy the painting undistracted as well as admire the décor of the room itself. Elizabeth pulled out a photo she had printed off the internet of a painting of a Regency exhibit in these rooms that must have been much like the one Jane attended. The bare wooden floor, swept by the trains of the ladies' clinging, high-waisted gowns as they gossiped with gentlemen in frock coats and military dress, must be the same as the fine oak flooring under her own feet.

In one room Elizabeth spotted a ceiling plastered in the same design of ornate squares as seemed to be in her picture. Nothing else, however, could be compared. In the Regency exhibit, paintings were hung floor-to-ceiling with their frames touching, five or six rows high. For just a moment Elizabeth imagined herself in an empire dress and ostrich feather adorned turban, looking for a portrait of a young woman with a fine pair of eyes, in a yellow dress. Sadly, Elizabeth had no more luck than Jane Austen had.

Elizabeth did smile, however, when she spotted the robed and bewigged clergyman holding center stage in the middle of her picture of the Regency exhibition. Mr. Collins or James Stanier Clarke? Surely either one could have been in the artist's mind.

Enough of such daydreaming. It was time to collect her companions and get on to her last museum of the day. Elizabeth was on the landing, ready to descend the stairs curving back down to the lobby, when she noticed a placard on an easel. In exquisite uncial calligraphy it announced a special exhibit in the South Terrace Room: "Frauds and Fakes: The History of Art Forgeries." Elizabeth was torn. She needed to get on her way, and yet this very topic had been so much on her mind in recent days.

She glanced at the floorplan of Somerset House on the leaflet she had been given when she paid her admission. Yes, she could go down to the courtyard from the south wing. If she didn't spend long looking at the display, she could peek in without making Babs and Jack wait too much longer. Her mind made up, she hurried down the corridor.

The first section in the presentation to draw her attention was the story of Han van Meegeren's faked Vermeers, perhaps the greatest art forgery scandal in the twentieth century. Elizabeth recalled learning about this as a student in an art survey class. As she looked at the reproductions of van Meegeren's forgeries, she had the same reaction she had had as a student: If he could paint that well, why not paint his own pictures?

Shaking her head, she gazed at the photograph of van Meegeren in court and at the reproductions of his "Vermeers" next to copies of the actual masterpieces he had plagiarized. Mystified, she moved on.

The next display was of Galileo's Moon illustrations which actually turned out to be such convincing forgeries that in 2005 they fooled a rare books dealer, a professor of astronomy and an art historian. Besides the forgery, Marino Massimo De Caro, director of the *Bibliotica Girolamini* rare book library in Naples, stole some 1,500 volumes of rare books, including works of Aristotle, Descartes, Galileo and Machiavelli. No Jane Austen first editions were listed. Still, it did make her wonder.

Elizabeth leaned closer to the display to examine the electronic reproductions of the forgeries. They were breath-taking in their beauty and in their apparent antiquity. An information board explained: De Caro and an accomplice aged several bottles of nineteenth-century ink and used a sheet of Galileo's own writing as a guide for the seventeenth-century astronomer's hand. After opening a bottle of red wine, the forgers traced the outline of the moons around the foot of the wineglass. They then baked the pages in De Caro's home oven to age them.

Besides the moon drawing, De Caro forged Galileo's 1606 *Compasso* to replace a stolen version. The account of his crimes went on, but the psychology of the perpetrator of such deceits interested Elizabeth more than the how dunnit of the acts themselves. A sign explained: "In the peculiar underworld of rare-book theft, De Caro joins a rogue's gallery that features flamboyant eccentrics, disgruntled employees, corrupt academics—even a serial killer. While the criminal personalities vary, they all share something in common: base greed and a knack for gaining insider access to the cozy, exclusive world of rare-book collecting."

Elizabeth considered the details of De Caro's life. Although the hoax certainly involved monetary reward—a rare book dealer bought the faked Galileos for half a million dollars and they were once valued at ten million dollars—it seemed that De Caro's story was a mixture of greed, envy and vaunted pride. As a college dropout, De Caro had a desire to prove himself to a field he felt did not recognize his talents. He held a grudge against people who had spent years studying in libraries.

Fascinating. Certainly a great deal to ponder. But Elizabeth needed to move on. She skipped a display recounting three examples of faked Modiglianis and turned to the door when one final exhibit caught her eye. Original manuscripts of Alexander Pope, Robert Herrick and George Herbert had all been sold as authentic by a world-famous art auction house in London in the 1950s. The Pope and Herrick poems were manuscripts of poetry actually published by the poets but the "original manuscripts" were sold as newly discovered. The Herbert poems purported to be an undiscovered volume titled *Temple Mount* which, unlike his volume *The Temple*, the dying Herbert had not placed in the hands of his friend Nicholas Ferrar.

Perhaps it was the name Herbert that first caught Elizabeth's attention. Was there any possibility that Sara Ashley-Herbert's brother ...? No, the account clearly stated that the forger and his co-conspirators had been jailed for fifteen years in 1957. She looked at the newspaper photo: two men and a woman, all appearing to be at least in their forties. That would mean they were in their nineties now, if they were still alive.

She turned away, chiding herself for allowing her imagination to run away with her. Then she turned back and looked again. This time focusing closely on the tall, distinguished man in the center—silvery hair, aquiline nose, hooded eyes, slightly supercilious smile. Is that really what the man on the stairway at the Lyceum Theatre had looked like? Or was she imposing the photo on her memory? Actually, it wasn't so much a matter of his features, but something about his square-shouldered bearing. As if these were men who had trained at the same military academy. Unlikely for an art forger, surely. Anyway, it was just an impression.

Fortunately, Jack was no longer playing in the fountains when Elizabeth found him and Babs in the courtyard a few moments later. He had been sitting in the sun long enough for his curly, sandy blond hair to dry, and Elizabeth judged that his clothes would be dry enough by the time they reached Sir John Soane's House that he wouldn't be refused admission to the museum on the grounds that he would dampen the carpets. "A twelve minute walk," Elizabeth consulted her faithful Google maps. "That should give you time to finish drying off."

Jack seemed happy enough with the plan as he skipped ahead of the women. Across the Strand Elizabeth directed, "Go around Aldwych, then up Kingsway. But don't get too far ahead of us." She wanted to think. Surely it was impossible that there could be a connection, and yet...

"You look troubled," Babs prompted, matching her step to Elizabeth's slower gait.

"Not troubled, really. Just puzzled. I can't figure out how

there could be a connection, and yet..." Elizabeth considered. Should she share her thinking with Babs? Why not? If Richard were here, she would certainly want to talk it over with him. As an independent observer Babs might be able to evaluate her ideas. "There was this display on art and rare book forgeries. I didn't spend much time on it, but this one display—" She described it to Babs.

"Okay. Interesting, I suppose..." Babs was clearly puzzled by her interest.

"No, you see, the thing is, there was a picture of the conspirators. This one man—Herbert—he looked so much like the man Sara told Andrew was her brother."

"I thought you said it was in the '50s?"

Elizabeth sighed. "I know, it's silly even to give it any thought. But it seemed like such a coincidence—the appearance, the name..."

Elizabeth said no more as they walked up the busy, but leafy street. How lovely to have trees growing along the pavement. A building looking like a gothic, grey stone version of Cinderella's castle distracted Elizabeth for a moment, but her mind quickly returned to its puzzle. If the man with Sara were the son—no, grandson, surely—of the forger in the photo. And he had inherited his grandfather's "talent," And Sara found out about it ... She attempted to explain her thoughts to Babs, but only wound up more confused.

Jack had turned the corner toward Lincoln's Inn Fields. The fact that Richard was just across the way, meeting with Andrew's lawyer, helped Elizabeth reach her decision. "Jack, come back. Let's skip the museum." She turned to Babs beside her. "I need to tell Richard all this so he can call the police. I can't make sense of it, but surely there's a connection—or at least, if there is they will find it."

"But aren't we here now?" Babs pointed to the gleaming Portland Stone edifice in the middle of the block, its double row of tall, arched windows topped with Roman statues.

Elizabeth considered. Just one more hour couldn't make much difference. Richard was busy now and she did want to see the museum. Apparently Jack did too, because a bright smile erased his look of disappointment. His expression morphed to one of interest as Elizabeth explained how this unique collection came to be.

Sir John Soane was the leading architect of Jane Austen's day—he designed the Bank of England and was Professor of Architecture at the Royal Academy—then housed in Somerset House. He had purchased three houses facing Lincoln's Inn Fields and, as something of an architectural laboratory, then redesigned them as home, office, museum and showplace for his theories of architecture. Jane would not have come here on any of her museum visits, because in her lifetime the museum aspect was only for Soane's students. Just before his death in 1837 Soane bequeathed his collection of antiquities and architectural salvage to the British nation by Act of Parliament.

But not even Elizabeth's explanation could be adequate preparation for the overwhelming creativity and jumble of objects that met them in each room, opening one upon another in a maze of dining room and library, study and dressing room, monument court, museum corridor, picture room … staircases curved from floor to floor and colonnaded galleries opened onto parlours and chambers, each filled—if not to say crammed—with paintings, art objects, statues, and bits of masonry from antique buildings. "A succession of those fanciful effects which constitute the poetry of architecture," the guidebook called it.

Soane had used his collections as "studies for my mind" and a museum for teaching. A central theme of his work had been his fascination with light. Every room seemed to be magically lit by natural light brought inside by domes, skylights, channels in the walls and a three-story open atrium which gave daylight even into the basement crypt, catacombs and sepulchral chamber.

Elizabeth found herself most taken with the picture room—again, filled with natural light from high windows. Ingeniously, Soane had devised hinged screens so he could hang his more than one hundred enormous paintings in this small room but enjoy each panel of paintings by the simple technique of opening the boards as desired. Elizabeth spent considerable time there, following the cautionary tale of the collection's most famous paintings, the series by William Hogarth of *A Rake's Progress*. The artist vividly depicted young Tom's demise, as the simple country boy inherits a fortune, abandons his sweetheart Sarah, squanders his fortune in London, marries a rich crone, gambles away her fortune, is arrested for debt and dies in Bedlam, cradled by the faithful Sarah.

The host for that room next opened a panel displaying the Canalettos Soane had collected, but Elizabeth reminded herself that they must get on. When she turned to go, however, Jack and Babs were nowhere to be found. Elizabeth looked at the floorplan. The basement with its crypt and monk's parlour seemed the most likely to have attracted an adventurous boy. Yes, the guidebook said the Sepulchral Chamber contained the sarcophagus of King Seti I, one of the most important Egyptian antiquities ever to be discovered. She would find Jack there and they could be on their way.

As she progressed to the stairs she passed the open four-story shaft where the overhead dome gave light for all the floors. She leant over the high railing, being careful not to dislodge any of the heavy antique urns lining the bannister, and looked over. If she could spot Jack in the basement, she could simply call him up and avoid going down to fetch him. She assumed Babs would be accompanying her charge as usual. Thank goodness for Babs.

Elizabeth couldn't see Jack, however, so she would have to go down to get him. She paused to admire the impressive line-up of sculpted vases and jardinieres around the balustrade, running her finger over a smooth, white stone urn encircled with dancing maidens. Next to it, a vase with a much rougher surface had been carved in patterns of looped flowers. Bits of assorted masonry adorned the walls around her: cupids' heads, scrollwork trellises, even body parts such as hands from statues ... Elizabeth gave a small shiver and descended the stairs.

Soane had converted the basement rooms, originally a wine cellar, giving them the atmospheric impression of a burial chamber. Elizabeth chilled, feeling like she was entering catacombs. "Jack, we need to go." She startled at her own voice which echoed in the chamber. Feeling she should tiptoe, she moved forward. The whole ambiance was one of hush and reverence. The dust of the ages was not to be disturbed. And it remained undisturbed by any reply from Jack or Babs.

Elizabeth made her way through the crypt, glancing at the architectural fragments gathered there. What a gold mine this must have been for Soane's students. If they couldn't go to ancient Greece and Rome to study classical architecture, their teacher would bring it to them. She walked toward the shaft of light falling on Suti I's sarcophagus at the far end of the basement. As far as she could make out she was alone on this floor.

A sense of rush seized her. What had she been doing dawdling among these ancient stones? Fascinating as they were, she needed to tell Richard of her discovery. They needed to ring the police. Actually, why wait? She pulled her phone from her pocket and clicked on Richard's speed dial as she continued to walk.

He answered on the first ring. "Elizabeth? Where are you?"

"I'm at Sir John Soane's House. I need to tell you..." The silence at the other end told her she had lost signal. Hardly surprising, deep as she was in the basement. Just as well, this wasn't a very good place to go into a lengthy explanation anyway. She would take a moment to check the sepulchral chamber to make sure Jack wasn't hiding behind a statue or pillar, then hunt the upper floors for him.

"Jack?" she tried again, somewhat louder. In the echoing silence she moved toward the atrium, then caught a shadow of movement behind one of the urns on the next level. She stopped and craned her neck upwards. "Jack? Wait there. I'm com—"

She heard the scraping of stone on stone, more sensing

the disturbance over her head than actually seeing the sculpture hurtling toward her. She jerked backward. Stumbled. And hit her head on the edge of the sarcophagus as she fell. The crashing of the urn on stone at her feet mixed with the explosion in her head as everything went dark.

Chapter 28

"ELIZABETH! ELIZABETH!" RICHARD'S FRANTIC voice was the first sound to pierce the darkness. She could feel his arms around her, struggling to help her to a more comfortable position. She tried to give him a reassuring smile. She must have failed. "Oh, God," his prayer emerged as a sob.

"Where did he go? Did you see him?" Babs screamed from the upper floor.

Through the dense fog around her, Elizabeth could make out a murmur of voices above. But there was only one voice she cared about. "Richard." There was something important she needed to tell Richard. But Richard wasn't here, was he? She had tried to call him ... She mumbled something but it was lost in a cacophony of voices and footsteps as the small space seemed to fill with people.

"We need to search the house. He may still be here. Didn't anyone else see?" Babs, now standing by Richard, repeated her plea, accompanied by frantic gestures. "I saw him. That man. He did it on purpose. I'm sure."

Her words finally had an effect. Richard placed his jacket under Elizabeth's head and turned to Babs. "What are you saying? Someone *meant* to push this on Elizabeth?" He pointed to the heavy chunks of broken stoneware scattered over the floor of the chamber.

"He was young—twentyish. Black jeans. Short black hair. Tattoos." Babs headed back toward the stairs, pushing her way through a ring of curious on-lookers. At the foot of the stairs she was met by a museum guard. "Lock the doors. Don't let him get away!" Her voice rose to an urgent shout.

"We've done that. And we rang the emergency services. They'll be here shortly."

By the time the ambulance arrived Elizabeth was sitting up, declaring that she was unhurt. Never mind the lump on the back of her head that was beginning to throb fiercely. An ice pack and a few aspirin would fix that. There were far more important things to be seen to. "Police. I need to talk to the police," she insisted.

The police arrived almost as she spoke. But she wasn't allowed to talk to them yet. First she had to be checked out by a young Asian woman in a dark green paramedic uniform. Elizabeth struggled to hear what Babs was telling the uniformed police officer, while she herself obeyed the medic's commands to blink, count the fingers she held up, open her mouth, hold out her arm. While the blood pressure cuff inflated she heard Babs explain, "I heard her calling for Jack. I was on my way, coming along the colonnade, when I saw that man shove an urn off. I yelled at him to stop, but he ran." She repeated the description she had given the museum guide. Elizabeth wondered why that sounded vaguely familiar.

Richard was the next to be interviewed. The police seemed skeptical about Richard's quick arrival on the scene since Babs had said he wasn't with them earlier. "No, I was with my brother. At his lawyer's office—er, solicitor—in Lincoln's Inn just around the corner. Elizabeth rang me, but we lost connection. She sounded worried so I rushed right over."

"And you didn't see anyone leaving the museum?"

"Not that I noticed, but I was hurrying. I was concerned about Elizabeth."

The policeman looked doubtful, but turned to Elizabeth.

At last. She had been wanting to talk to the police for hours. But first, she had to answer their questions—explain how she had been looking for Jack, saw the object hurtling toward her, jumped back and hit her head. "And you didn't see who pushed it?" the officer demanded.

Elizabeth shook her head, then wished she hadn't. Motion intensified the pulsing. "I just had a sense that someone was there." The officer started to close his notebook. "Wait! That's not what I wanted to tell you." She grabbed Richard's hand. "This is what I was trying to ring you about. And, yes, I am worried. Well, puzzled, at least." She explained about the exhibit at Somerset House and the photograph of the convicted forger.

The policeman looked puzzled. "Don't you see—if Sara and her brother were descended from this man, the brother might have inherited his ability. He might even have his tools—would know how it's all done..." The bafflement on the policeman's face irritated her. "The Jane Austen books!" She would stamp her foot if she were upright. The officer plainly thought the bump on her head had left her delirious.

Richard came to her rescue. He pulled out the card Constable Lambert had given him. "I believe the inspector on the case is named Fulsom. I know my wife sounds confused, but it does all seem to tie together. If you could ask someone on that case to contact us." He gave the officer his number.

"And are the Austen books fake?" The officer wasn't ready to let go yet.

"Well, our expert said they were authentic," Richard began.

"But so did the experts in the cases I read about at the exhibition," Elizabeth insisted. Then she suddenly realized who was missing in all this. "Jack!" She struggled to her feet, but didn't let go of Richard's hand for support. "Where is he?" She turned to the policeman. "Do you have men searching the museum? They need to be looking for Jack."

Again it was Richard who made the situation clear, explaining who Jack was and what he looked like. "Where did you last see him?" The officer pulled out his phone to alert those searching the house.

"I was in the picture room. We all were, but then he and Babs went on. I thought they came down here, but he wasn't with Babs. He must have gone up to the first floor." Now she looked around. Where was Babs? "Oh, it's all right officer. Babs must have gone to get him."

Considerably later, however, the entire house had been searched—attics, closets and crannies. Areas open to the public and those not. No spot left unturned where an eleven-year-old boy could be hiding. Nor an adult woman.

Jack and Babs had disappeared.

Had they been abducted by the tattooed man Babs saw? Perhaps Jack had been looking into the atrium from above and had seen the man push the urn on Elizabeth. Babs had reported shouting at him, so he knew he had been spotted.

When it became clear that nothing more could be done at the Soane House, Richard secured a taxi to take them back to College Hall. Elizabeth would never have thought the rather stark dorm room could seem so welcoming and homey. She nestled in the corner of her bed and pulled the duvet around her.

Richard gave her two aspirin and a glass of water, but she refused to lie down. She couldn't relax while Jack was missing. She remained propped in the corner between wall and headboard, playing the scene over and over in her mind and trying to figure it all out. "How could Jack have been taken out of the museum when the director said the doors had been locked?"

"I've been wondering the same thing. If they had left before that, surely I would have seen them. I left the chambers as soon as you rang. Lincoln's Inn is literally around the corner. You can see the front door of the museum from the gate."

"And you kept your eyes on the museum all the time?"

"Well, no, of course not. But I think I would have noticed."

"Then it had to be after they unlocked the doors." She thought for a moment. "If Jack, or Jack and his abductor," she shivered at the thought, "were hiding, they could probably have slipped out after the doors were opened for the police and medics to come in."

Richard was studying the floorplan in Elizabeth's guidebook. "This looks like a back door. I wonder if they remembered to lock it?"

Elizabeth groaned. Everything they considered made her feel worse. And where was Babs? Wherever Jack was, she could only hope Babs was with him so he wouldn't be so frightened.

At first Elizabeth thought the pounding in her head was her headache increasing, then she realized it was the door.

Richard opened it and gasped with surprise before stepping back to allow Andrew and a bedraggled looking Jack to enter.

"Jack!" Elizabeth flung her duvet aside and engulfed the small figure in her arms. "Where have you been? What happened? Are you all right?" She paused to catch her breath on a sob. "Oh thank heavens!"

"In my room." The muffled sound of Jack's voice made her realize she was stifling him. She loosened her hold. But only a bit.

"Under his bed," Andrew added, then explained how he had gone there looking for Jack, unaware that he was believed to have been abducted. "When he didn't answer I used my key. I had a book about Lamborghinis I wanted to leave for him. I heard a noise and thought the college had been infested with very large rats."

"I was afraid it was her." Jack remained in the circle of Elizabeth's arm.

"Her?" she demanded.

"Babs. I saw her push that stone vase on you." He suddenly pulled back and regarded Elizabeth. "You weren't hurt?"

"Nothing serious. Don't worry." Jack's lip began to tremble. Elizabeth understood. "You were worried about me, but you were more afraid of Babs, so you hid."

He nodded and sniffed. "I knew I should help you, but…"

"No, don't worry," she repeated. "You did the right thing. Where were you?"

"Upstairs, I heard you call my name. I looked over the rail. I yelled when she pushed that thing. She looked up and I saw her face. I knew she'd come for me next, so I hid. When there was all that confusion with the medics and police and everything I ran."

Elizabeth couldn't believe it. "Babs? You're certain? She didn't just run to the rail and look over after that man pushed the urn?"

Jack blinked. "What man? I didn't see any man."

Elizabeth scooted back up on her bed and put both hands to her head, trying to think. Babs? Could the boy have seen right? The atrium was high. Jack would have been looking over the railing into a shadowed area. Surely the man in dark clothing had disappeared into the shadows or behind a column seconds before Jack arrived to formulate a very different scenario.

And yet—was it possible?

Before any coherent pattern could coalesce in her mind, there was another knock at the door. Jack crouched against the bed when he saw who entered. "Babs," Elizabeth gasped.

Jeremy followed her in, his crutches clomping on the wooden floor. "This woman came to me with the most confused story I've ever heard. I insisted we come here to see if you could make more sense of it."

But Babs dropped to her knees and extended her arms toward Jack. "Thank goodness! I'm so happy to see you, Jack. Where did you get off to? We were frantic. Do you know the police are looking for you?"

They're looking for you, too, Elizabeth wanted to say, but kept quiet. Here was something else she needed to sort out. This must prove Jack was mistaken. Surely Babs wouldn't have come back here if Jack's accusation were correct. Yes, Babs' coming back had to vindicate her. But still—"Where were you?" Elizabeth demanded. "They searched the whole museum."

"I slipped out the back door. I was frightened." Babs looked shame-faced.

"Frightened?"

"I realized that man knew I'd seen him. He would come for me next. Then I thought, maybe he was after me all along. You were in the shadows. If that was the man Cranston hired to follow me and he saw us go in the museum...," her voice quavered, "I knew he would try again. When he found out he had the wrong person with Sara." She looked around the room accusingly. "No one would believe me, but I told you so. He won't quit until he gets me."

Chapter 29

FOR ALL THE VAUNTED value placed on a good night of sleep, things were no clearer the next morning. Nor was Elizabeth's headache much better. Richard handed her a morning cup of tea. "Will you be all right if I go to the Senate House?"

Elizabeth assured him she would. Quiet was really all she wanted. But Richard wasn't convinced. "I could ask the director to meet with my class. It will only be a wrap-up. They have essays to turn in and there will be evaluation forms to fill out. Then a panel of crime writers. I don't really have to be there for that. I'm not lecturing or anything."

It took Elizabeth two more times of insisting. And a promise not to leave her bed or to open the door to anyone before Richard would consent to leave. She finished her tea and sank back against her pillows, thinking she could easily spend the rest of the day in bed, when her phone rang. Her first impulse was to let it go. Whoever it was could leave a message. Then she looked at the name of the caller. Lenore. The editor from *Regency Realm* to whom she had sent the preview of her article.

"Hello?" She scooted upright in bed. Then, as Lenore spoke, she came to a fuller sitting position.

"Yes. Yes, I could do that. I'd love to. Thank you!"

They talked for a few more minutes. When they hung up Elizabeth gave a whoop to the empty room. The editor loved the material she had sent. They didn't want to cut anything. But they wanted more. A regular column. Fifteen hundred words a month on places Jane Austen lived, visited, vacationed in, used in her books ... the possibilities were endless. She could use all her material from the London research. Then go back and do the homes Jane had lived in that she and Richard had already visited. Then she could plan trips to the seashore and to stately homes and ... the list went on and on.

She leaned back with a sigh. Was it really less than a month ago she had been thinking her life just a bit empty? Thinking there should be something more? Well, be careful what you wish for, she reminded herself. You might get it.

Her mind filled with ideas for the future. She must make a list. But first, she needed to type up her notes from yesterday's visits. She slid out of bed to get her laptop. Recalling her time at Somerset House, however, brought the forgery and rare book scam issues back to mind. She would do just a bit of research before she turned to writing her article.

"Alexander Pope, George Herbert forgery," she typed into the search engine. There had been a third poet forged, but she couldn't remember who it was. Oh, yes, Robert Herrick. But what she had entered was sufficient. The first story that came up was about the exhibit at Somerset House, but a few listings down she found a blog that recounted the crime in greater detail. Indeed, as she had expected, they were all deceased.

The tall, silver-haired forger had died in 1979, five years after his release from prison. The woman, who had represented the auction house, had been only thirty-nine at the time and had lived until the year 2000. The short, mustachioed man, who had posed as an Oxford professor of literature and gone around speaking to literary societies about the value of the supposed newly discovered manuscripts and giving newspaper interviews to increase interest in the sale, had died in prison.

Other than the coincidence of the names of the poet of the past case and the present suspect, and a possible physical similarity between the men, Elizabeth could see nothing applicable to the present situation. She was about to shut her computer when there was a knock at her door. She set the computer aside on her desk. "Who is it?" She had promised Richard, but she needed to know who she was keeping out. Jack might need something.

"It's us." Sure enough, Jack.

"Just a minute." She pulled a dressing gown on and opened the door.

"We came to see how you are. And bring you these." Andrew presented her a handful of bright blooms, undoubtedly purchased at the newspaper kiosk in Russell Square.

"Thank you." Elizabeth's smile included Jack, who entered almost shyly a moment later.

The boy stood with both hands behind his back, shifting one foot. "Jack?" Elizabeth wondered if he was still upset about the day before.

He took a step forward and held out a lumpy brown parcel. Perplexed, Elizabeth took it. The wrapping fell away at a single tug to reveal a soft Paddington Bear toy in a floppy, red hat and wellies, carrying a battered, brown suitcase. The tag around his neck read, "Please look after this bear."

"I got it at the shop that day. Because you look after me." He said it without meeting her eyes.

"Jack, I love it." It was a good thing that was enough, because she couldn't have said anything else around the lump in her throat. For the second time in two days, she engulfed him in an embrace as if she would never let go.

The soft thud of crutches on the floor, however, made her relax her grip, and she realized Andrew's earlier "we" had included one other. "Jeremy. Why aren't you in class?"

"More important things to do. Babs said she'd turn my essay in for me." He took the chair by Elizabeth's desk when the scene on her computer caught his eye. "What's that?"

She told him about the exhibit she had seen yesterday and the search she did this morning. "Unfortunately, I can't see anything much to it."

Jeremy frowned. "And when did you say this was?" He gestured toward the computer. "1957?" Elizabeth nodded as he turned again to the screen. "But that's the forger I've been tracking." He thought for a moment. "No, it can't be. It must be his grandfather."

"Tracking? What are you talking about?" Elizabeth's head had begun pounding again.

Jeremy sighed. "I suppose I should come clean with you. I mean, I haven't lied or anything—you just never asked me about my day job."

"I thought you were a student, doing an internship at Hatchard's."

"True enough. A starving student doing an unpaid internship in London. I finance this exotic lifestyle moonlighting as a private investigator."

It took that a moment to register with Elizabeth. She had assumed Jeremy's family had money. She could see he would need something to live on. Still—"Private investigator?"

"My uncle is a former Chicago cop. After he got shot in a drug raid he decided to go in for something less dangerous, so he opened a private firm. He often hires me to do jobs that require a lot of legwork." He grinned ruefully at his cast. "Well, you know what I mean."

"Archie Goodwin," Elizabeth said.

"No, Smith, I'm afraid. William Smith."

Elizabeth laughed. "No, I mean, you're Archie Goodwin to your uncle's Nero Wolfe." His blank look told her that wasn't a detective series he had read. "Never mind. So you came all the way to London to work under cover?"

"Yes, but also to get background for my English lit degree. That part's genuine."

Well, that did explain his proclivity for inquisitiveness she had noticed at times. "Okay, so what's your case?"

"My uncle was hired by an antiquarian book collector in

Chicago who discovered that his set of Jane Austen first editions had been replaced with forgeries. He occasionally displays them at rare book shows or Austen events. He took one to an exhibit in New York two years ago, and he's sure they were the authentic ones because so many experts examined them closely there.

"Then he took them to a Chicago event honoring Jane Austen's birthday last December and realized something seemed different. He said they felt lighter. So he had them examined and discovered they were forgeries. He didn't want to go to the police because he doesn't want public knowledge to devalue the rest of his collection. He just wants my uncle to recover them for him.

"Uncle Bill had reason to believe the books had been brought to England, so he sent me. It helped that he knew I had done a seminar at UCLA working with their set of Austen first editions."

Elizabeth shook her head as if to sort her jumbled thoughts. There had been so much in the last few days—revelations and contradictions. She wasn't sure what she could believe. "And your uncle believes the books Andrew bid on are the ones stolen from his client?" She thought more. "That would explain why the so-called owner insists on remaining anonymous. But there could be more than one set. What makes you so sure this is the right one?"

"Other than the too, too coincidental timing of the sale?" Jeremy cocked an eyebrow. "Remember that misprint you saw in *Mansfield Park*?"

"The catchword. It was 'of' when it should have been 'from.'"

"That's it. That was corrected after only a few were printed, so not even all first editions have that."

"So what—" Before Elizabeth could finish her question Andrew's phone rang.

After a short conversation Andrew turned to them. His wrinkled brow and reluctant smile were an almost comical contrast of worry and excitement. "Well, it looks as though

I've won the bid. The books will be delivered to the Russell Hotel by special courier from the bank in an hour."

Chapter 30

RICHARD RETURNED FROM THE Senate House, his mind on the armful of essays he needed to read and comment on before they could return to the peace and quiet of Oxford. What a blessing that would be, after the alarms of London. He opened the door of the dorm room and stopped still in his tracks. The faces that met him were a study of emotions: surprise, stress, satisfaction…

"Elizabeth? Andrew? Jeremy? Jack?" He looked from one to the other, trying to imagine what could have happened now.

"Uncle Andrew won!" Jack, who could see no reason not to be pleased for his friend, broke the news.

Richard turned to his brother. "Drew? The books?" He wasn't certain whether to offer congratulations or condolences. He knew he himself would have been relieved if the news had been otherwise.

But Andrew seemed to be cautiously happy. "I didn't think Caudex had a chance. Now we can go ahead with all those plans. I expect I should start with going back to Lincoln's Inn. I'll need a solicitor to help me negotiate the red tape to take the books out of the country."

Here was a complication Richard hadn't thought of before. He remembered reading about the American actress who bought Jane Austen's turquoise ring at auction a few years ago. There was such a public outcry against her taking the ring out of England that she wound up donating it to the Chawton House Museum. Would his brother now be the focus of a public clamor? But Andrew seemed so pleased, he hated to rain on his parade. He crossed the floor and shook Drew's hand. "Well done." The thing was settled. He might as well put a good face on it.

Richard turned to Elizabeth who looked frozen in anxiety. "Elizabeth?"

"Jeremy believes the books are stolen." She told Richard about his student's revelation.

Richard frowned. A million pounds for stolen books? Books that would have to be returned to their owner? Would Andrew get his money back? Caudex's money, Richard amended.

"Have you got anything here to eat?" Jack's very mundane question brought Richard back to the present. There was more than enough to worry about, and he would certainly be going with Andrew when he visited his solicitor. But at the moment, an empty stomach trumped everything else.

"Oh. It's Friday!" Elizabeth sprang off the bed, then flung out her arm when she swayed a little. "I've been looking forward to this for weeks—the Ritz. I have to shower."

Richard caught her arm. "Not with the state your head is in. Get back in bed. You almost swooned when you got up."

"Yes, from hunger. It's my stomach, not my head. You promised we'd celebrate when the course was over. What could be a better conclusion to the Queens of Crime than the hotel where Tommy and Tuppence stayed?"

There was no arguing with that. It seemed to Richard that it had been ages ago when he had made reservations for a party of five for afternoon tea—thinking then that Drew and Sara would join them along with Jack. "We have an extra reservation, Jeremy. Would you like to come?"

Two hours later, in deference to Jeremy's broken ankle, they took a taxi to the elegant French Chateau style hotel in Piccadilly. Not a sight Jane would have seen, Elizabeth explained. The Ritz opened early in the twentieth century. In Jane's day the site was occupied by the Bath Hotel—this was not a research moment. It was purely for pleasure.

And it was pleasure and delight from the moment the doorman, in frock coat and top hat, opened the glass-paned doors underneath the arcade to make way for them to step onto the pink floral carpet below the glittering crystal chandelier of the lobby. Richard smiled when Elizabeth gave a small, appreciative sigh as they approached the Palm Court. Her pleasure more than doubled his own.

She squeezed his arm as they went up the three steps to enter between marble columns flanked by palms. The headwaiter led them to a linen-draped, round table near the entry and held a pink velvet chair to seat Elizabeth. Richard chose the seat next to her, facing the mirror-lined wall, and Jeremy, to give room for his awkwardly protruding cast, took the chair by the top of the stairs. Their host placed a large, linen napkin in each lap, with special attention to Jack who looked unusually well-groomed in his school blazer and tie.

"Look!" Jack pointed to a couple on the far side of the room seated next to a golden statue in an alcove. "Auntie Babs. She'll be surprised when she sees us."

Richard agreed that she would, indeed, be surprised. But Babs was far too deep in conversation with her companion to notice the newcomers. To Richard that was the surprise. Babs was having afternoon tea with Bramwell Child. Of course, she had met him the day she went to the bank with Elizabeth, but Richard hadn't noted that either one seemed particularly taken with the other. They had no more than exchanged names. What could she be doing here with him now? If she was still investigating Andrew's business venture she was too late. That was done and dusted.

Richard couldn't help hoping Babs wouldn't notice them. He had been finding her rather tiring of late.

They settled on Ritz Royal English tea which arrived almost immediately in its silver pot, as did the bone china, three-tier cake stand of delicacies. The waiter pointed out each item, then departed. Jack fell immediately on the scones with Cornish cream and strawberry preserves. The adults were only slightly more restrained as they began with the tiny finger sandwiches. Elizabeth went straight for the smoked salmon. Richard hesitated, then chose the chicken breast with parsley mayonnaise while Jeremy began with ham and grain mustard.

"Now," Elizabeth turned to Andrew, "tell us about the books. Did they arrive?"

"Absolutely on schedule. Bonded courier—all efficiency. As promised. They're locked away in the safe at the Russell Hotel—by the personal hand of the manager." He gave a boyish grin. "I'll have to admit, now that it's done I'm delighted. I'd really abandoned hope of winning after all the anxieties of the past weeks."

"Yes, and I truly thought those Russian Oligarchs had carried the day. What a coincidence that was. I wonder what 'beautiful books' they bought?" Elizabeth emptied the tea pot and signaled the waiter for another.

The conversation turned to favorite memories of the past three weeks, with Jack recounting his outings with Andrew, especially Madam Tussauds and the London Eye. It was all light chatter as suited the surroundings, but when their initial hunger was assuaged, their eating slowed and their talk became more serious. "Do you think we'll ever know what's been going on?" Elizabeth asked.

Jeremy shook his head. "I hope so for Uncle Bill's sake—well, his client's really, of course. I sent him the information about that '50s case. It could be a useful lead, but I'm doubtful. At least you have your books, Andrew."

Drew raised his teacup in salute.

Richard frowned. It all sounded so settled, and yet nothing was. Had Andrew bought stolen books? Or perhaps the Russians had? Would they ever know for sure?

"I expect the police will catch Sara's murderer—or prove it was suicide." Elizabeth seemed to misinterpret his frown. "Or an accident like poor Clive Kentworth," she added. "At least we're out of it now."

Richard fervently hoped so, in spite of lingering uncertainties. As much as he had enjoyed teaching his course, he couldn't wait to get back to their rooms in Headington and start on his next book—although he had yet to decide on his story. Perhaps something set here at the Ritz. All this refined elegance would give a fun counter-foil to a murder plot. He was reaching for a meringue from the top of the cake tray when Elizabeth's murmur of surprise made him look up.

The trendy-chic man, with tattoos around the scalp of his close-cropped hair, now being greeted effusively by the head-waiter, was the man they had met in the bank—the one who had declared his would be the winning bid. And he fit Babs' description of the man she had seen hurtling a stone urn over the atrium. Had he thought killing Elizabeth would eliminate the competition on his bid for the books? How would he re-act if faced with his intended victim?

Two fashion-model-thin women in miniscule skirts, clunky shoes and whirlwind hair waved the newcomer to their table. But Richard rose and stood in his path.

The man blinked with a puzzled look on his face, then broke into a broad smile and extended his hand. "Well, hul-lo." His gaze extended to the table next to them. "A party. To lick your wounds? Let me host you. George," he turned to the headwaiter. "See that their bill comes to me."

"Of course, Lord Egleton. My pleasure." The waiter sketched a bow.

Egleton turned back and held up his hand at Richard's protest. "No, no. It's the least I can do. If you don't mind my being the teeniest bit chuffed, of course. But I promise to try to control it."

Richard couldn't make sense out of anything. "Lick their wounds"? Did he mean Elizabeth's injury? "What?"

"Why, winning the auction, of course. No hard feelings,

I'm sure. But, you understand, I had my heart set on those books, so I did bid rather on the high side. I don't like to take chances on something I want." He smiled at the women waiting for him and strode to his table leaving Richard slack-jawed.

Richard sat down. "Did you all hear that?"

"He's a nutter. He can't have won. Uncle Andrew won." Jack insisted.

Elizabeth counted on her fingers. "The Russians. Lord Egleton. Caudex House. Just how many people won that auction?"

"And how many security deposits did the bank keep?" A dark understanding flooded Richard's mind.

"But we have the books," Andrew insisted.

"I'm not so sure." Jeremy spoke for the first time. "If they made copies—"

"Yes!" Elizabeth leaned so far across the table she almost brushed the chocolate ganache on her fudge slice. "Like one of those scams I read about at Somerset House. They replaced the stolen books with forgeries. And this auction was all so private and hush-hush. Who would know?" She thought for a moment. "They had authentic first editions for the experts to examine—the set stolen from your client, Jeremy. Then a forger made copies so they could notify everyone they had won and give every bidder a fake set of books while they keep the originals and all the money.

"Everyone wins. Everyone's happy."

Andrew groaned. "Ohhh, it's brilliant. Who's going to bother examining winnings that have already been authenticated? They could easily have gotten away, with no one ever suspecting there was a problem."

"And if anyone ever did discover they possessed fakes, the criminals would be long gone by then."

"Exactly," Elizabeth agreed. "The winners would just all go off and celebrate." She looked toward Lord Egleton who was pouring champagne from an iced silver bucket.

But Jeremy was occupied watching a newcomer cross

the room to the table where Babs and Bramwell Child sat. "I don't think it's only the bidders who are celebrating."

Elizabeth followed his gaze and gasped. "Sara's brother? What's he doing with Babs and the banker? Do you think Babs is in danger? If he killed Sara—"

"I don't think she's in any danger," Richard commented, as he observed the man greet Babs with a kiss on the cheek, then take the chair next to her.

"Wait." Jeremy pulled his phone from his pocket and scrolled to read a text. "From Uncle Bill, I asked him to follow up on questions about the goings-on here. You won't believe this." He held his phone so Elizabeth and Richard could see as he read out, "Julian C. Herbert—who goes by his middle name Cranston—"

"*Cranston* Herbert!" Elizabeth and Richard read aloud together.

Elizabeth clapped her hand over her mouth. They had both spoken too loudly for their genteel surroundings. "There can't possibly be two Cranstons, can there? That must be Babs' husband. But she doesn't seem to be the least bit frightened of him."

"She certainly doesn't," Richard agreed, observing Babs' hand rubbing the man's arm possessively.

"What's going on?" But before anyone could answer Jack's question, he brushed a crumb of lemon bombe from his mouth with his napkin and asked, "Can we get another plate of cakes?"

Richard signaled the waiter, but it was Jack's first question he was focusing on. A pattern was forming in his mind. "So someone with connections in the rare book world—someone like Clive Kentworth—"

"Or Sara," Elizabeth added.

Richard nodded and continued. "Someone like one of them, attends that exhibition in New York where Jeremy's client was showing his books…"

"And takes a fancy to them," Andrew prompted.

"Exactly. Someone with connections to rare books and

to the shady side of the market as well," Richard continued.

"Sara, then," Elizabeth said. "Or Cranston Herbert. Or Babs, if he's her husband."

"We don't have any indication Babs has any background in rare books. She said she was an investigative reporter," Richard reminded her.

"Which could have put her in contact with the criminal world," Richard continued after a moment's pause. "Do you think she was making up all that about Cranston being a judge in Evansville?"

"Apparently she was." Jeremy looked up from the small screen of his phone. There are no Cranston Herberts or Cranston Ellingtons listed as judges in Indiana. I'm convinced he's our forger, but Uncle Bill is still working on that connection."

"Right." A very plausible scenario was becoming clearer to Richard. "Sara, say, spots the books—it should be possible to find out who attended that exhibition. Hopefully she bought her ticket with a credit card or signed a guest book or something. It was apparently a pretty select group, wasn't it?"

Jeremy agreed that it was.

"Then someone steals the books, and your forger makes multiple copies. They hire an exclusive art auction house to handle this very specialized sale. Clive Kentworth gets the short straw for Legacy House. He must have suspected something was wrong—perhaps he got wind of the stolen set of books—and told the wrong person of his suspicions."

"Bramwell Child," Elizabeth broke in. "Remember that day—lunch at the Old Bank of England Pub? Child introduced us to Kentworth. I recall thinking at the time that Kentworth's reactions seemed odd—a little forced."

"Yes, of course. He was worried, so he talked to the banker handling the transaction. Natural enough," Andrew said.

"Not realizing," Richard continued, "that for such a scam to work there would have to be someone inside the bank. Someone who would take the money for the bids."

"And keep it all, after notifying all the bidders they had won."

"Bramwell Child," Elizabeth mused. "I wondered at the time why he wasn't working for his family bank—if he is from the same family. Maybe he's bitter about not owning what he sees as rightfully his."

Richard considered this. It was supposition, of course. But they had evidence for a lot of it. And it did seem to hang together. A ring like that one last century: a thief, a forger, a banker—and a mastermind who was most likely the one to have turned murderer. And there were three of them—sitting on pink velvet chairs across the room, sipping tea from white and gold china cups.

Should he challenge them? Should he call the police? Then Richard saw that his brother had chosen to take matters into his own hands and was going to confront the culprits. But no ... Andrew veered to the other side of the room and approached Lord Egleton's table.

Then Richard realized he had been wrong about his suspects sitting and drinking tea. They were moving hastily toward the palm-flanked exit. If they had seen Andrew and Egleton together they must know the game was up. They would flee the country with their ill-gotten gains if they weren't stopped. Richard stood to block their way.

Babs gasped and pulled back, but Bramwell Child forged ahead at increased speed. Jeremy, sitting near the top of the steps, stuck out his long, plaster-encased leg. Child pitched head-first down the steps.

Cranston grabbed Babs' arm and spun her around, apparently looking for a rear exit. But he whirled without looking—crashing them both into a waiter carrying a tray laden with cakes, sandwiches and scones.

Andrew sprang forward and grabbed Cranston. A horrified headwaiter rushed in, wringing his hands, but Lord Egleton cut him off. "Ring for the police, George."

Understanding replaced dismay on the host's face. "Very good, my lord."

"No! No one is ringing anyone."

Richard froze when he saw that in the mayhem Babs had

grabbed Jack. Before Richard could react Babs pulled a thin, sharp knife from her bag and held it at Jack's throat with one hand while clasping him to her with the other. "Now back off. All of you."

They did.

Pushing Jack in front of her, she backed down the steps and turned toward the door.

As soon as her back was turned, the room that had been frozen in shocked silence sprang to life. Near-to a hundred mobiles sent 999 calls. But there was little hope of the police arriving before Babs had made her escape—taking Jack with her.

At least her conspirators would not be absconding with her. Jeremy stood over the dazed Bramwell Child, the ferrule of one crutch digging deep into his chest. Andrew held Cranston Herbert in an armlock.

Richard took the three stairs at a single leap and headed down the hall, feeling the inadequacy of only being able to observe. He wouldn't dare attack Babs. Anything he might do would trigger her jab of that stiletto blade deep into Jack's throat. Richard shivered with horror at the thought.

Richard couldn't hear what Babs barked at the doorman, but his shock showed in the jolting motion with which he opened the door. Once they reached the street Babs would melt into the throng of shoppers. Richard broke into a run. She could take a bus, a taxi, steal a car. They would never see her again. Or Jack.

Then he heard a footstep running beside him. Lord Egleton held a small object in his extended hand. Richard and Egleton exited the hotel side by side just as Babs pushed Jack through the central arch in the arcade onto the pavement.

Package-laden shoppers, camera-wielding tourists and assorted humanity crowded the walk on both sides. Babs glanced over her shoulder and saw Richard.

"Keep back!" she shouted, then indicated the crowd around her. "Tell them to keep back." To be certain Richard obeyed, she whirled to face him. He could see a tiny trickle of blood on Jack's pale skin and a few bright red drops on his white shirt.

Richard held out his arms. "No! Please! Stay away!" He shouted to the crowd.

Babs backed across the pavement toward an electric purple sports car. Could she have had a getaway car parked there?

In the next moment it became clear that the car was not Babs' but Egleton's. A small click told Richard that Egleton was by his side and had activated his remote. Just as Babs reached the edge of the pavement and looked ready to run, the falcon wing door behind her swung up and out, knocking her sideways away from Jack.

Richard sprang forward to clasp the boy, and Lord Egleton grabbed Babs. Only when he turned with Jack in his arms did Richard realize the crowd was applauding and cheering.

Chapter 31

"A RIDE IN YOUR Lamborghini? Oh, yes, please, sir!"

Egleton ruffled the boy's sandy curls. "Don't call me that. You make me feel like my grandfather. My friends call me Bo."

Richard gave consent for the outing and, shaking his head at the resilience of the young, watched Jack almost skip down the pink carpet beside his new friend.

The police had conducted interviews and carted off the criminals, a paramedic had bandaged the scratch on Jack's neck, and the headwaiter had overseen setting the Palm Court to its pristine order. Elizabeth had ordered another pot of tea.

Richard smiled at the re-established calm as he entered the room. "Order out of chaos," just as P.D. James said. Except for his still-elevated pulse one might think nothing had happened. He gratefully accepted the cup Elizabeth offered him. "Can you believe our innocuous airhead Babs was a master criminal?" Elizabeth asked. "What an actress."

Jeremy rejoined them in time to hear her comment. "I just spoke with Uncle Bill. He's delighted with our results, of course. And amazed at the scope of the operation. He and his client thought it was a straight-forward theft. Apparently

Barbara Ellington is known to the Chicago police. She's been suspected of being involved in thefts of art objects before, but they never could prove anything."

"But why did she latch onto us? Why even take my course?" That was the most incomprehensible part of it all to Richard.

"I suppose she needed a cover for being in London— something intellectual and bookish. Then, when Andrew Spencer registered Caudex House to become a bidder and she saw another Spencer who publishes with them, it was easy enough to put together. It offered a good vantage point for her to keep an eye on everything, and I imagine she enjoyed staying close to you and watching it all unfold." Jeremy spoke slowly as if working it out as he went.

"When she found her sister-in-law was dating one of the bidders she must have been horrified, though," Richard said.

"What do you think Sara's role was? Was she involved?" Andrew's voice showed how much he would rather not ask that question.

Elizabeth answered, perhaps a little too quickly, "I'm sure she was sincere in her attraction to you, Drew. If she was involved in the scam, I believe she had a change of heart."

"Why didn't she tell me, then? That last evening—we were so close…" Andrew's voice cracked.

Richard gave him a minute before he spoke. "My guess is that she confronted her brother—told him to call off the swindle or she would go to the police. So she was giving him time to make it right."

Andrew shook his head. "If that's true, I caused her death."

Elizabeth was quick to reassure him, but it was several moments before the conversation resumed. "I'm still trying to figure out how Kentworth's killing was rigged." Elizabeth thought for a moment. "If he mentioned to Child he was going to talk to Sara—without explaining it was about a completely different sale—Child would have been terrified Kentworth was going to spill the beans."

"You think it was Child on the roof?" Richard asked.

"Waiting for Babs to signal him on his mobile? Looking back, it does seem Babs knew what was coming. Later she must have regretted stopping Sara. It would have saved her the trouble of dealing with that problem."

"I'm sure the police will get to the bottom of it." No one seemed to have anything to add to Elizabeth's comment. Silence ensued while she refilled their teacups.

"I spoke to one of the officers." Andrew spoke in a brisk tone that showed he was struggling to move on. "He says it's likely they'll recover our money. They will want our forged books to use as evidence, but they'll be returned after the trial. As will my passport, forthwith. What a relief!"

He pushed up his glasses with a purposeful gesture. "I've been thinking. There's no reason for Caudex not to go ahead with our plans to publish the facsimiles and promote them with a traveling exhibit."

"Of forgeries?" Richard was skeptical.

"Certainly. That ensures the success of the project."

"I don't follow you."

Andrew smiled at his brother and lifted his teacup. "Because now our Enigma imprint will have the latest Richard Spencer mystery novel telling the whole story. The entire venture will be a publishing sensation."

Richard smiled. He did like the idea, but ... "I think we've had quite enough sensationalism for a while."

References

— "Jane at Prayer", adapted from "Prayer II," *Three Prayers and a Poem by Jane Austen*, Friends of Godmersham Church, Kent.

— *Jane Austen's Letters*, 4th ed., Deirdre Le Faye, ed., 2013. Oxford University Press, Oxford.

Allen, Louise, *Walking Jane Austen's London*, A Tour Guide for the Modern Traveller, 2013, Shire Publications, Oxford.

Austen-Leigh, James Edward, *Memoir of Jane Austen*, 1871, Richard Bentley & Son, London.

Chapman, R. W., *Jane Austen*, Facts and Problems, 1948, Clarendon Press, Oxford.

Chesterton, G. K., *The Complete Father Brown*, Penguin Books, 1935, London.

James, P. D., *Talking About Detective Fiction*, 2009, Alfred A. Knopf, New York.

Tomalin, Claire, *Jane Austen, A Life*, 1997, Vintage Books, New York.

Watson, Winifred, *Jane Austen in London*, 1960, C. Mills & Co., Alton, Hampshire.

READ ALL THE ELIZABETH & RICHARD LITERARY SUSPENSE MYSTERIES

The Shadow of Reality, Elizabeth and Richard confront murder and find love at a Dorothy L. Sayers mystery week high in the Rocky Mountains

A Midsummer Eve's Nightmare, Danger interrupts Elizabeth and Richard's honeymoon at a Shakespeare Festival in Ashland, Oregon

A Jane Austen Encounter, Elizabeth and Richard, on sabbatical in England, discover that evil lurks even in the genteel world of Jane Austen

The Torch Ignites, Elizabeth and Richard face danger from the past as they explore letters from the beloved romantic novelist Elswyth Thane and visit Rudyard Kipling's American home

ABOUT THE THE AUTHOR

Donna Fletcher Crow is a former English teacher, a lifelong Anglophile and Janeite, and a Life Member of the Jane Austen Society of North America. She is the author of 50 books, mostly novels of British history. The award-winning *Glastonbury*, A Novel of Christian England, is her best-known work. Where There is Love is a series of historical romances set in the Church of England of the eighteenth and nineteenth centuries. Besides her Elizabeth and Richard literary suspense series she also authors The Monastery Murders, a clerical mystery series, and The Lord Danvers Victorian true-crime novels. Donna and her husband live in Boise, Idaho. They have 4 adult children and 14 grandchildren. She is an enthusiastic gardener.

To read more about all of Donna's books and see pictures from her garden and research trips go to: http://www.donnafletchercrow.com/
You can follow her on Facebook at: http://ning.it/OHi0MY

Made in the USA
Middletown, DE
08 January 2020

82861420R00159